The Rebel Christian Publishing

Copyright © 2022 A. Bean

All rights reserved. No part of this publication may be reproduced, distributed, or transmitted in any form or by any means, including photocopying, recording, or other electronic or mechanical methods, without the prior written permission of the publisher, except in the case of brief quotations embodied in critical reviews and certain other noncommercial uses permitted by copyright law. For permission requests, write to the publisher, addressed "Attention: Permissions Coordinator," at the address below.

ISBN: 9781957290324 (eBook)
Print: 9781957290331

This is a work of fiction. Any references to historical events, real people, or real places are used fictitiously. Names, characters, and places are products of the author's imagination. Inclusion of or reference to any Christian elements or themes are used in a fictitious manner and are not meant to be perceived or interpreted as an act of disrespect against such a wonderful and beautiful belief system.

Cover image provided by Envanto Elements
Cover designed by Valicity Elaine

The Rebel Christian Publishing LLC
350 Northern Blvd STE 324 - 1390
Albany, NY 12204-1000

Visit us: http://www.therebelchristian.com/
Email us: rebel@therebelchristian.com

Contents

One 1

Two 9

Three 23

Four 31

Five 40

Six 52

Seven 57

Eight 63

Nine 74

Ten 84

Eleven 93

Twelve 101

Thirteen 113

Fourteen 127

Fifteen 135

Sixteen 141

Seventeen 150

Eighteen 157

Nineteen 171

Twenty 183

Twenty-One 191

Twenty-Two 200

Twenty-Three 206

Twenty-Four 213

Twenty-Five	222
Twenty-Six	235
Twenty-Seven	250
Twenty-Eight	262
Twenty-Nine	277
Thirty	295
Thirty-One	304
Epilogue	320
Thank you for finishing the series!	328
ACKNOWLEDGEMENTS	329
The Rebel Christian Publishing	330

Series Order:

The Woof Pack

The Beta Rises

The Bite of the Alpha

Other Books by A. Bean

The End of the World Series (End Times Fiction)

Too Young (Children's Fantasy)

The Scribe (Fantasy)

The Living Water (Contemporary Romance)

When he broke the shelf and pieced it back together, I knew I was in for a wild ride. So this time, I tried to break the shelf and piece it back together.

The Bite of the Alpha

Book III in The Woof Pack Trilogy

By A. Bean

A Rebel Christian Publishing Book

One
Alex
Jan. 3rd | 2:05 am

"Now," Brandon said, "go get the hose from the back, and don't even think about running." He shoved my head once more into the ground, rocks scraped my face and dirt filled my mouth.

With trembling hands, I lifted myself to my feet, and stumbled to the back gate.

"Hello? Yeah, I need a favor…" I heard Brandon's voice behind me as I unlocked the gate. For years, he's hidden his life from me, and the few times I dared to asked, I was silenced. The miscarriages I had were both by Brandon's own hand. After the second one, he started keeping me inside more. He didn't want people questioning me, and he didn't need anyone getting suspicious of him.

We moved here to avoid neighbors. I guess that was all he was concerned with—other people knowing what he did to me behind closed doors. He didn't care that his son sometimes wondered why I had so many bruises and cuts, scars and scrapes. I told BJ the same thing every time, that I was clumsy, and I was foolish.

It was the truth. I'd clumsily fallen in love, and foolishly stayed with a man who didn't seem to love me back. Whatever it was that I told BJ, whether it be a lie or the truth, it held up for a while.

One night, Brandon lost his temper, and my screaming woke BJ. He's a bright boy, so I did what I could to keep him from putting things together in his head and discovering that I'd been lying to him about the bruises, and the blood stains on the carpets. Living with Brandon had been hard, it'd been scary at times too. It'd been scary enough not to ask him anything that would anger him.

Somedays, my own anger got the best of me but, thankfully, Brandon didn't always react. I was tired of it though, wondering if things would ever get better. I was tired of walking on eggshells, but I knew Brandon's work was hard, so I put up with it all. Until I found out that Brandon's work wasn't what I thought it was. My mind has been spinning these last two weeks, and I just haven't been myself. He hadn't noticed though, only little BJ had.

I held my belly as I leaned over and unraveled the water hose. Twisting the handle on the spout in the night, the squeaking rang out. I dragged the hose through the gate, wondering what to do next. He didn't know that I knew the truth, he didn't know that I was seriously considering calling that girl from the diner. I wanted to get away when I first learned the truth, but I didn't know if running would be good for BJ. But now, I knew I had to get away.

When I fell and saw the grill of his truck covered in blood and dust and glass, there was something else there, something else that didn't belong to an animal. There was something that looked like clothing, purple clothing, and animals don't wear clothes. Not deer at least.

As I came back around the front, I heard Brandon yelling into his phone, "No! Just reconnect me to her."

Silence.

"What do you mean, you can't? I was literally just talking to her, and the phone went dead." His back was to me as he tossed a hand into the air in frustration. "Just tell her that's the payment and tell her to get there before anyone else does and lock it down. She knows what to do. Alright? Bye."

Shakily I lifted the hose and swung it. With a loud thud, Brandon dropped his phone and crashed to the ground. I covered my mouth as I stared at his still body. He wasn't bleeding, but he was out.

Nervously, I dropped the hose and raced into the house, rushing to lock every window and door. I didn't want Brandon Sr. getting inside, or Junior getting out.

"BJ! BJ! Get up!" I screamed.

I jogged up the stairs, holding my belly, feeling panicked and nauseated, but I tripped and slammed down on my knee, making me holler out. Thankfully, it was the last step, and I was able to keep myself from falling on my belly.

"Mommy?" BJ called sleepily. He stepped out his room, blinking back the light and rubbing his eyes.

"BJ, I need your help, alright?"

"Where's Daddy?"

"Never mind Daddy right now." I swallowed.

He finally stopped rubbing his eyes as he sleepily turned his head to look at my knee. "What happened, Mommy?"

I gritted my teeth against the throbbing pain. "I told you, I'm clumsy. But I need you—"

"I'm hungry, Mommy."

"I know, but we need to pack. We're going on a trip," I said as I slowly got to my feet.

"A trip? To visit Daddy?"

"Yes." I paused, watching BJ dance around gleefully. I didn't want him worried, so I changed my mind and said, "You know what, BJ? It's going to be a long ride, so I need you to eat something."

"Can I cook this time?"

"Sure, but only boil an egg, like I showed you, ok? Hurry up."

He nodded and raced down the stairs and I limped into his bedroom. I grabbed his sports bag and dumped all his cleats and sneakers out onto the floor and started shoving what I could inside. From his bedroom, I raced to the bathroom and took soap, toothbrushes, and paste. Then I grabbed all the medicine I could from the cabinet above the sink and shoved it into his bag before zipping it shut.

I moved to my bedroom and gathered my clothes, digging through the closet for my shoes and flats. I couldn't wear heels, which was fine for now since we'd be on the run. I reached up top for a box, and when I pulled it down, a big duffle bag crashed to the floor.

I jumped back and stared at it. Slowly, I opened it, finding that it was stuffed with money and a gun sat atop an envelope. Carefully, I took the weapon out and laid it beside me to find passports and IDs inside the envelope. One belonged to Brandon and one belonged to…

I gasped at the image of the woman. It was the woman Iyana said was BJ's mother. The ID read *Jewels Jefferson*. I could feel bile clawing up my throat.

Bursting into the bathroom, I hurled into the toilet. My eyes stung as I wiped my mouth clean and flushed the toilet when I heard Brandon Jr. squeal.

"Brandon!" I screamed. I nearly slipped as I scrambled to my feet and rushed downstairs to find a young man in the middle of my kitchen … Holding a gun to BJ's head.

"Please!" I screamed. "Don't hurt him!"

"I won't," the young man said. "But I will if you don't tell me the truth. Let's start with something simple, what's your name?"

"Alex," I said shakily.

BJ's eyes were large and filled to the brim with tears.

"Very good. Now, what is this place and why does Brandon come here?"

"How do you know Brandon?" I whispered.

"*I'm* asking the questions!" he snapped.

I cowered at his voice and nodded. "I'm sorry, just please don't hurt him."

"Just answer my question."

"I'm his wife, this is our home. That's our son, so please," I begged.

"Brandon's married? I thought he was with Jewels." He sounded confused, and shocked. But before I could register anything, a man came up from behind and wrapped an arm around me. Panic shot through me, but not at the roughness of his touch—it was his *gentleness* that stunned me.

Slowly … he began to caress my belly, making me squirm against him.

"Calm down," he said, swiftly lifting his hand to my throat. "I won't hurt you."

He smelled like cigarettes and alcohol.

"What do you want?" I asked.

"I see Brandon's been awfully busy." His hand slowly traced over my breast, and back to my belly. "You are a very fine woman."

I swallowed thickly, squeezing my eyes shut.

"What do you want?" I repeated in a shaky voice.

"I want to get to know you a little better." He grabbed my hips and adjusted them forcefully against him. "I want to know why Brandon's been keeping you a secret."

"Get off my mom!" BJ screamed, but the young man shoved the gun harder into his head, making him squeal in pain.

"Please!" I cried.

"Dahodda, cool it," the older man said. "He's doing what any good son would do. Protect his mother."

"The couch," I swallowed, "it's through that doorway, we can go right there."

"Why not here? I'll lean you over the table and get a good look at you."

My breath hitched. *My God, he's serious. He's going to assault me right here in front of my own son.*

"Please," I begged, "not in front of my child."

He was silent for a moment, and I was pleading with God in my heart that the old man would take the bait.

"Fine," he said. "Lead the way."

I nodded and walked slowly by the stove where BJ's boiling egg was turning and flipping in the pot. With a sudden breath, I grabbed the pot and slung the hot water over my shoulder, making the old man holler in pain.

"Boss!" Dahodda yelled as I shoved past the man and grabbed BJ.

We ran through the living room as a shot fired off behind us. We both ducked, and BJ fell to the floor in fear. But we didn't have time for that.

"We have to move!" I shouted as I dragged him to his feet. He stumbled beside me as we made it to the top of the stairs.

"Grab your bag from your bedroom, and I'll grab mine."

BJ nodded and took off into his bedroom. I went into mine and grabbed the bag of clothes and the duffle bag full of money. Taking the gun from the floor, I met BJ at the top of the stairs and slipped a finger to my lips, signaling him to be quiet. He nodded as tears streamed down his cheeks, and we began to creep down the stairs.

"Find them both! Don't come back without killing them or I'll kill your brother. We're taking Brandon to the cove, meet back there when you've cleaned up here."

"Understood," I heard Dahodda say.

The front door opened, and I could hear the old man heading out the door. It sounded like Dahodda's footsteps trailed away.

"Come on!" I whispered, grabbing BJ's hand. We flew down the stairs and around the corner and slammed right into Dahodda. It didn't register to him what'd happened until I screamed and backed away in horror.

Gripping BJ's hand, we turned and headed for the front door, but a shot rang out behind us, and BJ hollered. His hand slipped from mine, and all the world was silent.

BJ hit the floor hard and began to scream in horror. I didn't know where he'd been shot, but Dahodda was frozen too. Just staring at my little boy weeping on the floor, reaching for me and begging me to make the pain stop. I scooped him into my arms and rushed out the front door. Placing him and our things in the backseat, I hopped in the front and took off.

Two

Vito

Jan 3rd | 4:29am

I stepped out of the elevator and walked through the quiet halls of the hospital. I'd gotten word that Gio Jr. didn't make it, and Emilia had suffered a heart attack from the news. I was numb when I received the report. Nothing felt real. I was losing the one family I wanted to protect, but I wouldn't allow myself to be hurt. I couldn't. Because if I let the hurt in, it wasn't going to stop. The only thing I could do to stop the pain was turn it into fire. Let it send me on a wild goose chase, anything just to keep my thoughts clear of reality for the time being.

I convinced myself it was a murder, and not a random drunken accident. The only person I was willing to blame was Brandon, but that was because I still hadn't forgiven him. I was still secretly fighting the way Brandon's betrayal made me sick to my stomach. The way I foolishly poured my trust into him. This was my retribution; blaming him would make me feel better. I called it justice, but I knew it was only vengeance. But

I didn't even want it to be vengeance because deep within, I didn't want to believe Brandon had truly turned on BT... had truly turned on *me*.

I hated this world because, in this life, even your enemies looked like you. When I looked in the mirror, there was no difference between Brandon and me, and that's why I trusted him. We both took lives, we both tried to protect what was important to us. It's just that one of us has morals and the other doesn't... but is that even true?

How am I moral when everything I'm doing now is for my own sake, and for Iyana? BT is the last thing on my mind, yet I boast that I would never betray the pack. But I betrayed the pack when I fell in love with Iyana. It was inevitable. Because I knew I'd do anything to protect her, even if that meant forsaking the Pack. Forsaking your brothers in this life was equivalent to betraying your family.

Everyone tells you that it's okay to fall in love, but they don't know how damaging it truly is. It tears things apart; it pits people against each other. Jesus said it Himself, that He came to divide the mother and daughter, the father and son. Because, although you love your family, you're supposed to love Christ more, and that can bring division.

It's funny because love can also unite people. But if one is not careful and there is confusion, the word *unite* can become muddled, and all you're left with is the word 'untie.'

Love unites while simultaneously unties. It's a beautiful thing. The way it makes you feel, the way it can make a boy grow up. But in this dark, crime-ridden world, you usually grow up without love, just some false sense of it to get you through. Really, it's loyalty that matters. Loyalty produces love, and loyalty is what makes that boy a man.

"Excuse me," the kind voice of a woman behind a desk caught my attention. "Sorry," she murmured as I came over to her. "I didn't know you were coming. We've kept everyone away, all the detectives and visitors paying their condolences as you ordered."

"I ordered?" I squinted.

"Yes?" she said, reaching over and flipping through some folders. She opened one and read it over briefly. "Detective Murphy said you didn't need anyone else talking to Emilia. She said you wanted her left in peace, and no one was allowed to speak with her since she'd already given a statement to your detective. But NYPD said they'll only give you twenty-four hours since they'll have to conduct their own investigation."

I cleared my throat and nodded. "Yes, thank you."

I hadn't ordered a detective, or anyone, to see Emilia. Someone was trying to keep what happened a secret long enough to buy themselves time to get away. Which only further convinced me that it wasn't an accident.

"You seem lost," the young woman said, catching my attention again.

I sighed. "It's just, they were like family to me."

"I'm so sorry."

"Thank you."

"I know it must be hard. You just got married, and now in the same sentence we're saying congratulations *and* I'm sorry. It's such a horrible thing that's happened."

I looked her over, and then glanced at the two women sitting with their backs to us. Reading her name tag, I placed my hand on hers. "Syrene," I said quietly, "you really seem to care."

She nodded, her thick curly ponytail swaying behind her. "I do care. I lost my father two years ago, so I understand what it means to lose family."

"You understand what it means to be consoled too, I bet."

She took a breath, and I dropped my eyes to our hands. I played with hers for a moment, her honey brown hands were as light as mine, her fingers as slender as Iyana's, but for some reason, they just didn't fit between mine the way Iyana's did.

"Listen," I said as I slowly looked up from our hands, "I need a favor."

She leaned closer. "What is it?"

"I need those files. I want to look over the detective's report."

"Well," she paused. Took a shaky breath. I rubbed her hand a little more, and she swallowed nervously. "I can get you a copy since she's your detective, but the police will want to see the report too."

"That's fine." I nodded. "They should."

"I'm surprised she's not sending you the report."

"Well, this was out of the blue for her, so she did what she could in passing. She was on her way to another case but stopped to help an old friend."

She nodded, and I almost sighed a breath of relief that she believed my lie.

"Well, let me make that copy for you," she said.

I patted her hand and stepped back from the counter. She came around and gave me a small smile as she walked down the hall to a room. I waited at the desk, refusing to see Emilia. I hadn't come to visit her, just to learn what the police had to report from her. I didn't want to see her in this condition, but I was going to get justice for her no matter what.

Syrene returned and handed me an envelope.

"I didn't want to make it so obvious."

"Thank you." I nodded and turned to leave.

While on the elevator, I opened the envelope, shocked to find that Syrene had left me her number. I crumbled the small piece of paper and tossed it to the floor before pulling out the report. Beside the number left for Murphy, Syrene had crossed it out and written in black ink, **St. Sessa's Hospital**.

When the elevator dinged, I found Leo standing in the lobby waiting for me. He and Kat were head of security together because Kat was strong, but Leo was a genius. He was a technical engineer before crossing over, he's used his talents for me ever since.

"It's like I thought," I said as we left the hospital, "there's someone pulling strings, and they're trying to cover it up. From the look of the report, they didn't even talk to Emilia. It's a garbage statement saying Emilia didn't see or hear anything. Everything happened at once."

"But you got the name? You sure it wasn't a fake name?"

"Hopefully not," I said as we reached the car.

Once inside, Leo pulled out his laptop and scanned the documents in. He read them over in an aching silence before clicking around on the keyboard. "Alright, I was able to get into the hospital security cams while you were gone."

"Really? I didn't know you were that good."

"Kat's good, she taught me how to slip in and out of places and never get noticed. But tech stuff? I've got you covered."

I nodded.

"Anyways," he said, "I downloaded the last forty-eight hours of security, and there was a woman who came in and waved a badge around three in the morning. She did pretty good with keeping her face out of the cameras, but I caught an angle and I've got facial recognition going."

"What do you have?"

His light brows creased as he leaned forward while scrolling. "I've got a woman named Clemons Murphy. She was a detective for the Buffalo Police force, but she was killed in action."

"So she was taken in by a gang—if she's still alive."

"More than likely. I'm still working on her backstory. But you were right about the report. She came in, waved her badge, and had a folder in her hands. She disappeared for a few minutes and returned to pass off that folder."

"I knew it." I hit the steering wheel. "I don't care about her backstory, just get me an address. I need to know who she works for and why she left the number for St. Sessa's."

In the silence, he pecked the keyboard before I heard his computer chime.

"I've got an address."

—— BT ——

"Detective," I said as I stood on her front steps. Thick coils were pulled back into a messy ponytail as she held open the door to her small house.

"Well, if I knew all it took was a few dead bodies to get the prince on my doorstep, I would've killed them long ago," she teased.

"Then we wouldn't be having this conversation. This visit would be very different," I said flatly.

"Goodness," she placed a honey brown hand over her flat chest, "you actually cared about those people?" When I didn't respond, she chuckled. "I would hate for this to get back to Grizzly."

"I'm here to make sure it doesn't," I said.

"Really?" She crossed her slender arms and leaned against the doorframe. Her eyes shimmied over me quickly, and the delight in them made me believe she was pleased with what she saw. "Well," she reached out and stroked my cheek, "I can keep a secret if you can."

I stepped up the final step, standing over her as she straightened from the door post. "I can do whatever you want as long as this stays between us."

A smirk danced across her lips as she grabbed my hand and pulled me into her house. There wasn't much inside, which made the small place look spacious and inviting besides the piles of papers and folders laying around.

"Have a seat." She gestured toward a green couch in the living room.

"Can I have a drink instead? Scotch, if you have it?" I asked.

She nodded and disappeared into the kitchen. When she was out of sight, I slipped to the couch and began searching through the folders and documents sitting on the cushions. I was looking for anything linking her to Grizzly, Brandon, or anyone between my gang and Grizzly's. Old cases she worked, things she covered up, I wanted information to see who she really worked for.

I heard her footsteps rounding the corner and closed the folder and jolted to my feet. She appeared holding two glasses, one clear, one dark. "Here you are," she said as she passed me the scotch.

"Thanks," I muttered, taking a sip.

"So, my dear prince—"

"Vito is fine."

"I like calling you a prince, it's *so* fitting." She gazed at me from across the room. She'd taken a spot on her matching green chair and was watching my every movement over the rim of her glass. "How did you find me?"

I shrugged. "I'm the *prince* aren't I? There's not a lot that goes on in this city that I don't know about."

"I'd expect nothing less from you."

I raised my glass to her. "So then, you'd expect that I know you're not from here."

She smiled. "Of course."

"There's no Detective Clemons Murphy on this force."

"Very good, prince. You know I'm not from here, but you don't know who I work for?" I sipped my drink and she nodded slowly. "You're trying to figure out why Manhattan police would call in someone who's not even from the city?"

I shrugged.

She set her glass on a stack of papers. "Well, you should know I'm not Grizzly's girl."

"I've already checked Jersey and Maryland."

She frowned. "Maryland? How'd you know about that?"

"I thought you weren't Grizzly's?"

"Money is always green no matter who's giving it to you. I go where I'm needed. Now, you tell me how you know about Maryland."

I stirred for moment before answering, "A woman I know knew her way around men. There weren't many she couldn't coax information out of. She left me some of that information."

"She ran off?"

Trying not to think of Jewels, I set my glass down and replied, "Something like that, but let's skip the formalities." I took my jacket off and tossed it onto her couch before crossing the room to her. She smiled largely at me as she sank into the chair.

"Who do you work for?" I said as I leaned over her.

"Wouldn't you like to know?" she teased. Her eyes were wide and there was a wild look in them as I studied her. This was not a woman to be taken lightly. This was not a woman who wanted to be taken lightly. Not in any capacity.

I snatched her up from the chair, wrapping my arms around her waist. As expected, she squealed in excitement.

"Oh, Mr. Prince, you really want to know, don't you?"

My hand went to her hair, taking a fistful and tugging her head back. She giggled madly before sighs of ecstasy spilled from her lips.

"You like this?" I asked, scanning her blushing face.

"I love it," she whispered.

Her eyes rolled to the back of her head as I kissed her neck. She sighed in glee. My skin crawled.

"I'll tell you what want if you don't stop," she told me.

In one swift movement, I lifted her off her feet and carried her to her bedroom. Tossing her on the bed, I pulled my shirt off and stared down at her.

"I've wanted this for so long," she purred.

"Just tell me one thing," I whispered, leaning down so my words were spoken against her neck. "Tell me who did it."

"Give me more," she said lustfully.

I reached behind my back, gripping the gun tucked into my waistband. A moment of hesitation ticked by as I stared at this insane woman, wondering if I should even bother threatening her. She wanted only one thing from me, I doubted my gun would change anything at all. It would probably excite her.

It did.

As I yanked the gun free, she gasped and then batted her lashes, a flash of lust skirting over her face. God... of all the women to be holding on to information I need. It had to be the one who's absolutely nuts.

Oh well, nutty people are allowed their kinks. I won't judge. I promise.

Suppressing a sigh, I leaned down and ran the gun along the length of her slender leg. She shivered as the cool metal reached her inner thigh.

"It's cold."

"And stiff..." I whispered before kissing her neck again.

Leo had warned me this woman was a nut. She wouldn't be impressed with money or afraid of threats. But anything would set her off. Based on deleted private messages on social media Leo was able to recover, someone said she was a sex addict.

I really didn't care.

Nutjob or not, this woman was not loyal. I didn't care if I had to strip down and hang from the ceiling, I needed this information and I'd do anything to get it. That's why I asked Iyana to let me do this alone. I promised I'd get this done without breaking my vow, and I was determined to keep that promise.

"Detective," I whispered as I dragged my gun up her frame, "you've got to give me something."

"You're so frustrating," she sneered. "He was in a fit of rage over your wedding. Heck, I was too," she paused and licked her glossed lips, "for other reasons, of course."

"Very cute," I said.

"Well," she threw her arms around me, "as a bonus, since you've treated me so well, I'll tell you this: that man, Tim Walters, Brandon pulled the plug on his wife on the New Year."

"What?" I jerked away from her.

"Oh, please don't make me regret telling you." She sighed.

I tried to regain my focus, making sure my face didn't relay my emotions. "I'm just surprised he told you."

"If I tell you this, can we get back to us?"

I forced a smirk and leaned down to kiss her neck again. I couldn't get myself to kiss her lips, I didn't want to. It was enough I was here doing any of this at all with my guilty conscious.

"He only told me because he didn't have the money on him to pay. The money was going to come through a wire transfer from a woman named Jill at Saint Sessa's. She'd been the one collecting money to keep Tim's wife under."

My chest tightened and I buried my face in her neck, just so she wouldn't see the horror on my face.

"It's a pity," she whispered. "A woman like that has no idea what to do with you."

I raised from her and blinked in disbelief. There was a lot I was willing to tolerate, but belittling Iyana wasn't one of them.

I cleared my throat as I looked down at the wild woman. "I suppose you know what to do with me, then?"

Her hands slipped down my chest and over my scars as she smiled darkly. "I know how to please a man." She began tugging at the hem of my sweats, but I shoved my gun into her chest.

"Hold on," I said, pushing her back down into the blankets. The barrel of the gun remained sturdy, pressed her into her chest. "I want to get a better look at you like this."

"You're the dominant type? It fits your cool demeanor," she cooed.

"Hmph."

Her questioning eyes didn't look away from mine as I lifted the gun and tapped her jaw with it. "A gun this close to you doesn't scare you?"

She shook her head. "It makes things interesting."

"What does scare you?"

She rolled her eyes and grunted. "You wasting my time scares me. I told you what you wanted to know, now give me what I want, prince!"

I stared at her as I carefully put the gun to her lips. "You know something? I did care about those people who died."

"What a pity," she said flatly.

"And I love my wife, whom you just insulted a moment ago. What a pity."

Before she could speak, I cocked the gun—cutting off her next words.

She blinked up at me. Somewhere in her eyes there was uncertainty. She didn't want to be afraid, she wanted to believe this was all part of some sick sexual role play. It wasn't.

"I cared about those people," I hissed, my grip on the gun was so tight my hand was shaking. "And I told you I wouldn't let that fact get back to Grizzly. Or anyone for that matter."

Her eyes widened. Her nostrils flared as she took a breath. Her hand twitched as she tried to move, but I fired before she could get anywhere.

Three
Hardy
Jan 3rd | 6:01am

I don't think I've slept since Jewels died. I couldn't get her thrashing body and pleading eyes out of my head. She didn't want to die; she didn't want me to kill her. But I couldn't control myself.

I was hurt. I was angry. I was confused. And even after she was dead, I couldn't stop choking her. I couldn't stop screaming. But when I realized that she was gone, I panicked and ran away. Although, somewhere in my heart, I felt like she deserved what'd happened. She was going to leave me when she panicked and tried to run away with Brandon.

"Hardy, come on! Stop spacing out!" Kat whispered hotly.

"Sorry," I whispered as I grabbed the other end of Rion's body.

"You have to stop thinking about it or else we're never going to get this done."

"I just don't know why I have to help," I grunted as I struggled to walk with Rion.

"Because I couldn't let you keep sulking, and Iyana and Vito needed space. She just found out her mother is dead and had been kept in a coma by Brandon."

"I know that. But I wouldn't have gotten in the way."

"It doesn't matter because you're here now."

I dropped Rion's legs and Kat gasped. "What are you doing?"

"I can't do this! Jewels was just alive *hours* ago! I can't even think and we're out here carrying dead bodies onto Grizzly's property!"

She dropped his arms and pressed a finger to her lips. "Shh! Keep your voice down or we'll be caught!"

"Maybe we should be!"

"For what?" she snapped. "I don't think it's right either, but there's nothing else we can do. This is what Vito wants and we just follow orders."

"I don't care what Vito wants; I care about what *I* want. And I want to be caught so that I can pay for what I've done!"

"You want to throw your life away? Fine," she said sternly, "but do it after we've done our job."

"What life? What do I even have now that—"

"Are you serious?" The shock and anger in her voice shoved me into silence. Kat pressed gloved fists into her hips and said, "Your whole life is over because Jewels is dead? So, there's no other reason to live? Not even to protect Iyana or repay Vito someday for starting this war?"

I couldn't summon a single word in response.

"Or maybe you'll live to finally beat Logan in one of those matches? Prove to yourself and everyone else that you are smart and go back to school."

"Alright, I get it," I said weakly.

"Maybe you want to live another day to screw some chick at a party whose name you can't even remember."

"I said I get it!" I snapped.

"Or maybe you want to live just one more day because you mean something to someone! Because you mean something to *everyone* at BT! Because you mean something to the only person you've always disregarded." Her voice lowered, and in the low streetlight, all that was visible was our breath forcing its way out of our masks.

"Maybe," she whispered, "you'll live because you mean something to me."

"Kat," I started but she leaned down and began to struggle with Rion.

"The longer we wait, the more dangerous it is out here. We need to get these bodies in the trash before we're caught."

I nodded. "Alright."

We left Rion's and Jewels's bodies in garbage cans along with Rion's gun. It was decided by Iyana—who just wants to hurt Brandon for hurting her—that we would frame Brandon and Gang Grizzly for Rion's and Jewels's murders. That would give BT the leverage it needed to make a bigger attack on Gang Grizzly, and it would tear Grizzly apart internally, which is what we need more than anything.

We had a rat, and it caused quite a stir within our ranks. We needed to do the same, cause a stir and cause confusion within Gang Grizzly and with their clients. Jersey isn't far, and Vito was willing to make as many trips as he needed to secure new business from Grizzly's former clientele.

It was a dangerous and reckless plan, but Vito and Iyana were certain the plan would work. And even if the bottom fell out, there would still be enough time to weaken Grizzly. Besides, who would believe the Prince of the Apple framed Grizzly and didn't fight the war fairly? No one.

Silently, I sat in the darkness of Jewels's apartment. I stared at the wall as I cradled some of her clothes. I loved Jewels more than anything, more than anyone. The woman I swore to protect was gone by my own hand, and I couldn't take it. I couldn't stop sulking and mourning. I wanted her back. I'd do anything to bring her back. But there was nothing that could be done.

I wanted to apologize. I wanted to hear her say she loved me. I wanted another chance to kiss her, to sleep beside her. But all that was left was the coldness and stillness of her apartment. Nothing but tragedy echoed the halls of BT anymore. Everywhere you looked, someone was hurting. But there was no way to fix what had been broken inside of all of us. Iyana lost her mother and was losing her father. I lost Jewels, and BT lost Rion. Vito lost Gio Jr. *and* Sr., and Emilia was barely hanging on now.

"What is happening?" I whispered. "God... please, You're the only One I know Who can stop these tragedies. Why are You doing this to us? We're not bad people... are we? Is this all some punishment? Please... say something!"

But there were no remarks from God. Just the bitterness in my heart as I longed for Jewels. I wanted to hear His voice. I wanted everything to be okay. I needed Him to say something, but He was silent. I needed Him to punish me, for someone to scold me.

I just took someone's life, and no one seemed to care. Am I wrong for caring? *No,* I thought, *I only care because it was Jewels.* I didn't have this problem when I killed one of Grizzly's cubs. I hadn't felt bad at all, I only wished I hadn't started a war. *How can I be so cold?* We only care when it's someone we love. When will we stop being like this? I sniffled and pulled Jewels's robe into my face, inhaling her sweet scent.

"Hardy?"

I looked around because I hadn't heard the door open. Light footsteps and the smell of food flowed into the bedroom where I sat. A light clicked on, and Kat walked inside.

"Hardy? I've been looking all over for you. You need to eat something," Kat said as she set a tray beside me. It was soup with toast, and it smelled delicious.

"I know you haven't eaten much, so I thought a simple broth with some acini de pepe would be easy enough to digest."

I lowered my brows. "What is *acini de pepe?*"

"Oh," she laughed lightly. "They're the little pasta balls in the soup. They look like couscous, but they taste quite different."

"I see," I said.

Kat loved cooking and she was really good at it. She always made me food when she came to visit, and it never tasted homemade. It tasted like a professional chef was cooking for me. I think she enjoyed the cooking more than my conversation, but she never missed a date and never said no when I'd ask her for lunch. That's when things began to get complicated between us. I didn't know what we were, and I didn't even know if I should consider it anything since I still loved Jewels. But I didn't want to keep loving her, I wanted to experience something new.

I think Kat knew that too. But I didn't think she liked being my rebound, and I didn't think she ever thought more of me than a friend.

"Well, you should eat, and get some rest." She glanced around. "And turn more lights on in here. It was pitch black when I came in."

"I don't want any lights on," I said flatly.

"Well, you can't sit in the dark either. You'll never get any better. You'll always be stuck here in this limbo state."

"I don't want any lights on!" I yelled.

"Because you're a coward who's too afraid to face his own reflection, so you sulk in your shadow. How childish."

"That's not fair," I muttered.

"It's not fair that you get to sulk while everyone else is working relentlessly. Even Iyana is trying to get back to work and she just found out her mother died."

"What?" I looked over at her, and she shrugged.

"Vito tried to stop her, but she doesn't want to think about it. She wants to ignore her mother's death, and just keep working."

"She's not dealing with it."

"It's not like you are either."

"At least I'm trying," I said forcefully.

"Please." She threw her hand and headed for the blinds. "You're trying to feel miserable and sorry for yourself, not better."

I pushed from the floor before she could reach the blinds and hugged her. I simply wrapped my arms around her slender figure and pressed my face into her back. She was shorter than me, but I didn't care. I just wanted to hold her, to hug her, to feel anything besides lonely.

She stood perfectly still as I trembled against her.

"I feel so lost without her. What do I do? I've tried everything, even praying, but there was no answer. Please … help me."

"He will answer you when the time is right. For now, give Him your tears. He is listening, I promise."

Slowly, we shifted so Kat was facing me now. She caressed my cheek before dropping her hand to her side. A small smile was etched onto her lips, and she said, "I can't be her, and I can't replace her or who she was to you. But I can be here for you. I'll be right here with you every step of the way."

I grabbed her hand and pressed it to my cheek. "Thank you, Kat."

Four

Brandon

Jan 3rd | 9:45am

I snorted, jerking into consciousness. There was a bright light beaming down on me; I tried to blink away the light, but it wouldn't stop. I tried to lift my arm, and realized it was restrained. Shaking my head from the blurriness, I tried my other arm, and realized I was strapped to the chair. My legs, arms, and chest were all strapped to the chair.

"He's awake." The masculine voice was familiar, and when the blurriness finally subsided, I realized it was Brooke.

"Brooke? What are you doing? What's going on?" I groaned as a sudden flash of pain swelled in the back of my head. Fleeting memories of being at home entered my mind's eye, but Grizzly was standing in front of me now, grimacing fiercely, and it was a wonder my bowels weren't fleeting also. There was a burn twisting down his wrinkled face. Bubbling and frightening to look at, Grizzly's left eye looked lazy now.

"You look confused and horrified, and I don't know if it's because I caught you before you left, or because of the new burn." He stepped closer. "Interested in how I got it?"

"I don't know what you're talking about, Grizzly. I was drunk, I passed out, that's all I remember!"

"When did you pass out?" he asked calmly. "Before you killed Gio and his son, or after?"

The memories were flooding back now; I remembered my rage, the anger I felt. But it was nothing compared to the fear that poured into me now. Grizzly could kill me, or worse, get Jewels involved. Thankfully, he had no idea about Alex, but I couldn't remember how I'd gotten from home to here. It was fuzzy. I didn't like uncertainty, and not knowing whether I was away from Alex or not when he found me had opened a pit in my stomach.

"He hadn't even had that woman in his bed, and you killed his family with a car, Brandon!" Grizzly's booming voice caught my attention. He was shaking his head, arms over his chest.

"It was an accident!" I yelled back.

"An accident? Do you think he's going to think it was an accident? No! He's going to think we killed his family to make a statement on his wedding night! And what's worse, you killed them when BT hadn't even retaliated yet!" Wiping the slob from his mouth, Grizzly dropped his head, and in a low growl, he said, "It is an unwritten rule that you do not make any moves while the other gang is retaliating."

"Yeah, well I've never seen the rules, and Vito doesn't always play by them," I snapped.

"I don't care! He had been playing by them all this time and now he doesn't have to. Just when we had him," he lamented, "you picked him back up and set him right back on his throne!" A deep silence stretched over us for a moment. "Your actions are causing us more harm than good. And dead weight is better off... dead."

"Please, Grizzly, wait! I can fix this! I—" A fiery punch rammed into my face, knocking the words right out of my mouth.

Grizzly leaned down and screamed, "I'm tired of hearing that!"

I sat up, in total disbelief that he'd actually punched me, but I was met with another punch, and one more for good measure. Then he said, "Do you know how much blood will be shed over this?"

I spat a mouthful of blood onto the floor, eyeing Grizzly. He was looking at his knuckles, flexing his fingers opened and closed. I had no reason to be angry, but I was. I was so angry that I was sitting in a chair tied up, and all my mistakes were suddenly turning into failures right before me.

"I will have to shed men and resources I don't have and be prepared for an all-out shootout or an invasion at a moment's notice. And you want to know why, Brandon?"

I didn't answer.

"Because you've been falling behind Vito this whole time. You've been licking up the crumbs from his sofa that he didn't even know he dropped. You've done nothing but make Vito look better. You've done nothing but lie and scheme, and look how far that's gotten you." He paused. "You don't understand the weight of what you've done because it's indescribable. There's no good price on family, which you took from Vito." He shrugged. "So I took the liberty of taking *your* family."

My head jerked up. The burning in my cheeks intensified, and my chest began to rise and fall quickly. "What are you talking about?" For the first time since I woke up, Brooke looked at me. The eye contact was brief, his gaze snapping to mine and then going straight ahead. It was all I needed.

"What are you talking about!?" I screamed.

"I'm talking about your family, Brandon." Grizzly was suddenly the kind and cunning man I remember trying to schmooze over when I first arrived on his doorstep years ago. Now, I was here, still trying to win him over.

I thought things had changed, but they hadn't. I thought I had made moves, and that I was actually bringing a sense of security for Alex, but all I've brought to her is danger. I never wanted that. I loved Alex.

Weakly, I dropped my head and Grizzly started again in the silence, "I did an even exchange. Dahodda is going to hand deliver them to Vito as a gift from us. Hopefully, he'll call it a truce."

"My family," I whispered as tears rolled down my cheeks. "How did you get to my family?"

"Well," he chuckled, "really, they got to you. They were packing bags and trying to leave while your unconscious body lay in your icy driveway."

"No." I shook my head. "That isn't right. There's no way you know about—"

"Alex and your son? Yeah, we met."

I jerked in my chair, riling and screaming curse words at him. Grizzly only watched as I tried to break loose. He was leaning against his desk, watching me struggle with a ridiculous grin on his face. I was screaming, but I couldn't hear it. My mind had frozen and all I could see was Alex standing out on the balcony of our hotel room the first day of our honeymoon.

It was morning; our balcony overlooked the sandy beach and shimmering waters. The memory was an image I'd always kept in my head. Alex had looked so beautiful and kind, her bright skin and dark hair. A loose curl sat on her bare shoulder as she sported a long summer dress. She was glowing.

A noise behind me made me stop struggling, snapping me from the vision of Alex in my head. As I glanced around, I saw Brooke brighten a little.

"Well, well…" Grizzly stood from his desk, smiling. "Dahodda is here. Must mean our little penance gift is ready." He leaned down and mused my waves before passing by to greet Dahodda. "Dahodda, from the looks of things, it went well," Grizzly cackled.

"Yes, sir. It's done. I've left them at his back gate; there was no one home."

I went limp at his words, and I could feel the emptiness I'd been running from for so long begin to overtake me.

"I expected that," Grizzly said. "He's probably out mourning the death of his family. Hopefully, when he returns, he'll feel a little better with our gift. Now, Dahodda has proved himself."

His thundering footsteps crossed over to me, but I didn't care. I'd lost everything, and I knew Grizzly would never give me the pleasure of dying. I was destined to live in this misery forever.

Dahodda came around the desk with Grizzly. I could see bloodstains on his shirt. I began to tremble, and hunched over to vomit, but nothing came except the vivid memory of me shoving Alex into the ground when she tried to vomit. It was coming back, but I didn't want to remember any of it. Alex had dealt with my temper, my failures, my agitation without even knowing it. She'd been my punching bag and my pass time and the thing I used to make me feel good when Jewels wasn't around.

The abuse I brought her was more than physical, and yet, she stayed with me. She loved me and loved BJ. All I ever brought her was a life of pain and fear, and all that came of it was death.

I stared at the bloodstains, choking on the sob that was trying to escape. Dahodda only looked down at me, never blinking or faltering in his face. His expression was detached. Dead. But his eyes looked very much alive, like he was waiting for his next move. I'd given him and Brooke everything, letting them work for me and for Grizzly at times, but they betrayed me...

How could they?

Vito's face flashed in my mind, and my own betrayal became heavy on my chest. I began to strain against the ropes, heaving for air.

"Look at him!" Grizzly fell back in laughter. "He's having some kind of panic attack! Brooke, since you haven't proved yourself, I want you to do it right now. Beat him to a pulp and I'll let you both live and join my ranks officially."

I didn't know if Brooke ever said anything, but the next moment I was punched so hard I heard my jaw crack in my head. It wasn't broken, but the pain was horrible. A burn that shredded through me, making me cry out in agony. I couldn't even register what was happening when suddenly I was punched again and then kicked over backwards in the chair.

Laughter erupted from Grizzly, and as I lay there blinking back the darkness that surrounded my blurry vision, I saw him waving Brooke on. Just as Brooke landed a blistering kick to my face, I heard the creaking of the door. Someone came inside.

"Grizzly! Grizzly! There are bodies in the trash!"

"What?" Grizzly snapped.

"Two bodies! A man and woman!"

Grizzly rushed out with Dahodda behind him, but the young cub stopped at the door. A few moments passed as he peered outside, it wasn't until he suddenly turned back to me that I realized he was waiting—making sure Grizzly had gone ahead.

Dahodda ran to my side. "Help me get him up," he said to his brother.

"Some plan that was," Brooke complained. "What if we didn't have this opening?"

"What?" I asked weakly as the two boys pulled me up and began to untie me.

"We're getting you out of here, Brandon," Brooke said as he leaned down to cut the ropes off my legs.

"Why?"

"We don't have time to explain," Dahodda said as he freed my hands.

The ropes on my left leg were off and Brooke was cutting my other leg free when we heard screaming erupt outside the room. Glancing around at each other, Brooke clutched his knife and cut faster as Dahodda raced to the door to listen.

"You guys, you saved me and my family. I just don't know why," I whispered as Brooke cut me free. The ropes fell off as he pulled me to my feet, but there was a soreness ringing through my entire body. A loud bang rang out somewhere nearby, and Dahodda raced over to Grizzly's drawer and dug through it.

"Here," he passed his brother something, "now go."

"We can't leave you Hodda, you're my little brother. I *won't* leave you!"

"Grizzly trusts me the most," Dahodda said. "When he comes in, I'll tell him there was a struggle and you got away with Brandon. Just promise you'll come back for me." He glanced over at me, then back at his brother. "It didn't turn out the way it was supposed to. I messed up."

The chaos outside was growing louder and Grizzly's voice could be heard somewhere in the mix of it all.

Brooke gazed at his brother before nodding and pulling him into his embrace. "I'm coming to get you," he said, then he pulled away and grabbed my arm to drag me to the window, shouting, "Let's go!"

I looked back at Dahodda. "Thank you."

He shook his head. "You shouldn't thank me... I'm so sorry, Brandon."

Before I could ask what he was sorry for, Dahodda raised his gun and yelled in a voice that would fool anyone, "Help! They're getting away!"

I ducked my head and hopped out the window.

Five

Iyana
Jan 3rd | 10:36am

Just don't think about it, I told myself as I stared blankly at my computer screen. My mother was dead, and I never got to say goodbye, I never got to wake her up. The last memory of my mother was her seizing in a hospital bed. I wanted to remember her differently, but there was a searing pain in my chest keeping me from remembering her any other way. That pain wasn't guilt, it wasn't fear for what was coming, and it wasn't resentment for my father or hatred for Brandon.

It was a desire for vengeance.

My father has never been a good man. He's always been a coward. And Brandon was no man at all. I know I will make things right, and I know I will silence the bitter sob banging on my chest to be released. I will replace it with relief when I have killed my father and slaughtered Brandon and everyone he loves.

He took all that I had left. My life was given to BT, my mother was dead, and my father was lost. I was nothing more than a splotch of ink on paper now. A name that no one would remember, no one would care about. Death was much heavier for those with very little, because once you died, you'd be forgotten to the world.

My only hope was to try to make this marriage to Vito work. But I didn't even care about that. Despite the fact that he probably just slept with that detective for information. All I wanted was my revenge and, mercifully, I got it when my phone began to ring.

I stared at the small flat device sitting on my desk. It vibrated, buzzing around until I turned it over. It was Alex. Without hesitation, I picked up.

"Iyana!" she bellowed. "They shot him and he's still not up! My son!" She was weeping furiously into the phone, but my heart didn't break, and my tears had suddenly vanished. I couldn't even try to produce a tear for this woman. I couldn't even try to pity her. But that was because I had a plan, and she was part of it.

"Where are you?" I said plainly.

"I'm at Saint Sessa's Hospital." I could hear her pull the phone away to blow her nose.

"Stay there, I'm on my way." I hung up the phone before she could say anything else and stood to my feet. Gathering my things, I ripped open my office door and set a blaze for the exit.

"Hey, where are you going?" Vito said as he looked up from his phone. He sat on the couch, watching me as I darted across the room. "Hey!" he shouted again.

I whirled and snapped, "Brandon's wife just called. She's at St. Sessa's." I grabbed a pair of boots and stepped into them before quickly ducking into the closet.

"Why are you going, though? What can you even do? I mean, you shouldn't even be out right now."

I stepped out from the closet and slammed it shut. "I'm going to kill her."

"Iyana, wait," Vito called as I went for the front door. I heard him tripping over things as he raced to me, but I was determined to fuel the burning fire within me. I wanted the hatred to burn me, I wanted the hatred to be scalding so that I could feel something other than my heart throbbing.

"Iyana," Vito called as I tried to pull the door open, but he slammed a hand on it, and it closed.

"Don't try to stop me."

"You don't want to do this," he said sternly.

"Yes, I do. Now move." I tried to shove him, but Vito was stronger and sturdier than he looked, and he didn't budge. "You're supposed to love me!" I snapped.

"I do! That's why I can't let you go out there!"

"No! You're supposed to support me if you love me. Not stop me and save him!"

"I'm not saving Brandon, or even his wife, I'm saving *you*!" He paused, heaving an angry sigh. "I'm telling you, Iyana, you don't want to do this. It isn't going to make things better."

"She was my mother!" I screamed. It was so piercing even my own eardrums were rattling. After a moment of silence, Vito reached for me, but I shoved his hands away.

"*No*," I warned. "Don't touch me." The sob I'd been trying to hold in was breaking free.

"Please," Vito whispered. "Let me—"

"*Stop*." I jerked away as he reached for me again. His face began to blur behind the tears, but I could still see the pain in his eyes.

"Let me help you. I know it hurts, but this isn't the way to do things."

"Why? You got your revenge, but I can't get mine?"

"What I did was for the Pack."

"Screw the Pack, Vito! What you did was for yourself and you know it. And you know it felt good to frame Brandon like that. So don't try to act all high and mighty." I sucked for breath between sobs. "You satisfied your own pain, but you're making me fester in mine! How is that fair?"

"Iyana, what I did was for the Pack," he tried again. "To buy us—"

I slapped him.

I hadn't even meant to. I don't even know why I did. My hand moved without me commanding it, reacting to my rage.

I was just angry because he was right. Framing Brandon worked in our favor and gave us the time we needed to put together an attack if we even wanted to. We could do anything because the ball was in our court now and would stay in our court because of the body count. But we would still need to react, to assure our clientele that their investments won't go up in flames. However, no matter how logical, the pain was still there. No matter what the plan was for the future, what I felt right now was all I could focus on.

Vito's touch pulled me from thoughts. He was holding my trembling arms, his grip shockingly light—not firm or painful, like I would have expected. I'd just slapped a mafia boss in his face, and he was looking at me like I was the most precious thing in the world. The only emotion in his eyes was worry. For me.

Weakly, I gave in to him, falling into Vito's chest and weeping loudly. I wanted to hurt someone because I was hurt, but I knew it was wrong, and I didn't really want to do it. But it felt so right. I thought that making Brandon suffer the way I had would make me feel better, however, my mother would still be dead. And when the satisfaction of hurting Brandon the way he'd hurt me finally dissipated, I'd have to face reality, face my feelings, and there would be no one there to hurt or kill or exact my vengeance.

"We can't," my voice came out shakily, "we can't leave her there."

"I know, we'll go to her," Vito promised. "Let me get my things." He pulled away, and I watched him disappear into the bedroom. It suddenly felt cold, like the bitterness that had been swirling within me might return if he wasn't near me again. I squeezed myself in a hug, and closed my eyes, trying to hold on to his warmth.

"Ana? You alright?" Vito's voice danced over my ears, and when I opened my eyes, he was standing right in front of me.

"I'm sorry," I whispered.

He leaned down and kissed my cheek. "Me too. Now, let's go."

We rushed into the hospital, but we didn't need to go far. Alex burst from the red cushioned seats in the waiting area and latched on to me. Vito went to the front desk to sign us in, and I took Alex off to the side, away from the piercing eyes of a man in the waiting room.

Her hands trembled in mine, and she was heaving greatly as she tried to breathe through the tears. I wondered if she'd been crying this whole time, and then there was pity and sadness and embarrassment. She had no idea that no more than thirty minutes ago, I was planning to come here and lure her away to kill her. The thought almost dropped me to my knees, but I knew I couldn't crumble right now, or right here in this hospital.

"Alex," I whispered, "tell me what happened, slowly and quietly."

She nodded and took a shaky breath. "Brandon came home, and there was blood all over his truck, pieces of clothing, and debris. He wanted me to help him clean it, and he said if I didn't, we'd both go to prison." Her story linked everything together, giving us a timeline and clarity on what exactly had happened. We had the pieces from Clemons Murphy, and now with Alex, we had glue.

I cleared my throat, trying not to let my mind wander in her silence. "What did you do?"

She looked around, and then grabbed my hand and pulled me across the room to a corner. "I hit him in the back of the head and knocked him out."

I gasped, but she kept going.

"BJ and I were trying to get away when these men showed up. And… and…" her voice began to tremble, and her tears started again.

"Ok, you don't have to tell me. But what happened after that? How did you get here?"

"I drove in from the outskirts of Manhattan. It's a rural area over there, but it took so long to get here. I went to a different hospital, but they were packed. No one could see BJ, so I came here. The doctors were having trouble keeping him steady and removing the bullet."

"Have you heard anything?"

She shook her head. "They came out twice. Told me they stabilized his breathing, but the path of the bullet…" She fell forward into me and cried onto my shoulder.

The guilt and sorrow I felt was immense, but I swallowed it down as I hugged her and asked, "Who were the men that showed up? What did they look like?"

"I only saw one of them, but he was there with an older man." Alex took a shaky breath. "I'm positive both of them were wearing—"

"Brown fur coats," I whispered. I looked around, and the man who'd been sitting in the waiting room was gone now. "We need to go," I said, rushing to grab her things from the chair.

Alex frowned. "How'd you know what they were wearing? Where are you going?"

"Alex," I grabbed her shoulders, "you are in danger right now. We need to go."

"*No.*" She backed away. "I'm not leaving my son."

"You have no choice!" I snapped in a whisper. "You are in danger, and there's nothing you can do to help BJ. He's in the best and safest hands right now. But you're not."

"I don't care! I'm not going!" Her loud voice attracted attention and caught Vito's eye.

He nodded at the woman at the desk and came over to us.

"Get her out of here," I said to him as he came close.

"Why?"

"Because Gang Grizzly is involved. And the man who was sitting here before is gone now."

"You sure he wasn't waiting on someone?"

"I don't know." I glanced around, noticing a woman approaching us.

"I'm sorry," she said, "but you're going to have to keep it down."

I nodded, eyeing her nametag. *Jill.* I froze. Murphy told Vito that a woman named Jill was going to wire her the money, because she was the one who handled all of Brandon's payments.

She was the one who pulled the plug on my mother.

"I'm sorry," I said, interrupting Vito who was mumbling an apology.

Vito and Jill looked at me, and I stepped closer to her. "Is there any way we can see or get an update on her son?" I motioned to Alex. "She's been here for quite a while."

"Yes, they're working hard. His fragile body took a very bad hit with that bullet. It's a miracle he's even still alive."

"So there's nothing that can be done?" I asked.

"I'm sorry," Jill said in such a chipper tone, I almost punched her. "Right now, the best we can offer her is a private waiting room."

"We'd like that," I told her.

She nodded with a wide smile spread across her rosy, pink lips. "Follow me."

I walked without looking back, following Jill around the corner. She stepped to the side and picked up the clipboard attached to the wall, scribbling something down.

Vito and Alex filed in one behind the other, and when they were out of sight, I said, "Jill?"

She looked up from her clipboard, still wearing a smile as if she hadn't killed someone just two days ago. "I'll let the doctors know what room you guys are in."

"Thanks," I muttered, trying to put a plan together to keep her there longer. "Actually, if you don't mind, can you show me how to work the vending machine? I was here a couple weeks back for a family member and I think I was typing something in wrong."

She laughed lightly and reached to pat my shoulder. "Trust me, it happens all the time."

As her hand slipped down, I caught it in the tightest grip I could.

She gasped. "You're hurting me." Her eyes were the size of baseballs as she looked from her wrist in my hand to my angry eyes. All of a sudden, she looked petrified. The way her brows furrowed, and her mouth sagged. I knew she could feel the rage swirling around me.

I kept my voice calm. "I'm going to kill you if you don't come in this room with me."

"What? I'll call—"

"Scream and I'll break your wrist and tell them who's responsible for the death of Velma Walters."

The panic on her face softened, but the pain was still there. "You look just like her," she said softly.

"Get inside," I snarled, pulling her into the room. I shoved her through the door, and she stumbled over her feet, drawing both Vito's and Alex's attention.

"What's going on?" Vito asked.

I pulled the door closed behind us and lunged at Jill. We fell to the floor, scrambling and twisting. I rolled her over and punched her as hard as I could. She screamed and her jaw made a distinct *cracking* noise beneath my fury.

"Iyana!" Vito yelled.

"Stop it!" Alex screamed.

I didn't listen. I couldn't.

I ignored their protests and the redness and blood on Jill's face. She was kicking beneath me, pulling on my clothes as I punched her repeatedly. I felt Vito pulling on me, but I didn't want to let go.

He yanked me up by my waist, but I grabbed a fistful of Jill's blonde hair and dragged her with me.

"You guys have to be quiet, or someone will hear us!" Vito was shouting.

Alex was behind us crying loudly, and Jill was screeching as I pulled on her hair.

"Iyana, please!" Vito shouted.

"She killed my mother!" I stopped squirming and began to hiccup. "She killed my mother, Vee." He squeezed me tighter, and I let go of Jill's hair. He backed us away immediately, and I sobbed, "She killed her! She pulled the plug on my mother!"

Through the tears, I could see Alex staring wide-eyed at Jill who was sitting on the floor panting and bleeding.

"I'm so sorry," Vito whispered against my neck. "I'm so sorry, Iyana." His pleading apology soothed me, and I sank into him. Without thinking, I twisted in his arms to see him, latching my own arms around him as I cried.

"I need you to be strong, Iyana," Vito whispered as he gently stroked my back. "I need you to be strong. We have to get out of here. We'll take Jill with us, alright? You can ask her whatever you want when we get home, but we need to leave now."

I took a breath, nodding against him. "Ok." My grip loosened as I made my decision. Gently, Vito helped me to my feet. And quickly turned into the gang leader I remembered.

In one swift motion he pulled his gun from his waist. Alex screamed and covered her mouth, but Jill only lifted her head weakly.

"Both of you are coming with us," my husband ordered.

Six

Iyana

Jan 3rd | 12:00pm

"Thanks," I said, taking a glass of water from Vito. He crossed the room and disappeared for a moment. I sipped from the glass, but I wasn't thirsty. I wasn't hungry. I didn't know what to feel after attacking Jill besides embarrassed. I couldn't stop myself from feeling like I'd made the worst mistake ever. We didn't need to take Jill because we already knew she was working for Brandon. But, when I saw her, I got so angry, I just acted irrationally.

How can I lead the Pack if I'm irrational? Maybe the Pack would be better off without me. *Vito is clearly the better leader.* He's always been able to keep his emotions in check, while I flew off the handles.

Vito reappeared in a green tracksuit with a suitcase. He set it down as he stepped into the living room. "Iyana—"

"What's that for?"

He took a breath. "It's for you."

"Why?"

"Because you're fragile right now and I—"

"You think I'm weak? You think I can't handle this?"

"Iyana, please, let me finish."

"No." I stood so quickly water escaped the glass. "You're trying to send me away to counseling or something. But I don't need it! I'm hurt, Vito! It's been hours since I found out that my mother is dead!"

"Which is why I'm sending you away! You can't do anything when you're like this!"

"Like what?!"

"Broken!"

I sank into myself and blinked at him. *Broken? Me?*

There was nothing but the sound of Challa's soft snoring on the living room floor. I could admit to being irrational, but broken sounded so damaged, so irreparable. Had I truly reached that point?

Vito stood there, he was an arm's length away, but he seemed like he was across the sea. Like even if I yelled, he wouldn't hear me. What was wrong with me? It was all too much. My mother, Gio, Junior, Alex and BJ. Jewels and Rion. I wasn't okay, but I wanted to be because Vito was okay and I didn't want to be weak.

"It's not fair," I whispered. "You've got experience in this. I don't. I'm just someone swept up in all this mess, but I'm losing everything."

"I'm going to make things right for you. For us. When you come back, things will be better, they'll be easier."

"Why? Why can't I stay?"

"Because you aren't like me, Iyana. You're not one of us."

I was ready to feel indignant, but he continued talking before I could comment.

"And that's a good thing. You don't want to let this world overtake you. It makes you forget who you are. But I don't want you to change."

"So you're sending me away for your sake."

He shook his head. "For your sake, Ana. Because you wouldn't change, you'd be consumed."

I was silent because he was right. I wanted to kill Alex and I'd tried to beat up Jill. Anger was a consuming flame. Anything could make me tick right now, and it would only cause myself, Vito, and BT more harm than good.

"Do I really have to go? I can't just stay here?"

Vito moved to close the gap between us. He took my glass and set it on the coffee table before pulling me into his chest. I could feel myself wanting to cry, but I'd never be strong if I let myself cry every time I felt the urge.

"I have to protect you, and this is the only way I know how," he said into my hair. He began to sway, rocking us back and forth to a rhythm only he knew. But it was alright because, as I leaned against his chest, I could hear the rhythm of his heart, and I let that guide me with his swaying.

"Do you really think I'll get better?"

"Yes."

"How can you be so sure?"

"Because where you're going is not a training camp or a counseling center. It's a place for you to live a normal life for a little while. Recover, grieve, cry. Do what you need, so that you can heal."

"I really am broken."

His chest lifted, expanding largely before slowly deflating. "You've always been fragile, Ana."

"I know," I whispered. "Because you saw me crying in my sleep."

"I knew then that this day would come. That someday, I'd have to protect you, but it would be from a distance."

"Do you want me to go?"

"Yes."

"Will you miss me?"

"Yes."

"You won't call me, will you? It'll be like I disappeared until I come stumbling back into your life like I did seven months ago."

He didn't speak, but he didn't have to. Going away meant Vito and I wouldn't have any communication. It was safer that way. It was enough he'd know where I was but communicating might allow my location to be found by someone tapping the towers. With a war that went from political to bloodshed in one night, I knew this was the best way. I just didn't want it to be.

I knew I could never clear my head completely here, and I'd always do things out of anger, or hostility. Going away would be like a retreat. I'll go there, and I'll find myself. I'll get stronger, and when I return, Vito and I will tear BT and every gang in New York to the ground.

"Vito," I whispered as I leaned against his chest. "How long will I be gone?"

"One month."

I sucked in a deep breath, trying to hold in my sob. Vito has been gone before, for a week at most, but we've never been apart for an entire month. Not in the seven months that I've known him. Not only that, but we also just got married.

So much could change in this world in one month.

Would Vito be the same when I returned? Would he still love me? What if I'm too different when I get back? What if he's too different? What if our marriage becomes the sham everyone believes it is?

I didn't want that, but I didn't know how to speak up.

"It's not going to be easy," he said calmly. "I'm so used to you being here."

"Vito, when I return, let's go home."

"Yeah," he whispered, squeezing me a little tighter. It was like the realization was settling on us, and neither of us wanted this to be real.

"You find us a place, and when you come back, I'll be ready."

"I love you, Vito."

"I love you too, Iyana."

Seven
Hardy
Jan 4th | 11:15am

I sat on the plane between Alex and Iyana. Iyana took the window seat because she was moping about leaving Vito and only wanted to look out the window. Alex took the aisle seat because she needed to use the bathroom a lot. Vito decided to send Alex and me with Iyana on this grieving trip because I was her guard, but it was safer for Alex this way. Being as far away from Brandon and New York was the best thing for her right now, possibly forever. I didn't care either way, but it was annoying that I was the one left to fight Alex to come with us and mop up a melting Iyana.

Flying coach wasn't my idea either. But if anyone saw one of Vito's planes leaving, they'd know it had something to do with Iyana, since the death of her mother was made public because of Tim's running for mayor. Plus, her leaving right now would make BT look weak. Or worse, someone would tip off Grizzly that the tower was open and available for invading. We had to keep a low profile, and that meant flying like we weren't part of the richest gang in New York State. Nonetheless, Vito said where we're going, we won't need money. Everything will be taken care of for us. Again, I didn't care. I didn't even want to go. But it was better than sulking and forcing Kat to cheer me up.

"Hardy," Alex called as we stood around the carousel waiting for our bags.

"Yeah?"

"I'm going to the bathroom again. Do you mind getting my luggage?"

I sighed and waved her on. Iyana tugged on my sleeve. "I'm going with her."

"Fine," I said flatly.

The two walked off to the bathroom, shoulder to shoulder. They didn't chat with each other or laugh the way women did. But so much had happened in the last day, I shouldn't even expect either of them to smile for the next month while we're here in Los Angeles.

Once the two of them returned, we headed outside where we were greeted by a slew of drivers and families. Some were holding signs, others were looking nervously for their loved ones. I didn't know who we were looking for, but Vito said Iyana would know who to get a ride from, and thankfully she did.

"Henry!" Iyana called, waving a hand frantically at a slender Hispanic man. He waved back, flashing a wide smile, and came over to us.

"Ms. Secretary, it's nice to see you again."

Iyana blushed. "I'm actually Mrs. Ortega now."

Henry's eyes widened, and then his smile did too. "Well, I'll be! Cortez went and finally got you for himself! Many congrats, Mrs. Ortega."

Iyana was smiling now, and it was nice to see since she hadn't smiled all morning.

"Thank you, Henry. We're going to go to the truck if you don't mind. Can you get our things?"

"Of course. Mr. Gerardo had very stern instructions to do everything you say for all parties travelling with you."

"Very well." She nodded, then waved us on. We followed her, both inclining our heads to Henry before climbing into a black truck.

"It's so hot here," Iyana said, fanning herself.

When Alex didn't speak, I said, "Yeah, it's hot. I think it seems hotter though because it was so cold in New York."

"That's true," Iyana agreed absently.

Alex still didn't speak. She flashed us a quick smile before returning her focus to the window. My gaze lingered on her another moment. Alex was broken, and I didn't know if she could be fixed. Vito told me before we left that he was worried about Iyana because she'd lost her mother, but he knew she would recover. He was most worried about Alex because he'd gotten news that Brandon Jr. didn't make it. No one had told

Alex, but there hadn't been a chance to. Now, I was tasked with breaking the news and I dreaded it.

Henry's door opened and caught my attention. I glanced over at him as he climbed inside. "The traffic isn't heavy today, so we'll be there soon."

"Where are we even going?" I asked.

"To Vito's parents' house," Iyana responded.

"His parents? You mean like *Mr.* Gerardo?"

Iyana quirked a brow. "How'd you know about him?"

As if she should know. She's only been here seven months now, and if it wasn't for her and Vito getting married, she wouldn't know a thing about Mr. Gerardo at all. But I decided not to say anything to that extent. Instead, I said, "I heard from Jewels."

That sufficed. It made Iyana turn in her seat and watch out her window. The lonely look she wore on the plane had returned, and I settled into my seat to watch absently as the traffic passed by.

—— BT ——

"Iyana! Welcome home!" A woman who looked young but sounded old greeted and hugged Iyana while a tall man with black and white hair all over stood behind them smiling and nodding. The woman, who I assumed was Vito's mother, was identical to him. It was almost uncomfortable how much they looked alike.

"These are friends of mine." Iyana looked over at me. "Well, he's my guard, but she needs a safe place to stay for a while." She gestured to Alex.

"Of course," Vito's mom said, moving to grab Alex's hands. She looked down at her very pregnant belly and then back up at her. "Are you alright?"

Alex nodded sheepishly. "Thank you for your hospitality."

"Anytime. But I didn't get your name."

"Alexandra," she said.

"Alexandra. May I call you Alex?"

She nodded, and Vito's mother pulled her into her embrace. Then she stepped to me. She was a short woman, honey toasted skin and dark hair like Vito. She took my hand and said, "You've got to protect two very pretty ladies."

"Yeah." I chuckled awkwardly. "I guess so."

"And your name?"

"Hardy," I said.

"You are very handsome, Hardy." She reached up and touched my face. "But you look just as broken as those two women. How will you protect them if you haven't fixed what's wrong with yourself?"

I couldn't come up with a response. I stood there, feeling every hair on my neck raise. Suddenly I became viciously aware that I was still hurt over losing Jewels... Over *killing* Jewels.

"Come on, Dafni," the man behind her finally spoke up, and I snapped my eyes to his. "Cortez said to let them rest their first few days here."

"Alright," she said. "Well, I'm Dafni and this is my husband, Tobias. Please feel free to call us for anything at all. Your rooms are ready; dinner is around seven. If you get hungry before then, just come on down and I'll fix you something."

We all nodded, and Iyana stepped forward to give Dafni another hug before leading us upstairs to our bedrooms.

Eight
Vito
Jan 6th | 10:00am

The world seemed quieter without Iyana. She wasn't a noise maker, rather, she was the 'thing' that filled the room. The joy, the light, the tension or the ease. Everything was based on her, and when she wasn't there with me—where she'd been for so long now—I felt strange. I didn't know just how much I'd gotten used to her. The tower seemed to be rigid and cold without her. I missed her to say the least. I had expected to miss her. I just didn't expect to miss her *this* much.

"Vito," Logan called me.

I turned in my chair.

"She'll be back. She's not dying. And sending her away was *your* idea."

I sighed and extended a hand over the desk to him. "Just give me the paperwork."

"I don't have any."

"Then why are you here?"

"See, you're spacey without her, that's not good."

I dropped my hand. "Are you going to torture me or actually tell me something?"

He smiled devilishly. "Both."

"Logan…"

He laughed as he took a seat across from me. "Come on, boss, you've got Ana fever and it's written all over you. You should go out, do something to forget about her. I could call some girls?"

"She's my wife, Logan."

"I know," he waved a hand, "but she'll be gone for an entire month!"

"Sometimes I wonder why you're still single, and then you always give me a reminder."

He grinned as if this was something to be proud of. Shoving his dark hair from his face he said, "I'm single because I don't want to settle down yet. There are too many beautiful women to pick just one. I don't know how you do it."

I stood from the desk and began closing my books and folders. "When you stop thinking with that little thing between your legs, you'll find other organs to think with."

He leaned back and laughed so hard he turned a bright red, and it made me chuckle. Logan and I had always been like brothers, even closer than I was with Brandon. He was years younger than me, and he always reminded me of that fact. But I'd come to trust Logan; he's been very loyal the entire time he's been here, so I've never had a reason not to trust him or dislike him. He was funny, but not goofy the way Hardy was.

Both of them were like younger brothers to me, and I hoped that when this was all over, when BT finally fell, we'd all get away together with Iyana. But now things had gotten complicated with Tim running for mayor, Gang Grizzly having dead bodies that aren't there's, and Brandon still working for them. If any of us besides Iyana makes it out alive, it'll be a miracle.

"Alright, on a serious note," he said after gathering himself. "You've got that three o'clock meeting with Bridges, he wants to know when he can get a sample of the Malawi."

"I don't do samples. He knows that." I took some folders to my file cabinet.

Bridges was an old client. I started selling to him when I first joined BT and needed some assets in exchange for marijuana. He was good for his word and I found out why everyone called him, 'Bridges'. He made connections and brought people and things together. There wasn't a product or a person Bridges couldn't get to, so he was given that nickname. It was better than calling him 'Connection,' I suppose.

"I know. I told Bridges you don't do samples, but he insists." Logan shrugged. "No one can believe you've got that stuff. I kind of want a sample too, if I'm honest."

"Don't tell me you don't think I have any either?"

"No." I heard him yawning behind me, as if this was boring, which meant he really did think I had acquired Malawi.

When Logan got disinterested, it was because he'd put his full trust in whatever I was saying. He only pestered me when he was nervous about something, or when he thought I wouldn't come through, but I always have for him.

"Good," I said as I turned around.

Logan was eyeing me now as I leaned over and unlocked the bottom drawer of my desk. Taking out a silver tin, I set it on my desk and opened it.

"You're lying," he whispered as he stared at the plant in a tube, and three rolled blunts.

I passed him a blunt. "Try it and tell me what you think. I've got a desk full of these tins."

"Right now?"

"Yeah." I shrugged.

Eagerly, he dug through his pockets and retrieved his lighter. Flipping it open, he lit his blunt and took a deep breath. The smoke rolled out in clouds as he leaned back in his seat. He was quiet for a moment, squinting as he examined the roll. Turning it and looking it over, his dark eyes narrowed even tighter before replacing the blunt between his lips.

"I feel..." He paused, and his face lit up. "Really good." He took another drag and stood to his feet abruptly. I slowly sat back in my chair to watch him. He just stood for a while, inhaling and exhaling. His eyes began to brighten when the product started kicking in. "I'm going to do a handstand, because I can do a handstand," he said slowly.

"Alright." I nodded.

"VITO!" he shouted. "I am going to do a handstand."

Malawi makes a person focused, or sometimes energized. The coffee aroma over the fruity smell, with a lemony taste just on the exhale, Malawi proved itself to be a delicacy. It's not for someone who wants to relax or go to bed. Malawi has a long effect on its users, even some of the most experienced users can stay high for longer than normal. But it's a perfect combination for parties and outdoor events.

I'd gotten the report from my farmer that a few trimmers had used the product. The only reason they weren't fired was because I had no idea if this investment was even going to be worth it. But when my farmer told me the rundown of everything he observed, I decided to buy more land and plant more crops, especially since they take a while to harvest.

The doorbell to my loft rang, and I left Logan in my office, practicing his handstands and eventually his backflips. When I opened the door, Bridges was standing in my doorway. Tall, but lanky with long curls all over his shoulders. The dark brown man always looked sleepy, and I was happy he was interested in the product, not just because of his exhaustion.

"Vito, ya girl at the front desk… She free?"

"Unfortunately, she's not." I shrugged. That was a lie. Kat wasn't with anyone as far as I knew. However, I knew for certain she wasn't interested in anyone either, at least not a guy like Bridges.

He swore under his breath as he came inside, looking around. "So, Vee, you know what I'm here for. That little thang you married, is it for real or can I get in on her?"

I chuckled because I was feeling something between astonished and hot. I didn't like Iyana being referred to as 'someone to get in on.' But I knew what I was getting myself into when I decided to marry her.

"She's not open for business either."

"Dang, so it's serious?"

"Not in the way you're thinking," I said, crossing the room to the alcohol cart.

"Well in what way?"

"In the way that a man called a prince because of his dirty work will only wear a crown for so long. Someday, a dark knight won't be what the people want. They'll want someone who can run the city from somewhere other than his tower."

He was silent for a moment as I poured alcohol over ice in two cups for us. I didn't necessarily want to drink, if I was honest. But I needed Bridges, and he never drank alone.

"Oh, you mean you need her father. Tim Walters, who's running for mayor."

"Exactly." I turned and extended a glass to him.

Slowly, he approached with a frown. "So, what am I expecting?"

"I've got someone doing the political stuff for me, you don't have to expect anything."

"I mean, product-wise. I came for a sample."

"You know I don't do samples."

The room became stiff and quiet. Bridges slurped down the rest of his drink and dropped the glass on the floor. It shattered, sending ice and shards of glass everywhere. I didn't flinch or blink. I simply lifted my glass and took another sip from it.

"You know how I do business, Vito." He shrugged one shoulder. "We always play by my rules."

"Not anymore," I said, keeping my eyes straight ahead. He stepped into my line of vision, forcing me to look at him, to acknowledge him.

"You think because you've got a girl now business is going to be different? Nah, Prince. See ... you forgot what these streets really about."

"No, Bridges, you've just forgotten that we're not on the same level anymore. Princes *cross* bridges."

He chuckled. "Yeah, well they can't cross a bridge that doesn't exist."

"Of course not." I set my drink down and stepped closer to him. "We make our own."

Pushing by him, I walked slowly to the door and opened it. "I've got limited supply and a number of investors. I'll make do." I held the door open, eyeing him as he came closer. If he walked out, I'd lose my connection to a lot of clients, but if he stayed, I was going to make bank without taking another meeting today.

He came and stood before me, glaring down at me. Bridges liked having his way, and he didn't care about cutting people off because he had enough friends to replace the ones he lost. While I was the Prince, there was still a tradeoff. Not everyone likes princes ... like people who always get their way. Which is why I've always valued my clients.

Bridges leaned forward and pushed the door closed. A wave of relief washed over me as he folded his arms. He wasn't staying because I took a stand, he stayed because he'd probably already promised some people goods from me, which was a good thing. I could charge what I wanted, and demand payment up front if I wanted. I was now in a good position, one that would allow me to have the upper hand over Bridges for a while. The Malawi was rare, it'd be a while before my fields were replicated.

"Alright, little Prince, no samples."

"Good, I can—" my phone began to ring, cutting me off. I pulled it out and stared at the number. "I've gotta take this."

"You're wasting my time."

I headed for my office and opened the door. "Then stay entertained."

Logan stepped out, his eyes as red as a stick of dynamite. Raising his hands, he raced forward and did a front handspring into a backflip. I didn't know if I should be amazed or grateful that he was showing off to Bridges. He looked amused standing there watching Logan try to do another handstand. I stepped into my office and closed the door. I'd missed the call, but I quickly redialed and waited for an answer.

"Hello?"

"Hildago," I said, walking around my desk. "What's going on?"

"Well, boss, there's been a fire."

"What do you mean?" I froze just before sitting, blinking slowly, and trying not to overreact. I'd just convinced Bridges to agree to no sample, nothing could go wrong. I'd just gotten leverage on him.

I heard Hildago, my farmer, on the other end moving around. There was a dinging noise, then a thump. "I'm just getting in the car now. I'm going to the farm to assess the damage. But It's not good, Vee, the fire department was called."

I slumped into my chair, resting an elbow on the desk. I felt tense and numb at the same time, like in a moment I would explode because something's been festering somewhere I couldn't feel it.

"I'm sorry, boss. I'll give you a call when I know more."

"Alright."

I hung up the phone and put it on the desk. I wanted to throw everything off of it. I wanted to scream and run, because things hadn't been this bad in years, but now I was facing something I was not prepared for. I'd already made deals with others at my wedding for this product. I couldn't turn up emptyhanded. Some of those people even paid me in advance, I'd have to show something for our products.

Pulling open my drawer, I shakily grabbed my bottle of aspirin, but as I fumbled with the top, I shattered in anger and hurled it across the room. I swore loudly before dropping back to my seat. Hopefully, Bridges didn't hear me, but it didn't matter. I needed him out of my place so I could think of a way to fix this.

The only way to do that was to run away with my tail tucked or import a large number of crops from a different dealer. It was risky because half the plants could die on the trip if not handled carefully or imported at the wrong stage in their life. But in my fields, I'd worked that out.

Getting an import from someone I didn't know was too risky this late. Not only that, but for a plant this rare, it'd cost a small fortune, like the amount it cost to rebuild the basement and ground floor of BT as luxuriously as I did. And if word got out that I was making plans with another farmer, no one would believe I'd ever had the product in the first place.

I took a breath, running a hand over my hair before I made my way to the door. *God, if You're listening right now, I need a way out of this.*

Opening the door, I found Logan and Bridges sharing the rest of Logan's very small blunt. I could've killed him for letting Bridges sample the product. Now that he knew how good it was, he wasn't going to let it go.

"Vee, you were holding out! This is it." Bridges was standing up straight, bouncing on my couch.

"I'm glad you're pleased," I mumbled.

"Don't be sour because I got to sample the product! I told you we always do things my way. But don't worry, I'll pay you whatever you want for a boatload of whatever this is."

An idea bloomed in my head, and it made the boiling rage lower to a simmer. "I want half up front in five days," I said.

It wasn't fair that I was making a deal with him being stoned, however, business is business, and I needed this money. If I could get enough people to sample the product and agree to a contract once they've come down from cloud nine, then I'll be able to enforce whatever price I want on them because they wouldn't remember.

If this works, then I can pay to have some new products imported. Besides, I'm sure the entire field wasn't burned. I can have some people on back-order until the new shipment arrives.

I smiled to myself as I extended a hand to Bridges. He shook it quickly.

"Aye, man, you'll get your money. Just let me finish this and then I'll be out of your way," Bridges said with a goofy smile.

I waved him off as I said slyly, "Take your time."

Princes build their own bridges.

Nine
Alex
Jan 9th | 3:36pm

"Alex," Dafni called behind me.

"Yes?"

"What are you doing right now?"

I looked down at the chopped fruit on the counter and set my knife down.

"Nothing, just making a snack."

"Well," she came to the counter and handed me a slip of paper, "I want you and the others to go grab some groceries for dinner tonight. You guys have been here for three days and have literally done nothing but mope."

"I appreciate your kindness but—"

"No buts. I'm busy right now so I can't do it. Take Iyana and Hardy and get to the store, pronto." She patted my shoulder and left the room without another word. I sighed slowly and folded the paper, slipping it into my pocket before I headed upstairs to grab the others.

It was a slow climb to the top of the stairs. Every time I climbed one, it reminded me of the day BJ was shot. How I raced up the stairs to pack his clothes. I missed him dearly. I wanted to see him again. There hadn't been word on his progress since I left the hospital, but I didn't know if I wanted to know what happened. Because if he woke up and I wasn't there, it would break my heart. But if he didn't wake up at all, I would be shattered. Crushed, even.

"Alex?" Hardy's voice rang out, drawing me from my thoughts. He was walking down the stairs, extending a sugar brown hand to me.

"You were spaced out, just standing there."

"Oh." I took a breath and then his hand. I stared at mine in his, it was small and that surprised me. My hands were small in Brandon's too, but he was a man. Hardy was young and he looked like it. A goofy smile, a happy demeanor. Such youthful energy, youthful confidence and maturity. He was a man in many ways, just not in the ways anyone would think. Just from spending time with him the last few days, I'd found that Hardy was extremely intelligent, and he was also kind. But just like me and Iyana, he was broken.

It kind of hurts to look at him, knowing there was something tormenting him at such a young age. This life wasn't one for someone like him, and it showed. But what could I say? I barely knew what life I was even talking about, and Hardy and I weren't too far away in age.

I was twenty-seven, and he was twenty. I was still young and didn't need to experience this kind of heartbreak either. Well, no one should experience this. It just seemed more appropriate for *me* to suffer. I'd been an idiot for letting Brandon rule my life, it was only right that I'd be punished somehow.

"You're spacing again," Hardy said, tugging on my hand.

"Sorry, I've got a lot on my mind."

"I do too." He shrugged.

I studied his eyes for a moment, searching for what could possibly be on his mind, and then I realized he was searching me as well. His dark eyes looked intensely at me—almost *through* me.

I suddenly dropped my gaze to the floor.

"I-I… Dafni said we have to go shopping."

"Shopping?"

"Groceries. For tonight."

He helped me up the rest of the stairs and said, "Well, it'll be just me and you, then. Iyana is asleep right now."

"I see."

"Well," he shrugged, "let's hurry up and get this done."

"I just need to grab my jacket," I said before slipping into my room to grab it.

Hardy followed me to the room and stood in the doorway to wait for me. Iyana took the first bedroom, I took the second, and Hardy took one of the bedrooms further down the hall without a connecting bathroom to give Iyana and I space.

As I grabbed my jacket, there was a loud chirping noise that cried out from my window. I moved to investigate, realizing it was actually a child, two to be exact. There was a little boy holding the hand of his little sister, chirping at a bird in a tree. The bird continued looking in the opposite direction, completely unfazed by the boy and his sister. The two children were smiling and laughing, and I felt my walls coming down. I felt weakness settling in, and tears pricking my eyes. Shakily, I raised a hand and placed it on the window.

"He didn't make it, did he?"

Hardy was silent behind me, and my breathing became labored.

"He didn't make it... did he?" I asked again.

"Alex, I'm—"

"He didn't make it!" I whirled around to find Hardy standing right in front of me.

I don't know when he moved or why, but I was glad he did. Because I collapsed into him, wailing loudly and tugging on his shirt.

"My son," I hiccuped, "he's gone! Brandon Jr. is gone!"

"I'm so sorry, Alex," Hardy whispered as he rubbed my back. I could feel his hand circling against me, I could feel his chest rising and falling slowly as I cried against him. I could feel myself gripping his shirt even tighter. I could feel everything, yet it felt like none of it was real. Like, somehow, the bad dream would end, and I'd wake up beside Brandon on the day of our honeymoon. I wanted the pain to stop, the aching to be washed away. I wanted something, anything, to take away the anguish, but the throbbing in my chest was unbearable.

"*Please*," I cried, "tell me it's not true!"

He didn't speak, which made me angry. It made me furious … and sad. Because it was true, my son was dead. But it was also true that Hardy had known. *Everyone* knew my son was dead, but no one had told me.

I shoved him away with all I had, sending him stumbling backwards into my dresser.

"You knew! And you didn't tell me! All of you are liars!" I heaved a thick breath and began to choke on it. Hunching over, I gasped for air, trying not to let the world crush me.

"Alex, please—" Hardy was reaching for me, and I found my strength. Slapping his hand away fiercely, I rammed myself into him. We crashed into the dresser, and the lamp and other whatnots fell off it. But he was there, Hardy was still there, holding me tightly against him, giving me a false sense of security, but that was better than nothing. In Hardy's embrace, trembling against him, I cried hard. We sank to the floor, where I cried even harder and louder than before. I wanted this pain to end, but it wouldn't… it just wouldn't.

When I woke, Hardy was gone, and I was lying in my bed. When I rolled over, I found a note on my nightstand from Hardy.

Went to the store alone, thought you could use the rest. But I picked you up some flowers. Hope you feel better.

I looked over at the arrangement of flowers in a vase on the desk and felt tears swelling again. Brandon Jr. was actually gone, and Brandon Sr. was out there somewhere too. I had nothing now but the clothes on my back and the baby in my belly. I set the note back on the nightstand before rolling out of bed.

Moving to the flowers, I stared at them. It was so permanent when someone died. That was just it. However, the death of a child was more permanent than any other death because that was the end of their potential. They were taken before they could become something. They were killed or died before they even had a chance at saving the world. And all you were left with was what ifs, wondering what that child would have become.

There was no joy in death; only memories that got harder to remember every year that ticked by. That's why the pain lingered, because you start to forget the things you don't want to in an effort to move on.

I stared at the flowers a little longer. They were beautiful yet they were so ugly. Just a reminder that I was the only one who didn't know the truth. Turning away, I marched out of the room and went next door to Iyana's room. I walked in without knocking, catching Challa's attention in the corner. He looked at me, ears perked and blinking sleepy eyes.

I remember when Henry picked him up from the airport for us. Challa wasn't allowed to ride on the plane with us, he rode underneath in a deep sleep. When he woke up, Henry was notified and retrieved Iyana's pet.

I moved past the watchful eyes of Challa and leaned over the bed to shake Iyana.

"Iyana," I called.

She groaned as she rolled over, blinking slowly. "What, Alex?"

"Why did my son die?"

"What?"

"Who were the men that came and killed my son? Why did they come and kill him?"

She was trying to sit up, lazily waving a hand. "Hold on, Alex. I'm just waking—"

"I don't care! My son is dead! His father is somewhere out there and you're sleeping!"

"Alex, calm down."

"No! Not until someone starts telling me the truth!"

"Alex!" she barked. "I told you I'd tell you everything, didn't I?"

I nodded.

"Close the door," she said as she sat up.

I raced over and closed it as quickly and quietly as I could before taking a seat at her desk. Challa lazily crossed the room and hopped onto the bed. He turned a circle beside her before focusing his attention on me as he lay down.

"The name of the people who," she paused, "took your son from you, is Gang Grizzly. I don't know why they were after Brandon or what's going on between them because they're a different gang from us."

"A gang," I said, mulling it over. "Brandon was part of a gang?"

She nodded. "You didn't believe me when I first told you."

"It's not every day that you find out your husband is part of a gang. That's an accusation that's just—"

"If you keep thinking that everything I'm telling you is just an accusation, they'll never leave you alone because you'll keep walking into their traps. You'll always be fooled by the men in these gangs. By your own husband."

I stiffened in the chair. I didn't want to believe the reason behind Brandon's lies all these years was because he was in a gang. But who else would come into your house, try to rape you and kill your son if they weren't gang affiliated or racially motivated?

"You're going to need to be a lot stronger if you want the truth. You're going to have to stop grieving your son. You're going to need to be callous."

"Like you? Because you were so callous and strong when you saw the woman who killed your mother? You got to get some kind of revenge. But I didn't. So excuse me for wanting to grieve my son!"

"He wasn't your son. He had a mother who's dead now because of your husband."

"Don't you *dare* speak about Brandon Jr. that way," I hissed. "Or his father. He is not to blame for that wench's death!"

"Are you seriously protecting this man? He got a boy killed!" she yelled. "What part of that don't you get? Those men came to your house after *Brandon*!"

"He was protecting us!"

"He was protecting *himself*!" she snapped quickly. "Having somewhere to hide when things go wrong is all part of the plan. Why do you think we're here?"

The room began to blur, and I dropped my head. Grabbing my belly, I tried to hold in the aching sob. Even though I was planning to run away from Brandon, somewhere in my heart, I always hoped that the distance would finally bring us together. That Brandon wouldn't really be caught and imprisoned, just that he'd figure a way out of his mess that wouldn't involve BJ and me. But I never thought it would come to this. I never thought I'd be sonless and empty inside.

"We're here," Iyana started again, "because this place is safe. It's protection from all of New York. When Tobias came here, he vanished without a trace so that the Pack and other gangs could never find him."

"Tobias?" I looked up, wiping at my tears, "He's part of the gang too?"

"Used to be. He got out when someone almost killed Dafni and Vito stepped up. They've hardly seen or heard from each other for the past six years—"

A loud crash outside the door cut Iyana off and made me jump. We exchanged looks, but before either of us could move, Challa was off the bed and sniffing along the floor at the door.

Iyana moved first, climbing out the bed and walking slowly to the door. I followed, and when the door opened, Dafni was standing there. A tray of food was on the floor, dishes broken and liquid running down the hall.

I heard Hardy call, "Iyana? What's going on?" His footsteps thumped against the wooden floor as he approached. "What happened?"

"Tobias, is part of a gang?" Dafni asked weakly.

Iyana's eyes widened, and she looked like something terribly wrong had just happened.

Ten

Vito

Jan 10th | 11:00am

"Logan, get up," I said, snatching the blankets off him. He was staying in the guest bedroom of my loft, despite my wishes for him to stay elsewhere. But he's been tense ever since we dumped those bodies, so he's sticking closer to me than usual.

"What time is it?" he groaned as he rolled over to look at his watch.

"It's eleven in the morning, you missed my morning calls."

"Did Hildago call back?" I looked away from his sharp eyes, and he shifted in the bed. "What are we going to do?"

"We're going to make money," I said.

"Vee," he sat up, swinging his legs to the edge of the bed, "you can't be serious?"

"What choice do I have? It was an accident that's costing me millions to fix and cover up."

"Cover up? What happened?"

I rubbed my face, taking a deep breath. I was preparing myself to say it out loud since I hadn't mentioned a word about the follow up phone call from Hildago in the last few days.

"One of the trimmers didn't smoke weed, he smoked cigarettes."

"No..." Logan's eyes widened, and I nodded.

"He tossed it down and it started a forest fire. We owe a lot of money right now to the government since it burned through my field and further." I sighed. "The fire burned some protected land."

"The costs, they'll keep climbing, won't they?"

"Yeah."

Logan silently thought it over. His leg bounced as he stared at the floor, trying to come up with a solution, but there wasn't one. No matter what, we would owe that money to the government. Even if we kept it quiet, our billings would be split. We'd have to cut back on everything, probably even sell the tower. *But then everyone would know that BT is...* my thoughts stopped.

BT is falling.

"What?" Logan said. "Did you think of something?"

"What? No."

Logan wasn't a Believer like Iyana and me, he'd never understand what was actually going on. I didn't even fully understand it, but I knew that this was the beginning of the end. Which meant I needed to prepare for the fall of BT, needed to prepare for having a life again. I almost felt relieved, but what would Logan think?

BT has been his life for a while… who would he become? He joined the gang six years ago when he was only sixteen. And he spent a few of those on the streets. This was the most structure Logan has ever had, losing this might change him or break him. I looked over at him as he sat on the bed.

He'll be fine, I convinced myself.

Clearing my throat, I said, "We need to get as much money as possible and the only way to do that is by getting paid up front. I have a friend I can start sending money to for what we'll owe the government instead of imprisonment. They're my fields, but Hildago's name is still on the deeds. I gotta help him."

"You never signed the deeds? So, technically, this isn't our problem."

"Yeah, but Hildago's been my guy for too long. I won't let him get imprisoned for me."

"So, we demand that everyone who wants to buy product, which we don't have, pay us up front for *Hildago*?"

"For us too, but yes. They don't know that we don't have any product. But it'll buy us some time to get things figured out."

He sighed with a nod. "Alright, so what's our security price?"

"Since this is rare, we'll go high."

"How high?"

"Fifteen hundred for an ounce."

"Vito—"

"No one can buy anything less than ten ounces."

"Vito, that's fifteen thousand dollars up front."

I shook my head. "No, it's a quarter of whatever amount they want to buy up front."

He gasped. "So if I wanted to buy a hundred ounces," he paused and chewed his lip as he tried to do some mental math.

"It'd be one hundred and fifty thousand dollars. And a quarter of that would be—"

"Thirty-seven thousand, five hundred dollars, right?"

I smiled. "Right."

"And if just ten people buy it…" he trailed off.

"We'll be almost to a quarter of a million dollars with just ten buyers. We've got states full of people wanting to buy, *willing* to buy it with no sample. Convincing them to pay up front is the only thing we have to worry about."

"Then we shouldn't go into meetings together. We should take them separately so that we won't look desperate."

"Yeah, you'll go for Iyana. They'll be expecting her. Just tell them she sent you in her stead because of funeral arrangements."

"You sure?" He squinted.

"Yes." It was all going to be one great lie that would ruin BT forever. We'd never be able to pay these people back, not with the mounting debt and the government bills. But I could get us all out of here if I can take enough meetings and convince enough people to pay up front.

"The Prince himself is gracing my home, how can I help you?" Bridges laughed maniacally as we walked through his apartment. White walls and golden floors, his place looked more like a palace than the dark tower I lived in.

"I came to get my money," I said plainly.

He stopped his casual stroll and turned to face me. A high brow and a crooked smile took over his face. He was confused, which was good. I was banking on his foggy memory.

"I'm sorry, what did you come here for?"

"You heard me," I said, putting my hands in my pockets. "My money. I'm here for it."

"What money?"

"You promised me half a million dollars up front five days ago."

"What? No, I didn't."

"Yes, you did," I said as I shrugged. "You sampled even when I told you I wasn't sampling."

"Come on, what is this—some kind of fee? I bring you a lot of business. Five hundred up front is a lot of money."

"You should be careful not to mix business with pleasure."

He stared, and his eyes darkened. He was finally remembering getting high with Logan, but I knew he couldn't remember making a deal, and not because he never made one, it was because the Malawi could also impair your memory and other cognitive functions. It's known to cause hallucinations for those extremely paranoid and could also cause anxiety. It was funny, everyone thought weed calmed you down but, depending on the strain, it could actually wreck your mind.

"You're seriously making me keep my word? I was high!" he shouted.

"And now you're not."

"Who else are you pulling this crap on? You know this'll ruin your reputation, right? No one's going to sample or want to buy from you."

"I beg to differ." I slipped my hands behind my back and walked by him. Slowly exploring his house, I said over my shoulder, "No one's going to want to buy from you if you're going to be making deals and not fulfilling them."

"They would understand that you're trash, Vito! Making me pay something I have no recollection of! What sense does that make?"

"But you're already collecting money from bidders, aren't you?" I finally turned to face him. He was glowering, ready to pounce at a moment's notice. "See ... You're the bottom of the barrel. I'm the one in charge of *filling* the barrels. No one's going to think the one who's giving out barrels is the scum of the earth like the trash that gets caught in his barrels."

"A man from Buffalo once said you were the nicest man in the world. He said you were loyal, the best man to do business with, and he couldn't believe you were the head of a gang. But he warned me. He said you were nice until you weren't. I thought that was obvious, everyone's like that. But now I know what he means."

"I'm glad you understand, which means you should pay me, because that man is dead. I assume you know why now."

Bridges flinched as I took a step toward him. It'd been a long time since I had to be this way. Callous, cunning, angry, afraid. I had to do this. If I could convince him, then I knew all I needed to do was tweak the conversation to convince others to pay up front too. A little intimidation and reminding everyone where they stood with me allowed me to always sit on a pedestal. But it's crumbling now, and I'd need to do what I could to collect what I could before I lost everything.

"Either give me the money, or I'm going to kill you and have my men raid this house before the stench can rise off your corpse."

"You think you can scare me? I'm not afraid of you, Vito. I'll kill you before you can even—"

I ripped my gun from my waist and fired three shots.

Bridges fell to the floor, gasping and heaving. It wasn't supposed to go like this. Bridges wasn't supposed to die. I was only supposed to convince him to tell the others I'd like an upfront payment.

I sighed as I squatted over him. His eyes were wide as he panted. Blood oozed from his lips, and he began to tremble as the air stopped flowing to his lungs. He was drowning right before me, and all I could do was watch. If Bridges was gone, which he was, I wouldn't have the bridge between some of my investors. *This could be good,* I thought. *I can schedule a sampling party. And everyone pays while they're high.* It wouldn't be my first sampling party, and probably not my last, at least for a little while.

Bridges began wheezing for air, the noise pulled me from my thoughts. The next moment, he was gone, and I didn't feel a thing. I hated killing people, but it was part of the job. *It is the job.* Anyone who didn't agree with me at this level, was a contender for death. I'd killed too many to feel anything, but that didn't stop the guilt when the moment passed.

Tonight would be one of the hardest nights of my life because I'd have to face reality alone. Iyana won't be there to keep me from hardening. She won't be there to make me hold onto Christ or my humanity. But I shouldn't force her to be my anchor. I shouldn't impose my problem with following Christ onto Iyana.

It was like I was making my lost salvation her problem, and I didn't want that. But I didn't want to walk away from BT with nothing. I know I'm supposed to value my salvation, value Christ above all else, but I can't right now... can I?

I hated this turmoil; it was always here when I took a life. It was always blaring at me because I didn't feel anything when I killed. I didn't even feel bad, just guilty. Guilty because I wish I hadn't acted so quickly, but not remorseful because it needed to be done.

Who am I without Iyana? I wondered as I stood to my feet. I didn't want to face the fact that I was different because of her. This monster existed because of BT, but when the Pack was gone, who would I become? Could I really let go of Vito Gerardo?

I closed my eyes tightly and took a deep breath.

I have to be Vito until BT falls.

Lifting the phone to my ear, I called Logan.

"Hello? Boss, I'm in the middle of something, this is a bad time."

"When you're through, come to Bridges's place. Bring a team. We need to get rid of the body and search this place top to bottom for money, safes, and whatnots."

I hung up the phone and strolled through the house to take a seat by the pool.

Eleven
Brandon
Jan 10th | 12:23pm

"We've been here for days, Brooke, where is Dahodda?"

"How am I supposed to know? All I do know is that I can't leave without him."

"My wife and my son are out there!"

"And so is my brother! He stayed behind because of you, Brandon!"

"I know." I sighed. "I know. I just…"

"Give him the rest of the day, then tomorrow we'll leave."

I nodded. He crossed the room to the fridge and called, "I haven't gotten word from Jewels yet."

We drove all around after our escape to make sure no one was tailing us, staying on the road until the gas ran out. Then we rolled the car into a ditch and walked the eight miles to my warehouse where, thankfully, Brooke and Dahodda had stashed supplies. They'd been preparing to run away for the last three months, saving every penny I'd given them to make an escape.

Dahodda had become too reckless, Brooke recalled to me on our walk to the warehouse. He told me his little brother was enjoying this life of crime, and he didn't want him to grow up like this. So, he planned to get them out. When they were told to prove themselves to officially join the gang, they decided to bump up their runaway plans. But I threw a wrench in their plans and Brooke didn't want to leave me for dead. Thankfully.

"Do you think she's avoiding you, or laying low or something?"

"I think she's probably tied up with Vito and the Pack. She's under twenty-four-hour surveillance, and with the death of Gio, his son, and possibly Emilia on his wedding day, he undoubtedly tightened security."

Brooke offered me a water bottle with a timid look. "Why'd you do it?"

I knew this was coming, it was bound to. Brooke had decided to save me, but I knew he was hesitant because of the car accident. He'd been shy about asking, even though we spent hours together in the car, walking for hours, and have been in this warehouse for days.

I opened my water bottle and took a sip. Brooke leaned against the desk, staring down at his feet. I wanted to tell him the truth, tell him that I was angry and wanted to take something from Vito for screwing me over. But how stupid was I? I'd betrayed Vito and expected him to wallow in that betrayal. I expected him to crumble, but he didn't. He was absolutely fine without me, and it wasn't fair. All my life I'd fought for everything, and every loss was detrimental. Yet, I betrayed him, and he acted like it meant nothing.

"What if we tried to rescue your brother?"

He blinked at me, and I continued, "We can get in the same way we broke out. Get into that window and sneak around until we find him."

"That's too dangerous," Brooke told me. "If they find us, they'll kill us and it'll all be for nothing!"

"He's your little brother. We have to—"

"Don't you think I know that?!" he snapped. "I'm scared, man." He dropped his head and stared at the floor as a new pain birthed within me.

"Scared of what?"

"Scared that I'll find his body, or worse…"

"What's worse than your brother's death?"

He looked up from his shoes and his face had shriveled into a melancholic distortion. His expression was somewhere between fear and brokenhearted, like he'd already known the answer to my question before I'd even asked, and that's why he was hurting so badly.

"Walking into Grizzly's cove and finding that my brother is perfectly fine. Finding my brother alive and well… as a Grizzly cub."

There was a pressing silence as I stood there clutching my water.

"You knew, didn't you? That your brother wouldn't come along."

I thought of Hodda's words when he told his brother he hadn't done something right. He'd made a mistake, and now there was a pit of fear widening in my stomach again. What if Alex and BJ didn't make it? What if Dahodda had actually hurt them to join Gang Grizzly?

Brooke sniffled, and I shoved the thoughts away. *No, Dahodda's buying us time right now to get away,* I realized. We needed to leave, and I needed to visit my home and then IncogVito to see if those bodies had been delivered.

"I was hoping he would," Brooke said, "but he loves the gang life, he loves the money, the drugs, every part of this dark world. He loves it like this is where he's belonged all along."

"Brooke, we need to leave."

He shook his head, but I tossed my bottle to the floor and grabbed his shoulders before he spoke. "Your brother is giving us time to go. We need to leave before he brings Grizzly right to us! You know Grizzly's going to come looking for us—for *me*. We have to go."

"I can't leave him," he said quietly.

"If you really believed that, why are you here and he's there with Grizzly?"

Clenching his jaw, he squeezed his eyes shut.

"I know it's not easy to hear, but you have to let your brother go. He's where he wants to be. You have to be where you want to be." I was saying whatever I needed to get his feet moving. I didn't think traveling alone was the best move right now, but I was willing to leave him if he didn't snap out of his daze. We'd all lost someone, or was away from the people we loved most, but we had to keep moving.

"There's a car I parked just before all this broke out. It's about a three mile walk towards the south of here. We can make it there and go somewhere safe."

"I need to go by my house," I said. "There may be something there that can help us."

"Like what?"

"Like my phone. I'll be able to call Alex and call Jewels on a number she recognizes. There's food, supplies, money. I've got a bag full of cash and a passport. We can swing by an old friend of mine and get you a passport too."

"What are you going to do if you catch up with Jewels and with Alex?"

I hadn't thought about that. The day had finally come; I'd have to choose between my wife and the mother of my son. I wanted Jewels in every way, but I didn't know if I should leave Alex. She doesn't know anything about gang life, and she would never understand being on the run.

"Alex needs stability," I said as I brushed by him to grab my jacket. "She'll never have that with me."

"So we go to your place and then to the tower to get Jewels?"

"Yeah," I said.

After finding the car, we drove for an hour before reaching my house. The front door was wide open, my truck was still parked on one side of the driveway, and there were tire marks I noticed as I got out the car.

Kneeling, I ran a hand over the freezing ground. It looked like someone was in a hurry when they were driving, but that wasn't the only thing in my driveway. There was blood on the ground beside the tire marks too. I closed my eyes, taking a deep breath. Then I stood and rushed inside, stopping when I spotted my phone on the concrete.

It hadn't snowed in the last few days, but my phone was still frozen solid. Slipping it into my pocket, I noticed the water hose was on the ground too. The back gate was open, and it brought back memories of Alex. She'd gone back to get the hose to rinse off my truck, and then everything went black. I shook my head. I couldn't believe it.

I raced up the stairs to my house, but I didn't make it far when I saw blood on the floor. I stood there and glanced around the open area. There was a trail of blood leading all the way back to the tire marks.

Clutching my head, I fought off the panic that threatened to send me spiraling into madness. That could've been anyone's blood. It didn't have to belong to my family. As I walked through the house, the eerie silence and the blistering wind allowed a feeling of unease to grasp me in its clutches. The entire house was cold. I could see my breath puffing into the air as I exhaled. That meant the heat hadn't been on in days which meant my family hadn't been here in a while.

A horribly foul odor smothered my nose as I rounded the corner to the kitchen. There was a cracked boiled egg, a pot, and frozen liquid on the floor.

"There was a struggle," I whispered.

I broke into a sprint, racing through the house, looking everything over in a panic. The back window was broken, possibly an entry point for the gang, and upstairs was a catastrophe.

Clothes sprawled all over, shoes, medicine in BJ's room and in mine. Standing in the entrance to my bedroom, I took a deep breath and stepped inside. This didn't look like a struggle, it looked like Alex was spring cleaning.

I froze when I made it to the closet. The bag was gone. My bag of money, passports, IDs, it was all gone. Which meant I had nothing, and no idea what to do. I had no money to run away, and no ID. No money to pay for a new ID either.

I dropped to my knees and began to weep. Now I had no idea of anything. I didn't know if I could run away, and I didn't know who'd taken my bag. If it was Alex or Grizzly. Neither were good choices because Grizzly would've kept the money, and Alex could be hiding somewhere with my and Jewels's passports.

She'll know...

Jolting to my feet, I raced down the stairs and back outside to my truck. There was a spare key inside I used to get the truck started.

"What are you doing?" Brooke asked as he knocked on my window.

I rolled it down. "I'm charging my phone. I need to make a call."

"To who?"

"You remember Jill?"

He nodded.

"She's got some money for me, and I need to find my wife and son. There's blood in there and I don't know whose it is."

"Blood? But why?"

"I don't know. But I'll get whatever money I have left from Jill and have her check the hospital database for Alex and BJ."

"Wait a second, I thought you had money?"

"It's gone. Everything is gone. Everything is wrong!" I pounded the steering wheel before gripping it tightly and dropping my head. Something was wrong. Something terribly wrong had happened, and I couldn't even remember it.

Alex could be dead…

The sound of screeching tires bellowed into the quiet cold, and Brooke and I stared at each other.

"Let's go!" he shouted. "They're here!"

Snatching my phone and charger, I jumped out the truck and raced behind him into the other car. Before my door could close, Brooke was backing out the driveway, twisting the wheel, and speeding recklessly down the street.

Twelve

Vito

Jan 12th | 9:02am

"*Jill...*" Logan groaned.

I shoved open the door and they both screamed.

"Vito! Privacy! *Please!*" Logan snapped.

"Get up," I seethed, snatching the blankets off them both.

Jill tried to cover herself with the sheet, but I was all out of patience. Last night, Jill's phone rang (which Leo and Kat had been using to gather information), and Kat told me it was Brandon. They didn't pick up, and he didn't leave a message either. So, I decided to screw Brandon the way he tried to screw me and hopefully get more than vengeance out of it.

I sent Logan in this morning to get information out of Jill since I knew she wouldn't talk to me. Somehow, he ended up in bed with her and I doubt he's gained any valuable information.

"Get your clothes on," I said to Logan who was holding a pillow over his lower body.

"You couldn't wait until I finished?" he whispered hotly as he walked by.

When he was gone, I turned my attention to Jill who was sitting on the bed. Dusty blonde hair against milky white skin. She was staring at me like a deer in headlights. Wide eyes, and panicky breathing.

"Why do you think you can come here and enjoy yourself after you killed my wife's mother? How many other lives have you taken?"

"I don't have to answer you," she said forcefully.

I lunged across the bed, and she screamed and backed into the headboard. I grabbed her by the wrist, and she clutched the bedsheet against her naked body, trying to fight my grip. I was angry and I didn't have time for her nonsense. I dragged her across the bed while she screamed and kicked. The sheet fell off as I snatched her to the edge of the bed.

"Let me go!" she screamed.

I shoved her into the blankets to make her stop squirming. Before she could recover, I wrapped my hand in her hair and yanked her up to my face. Tears and sweat made her hair stick to her face as she panted heavily.

"You're a *whore*," I snapped.

She didn't respond. Her fearful eyes pleaded with me to stop, but I couldn't. I'd come this far, and using Brandon was the best way to keep Grizzly at bay. It'd buy us time before Grizzly found out the bodies were placed there if I can somehow turn Brandon against him. All I had was his wife, Jewels, and Jill. If he cared enough for any one of those women, then I'd have something to work with. But Brandon was shallow, and it was a risk trying to force a selfish man to care for someone else.

"You think you can come into my tower and screw my men? You're the stupidest woman I've ever met." I dragged her by her hair off the bed and threw her to the floor.

"Please!" She sucked in a big breath as she lay on the floor, naked and cowering away from me. "I'll do whatever you want, just please don't kill me."

"Why shouldn't I kill you?" I asked as I pulled my gun out. I racked the slide just to scare her, and she shrieked for mercy.

"I'll answer all your questions and do exactly what you say. Just please don't hurt me!"

"Look at me," I said flatly. She lifted her head slowly, blinking back tears. Her flesh was met with my gun in an instant and she began to shake violently.

"I swear, I only got into this business for mother. She's sick and I needed money."

"Well, isn't that something? You want me to have mercy on you because you have a sick mother. But did you have mercy on Iyana's mother?"

She didn't answer and I pressed the gun harder into her head, making her squeal in anguish. "Answer me!"

"No! I didn't!"

"Then why should I ever consider your life?"

"Because Grizzly is after Brandon!"

I stared at her for a second, and then knelt in front of her. Keeping the gun to her head I nodded at her to continue.

"I was paid by Grizzly the week before your wedding to give him information on Brandon. He said Brandon's been costing him more than he's bringing in and he wants him dead."

"And what did you tell him?"

"That Brandon had money tied up in St. Sessa's system, but I never knew his whereabouts. He only called me when he needed me. I told Grizzly the next time he called I'd try to get Brandon to tell me his location."

"Did you?"

She nodded. "The next time he called me, he told me to pull the plug, and hung up. I told Grizzly who was checking in with me every day and he made me come in and put an inbound tracker on my phone."

"And when Brandon called again, his location was pinged to Grizzly, wasn't it?"

"Yes. Grizzly went after him and that's all I know."

"Why does this help me?" I wouldn't tell her that she just dropped a diamond the size of the largest golden nugget in the world in my lap, but I wanted to know what else she knew.

"Because there's a woman named Clemons Murphy who's worked for Grizzly too. She'll know more about him than I will, but I can get you to her."

"We've met." I stood and tucked my gun away. She looked relieved as she watched me lean against the dresser.

"I want you to get dressed. I need you to make a phone call."

She complied, slowly moving around the room to dress while I thought about what she'd told me. Brandon must've gotten away from Grizzly or Grizzly was the one calling her phone. Either way, I couldn't use her phone to call Brandon. But the situation hadn't changed. *If Grizzly hasn't caught Brandon, then I've got two dogs I can let into the ring to kill each other. Their fight would buy me the time I need to gather enough money and get away.*

"Does Brandon recognize your number?" I asked. My voice in the silence made her jump as she pulled the top to her scrubs over her head.

"Yes."

"He called you last night. What phone can I use that he'll recognize the number and pick up?"

She thought for a minute. "The hospital. Sometimes he calls me there."

"Fine, let's go to the hospital then."

We rode in silence through the city. No one wanted to speak. Jill was frightened, Logan was remorseful after I chewed him out about sleeping with the woman who killed my wife's mother. I just wasn't in the mood. But looking at Jill beside me made my stomach churn and I ached for someone to say something.

It was the same way Iyana rode back to the tower with us after visiting the Abletons. Somewhere along the way, things became twisted and disoriented, and I somehow fell back into the dark pit Iyana had pulled me out of. Without her, I had no boundaries, I had no reason not to be malicious and angry. Before her, I was able to be nice because I could afford to. Now, things were up in flames, so I had no reason to be kind. But it was still agitating to be in this state, to want to be someone else, but stuck in this role.

When Iyana was here, I only wanted to be the person she fell in love with. I didn't want to be the leader of BT. When she was here, I could remember that I'm a man of God and I don't have to do things the way I've always done them. But when will I stop depending on people?

I depended on my father for my name and to get a foothold in this business. I depended on Brandon to help me keep BT afloat, and I've depended on Iyana to help me stay sane, but in all three situations, I'm still weak.

Vito Gerardo spent his years cleaning up the mess his father left. Vito Gerardo was betrayed by his own brother. By the man he thought would always have his back. Vito Gerardo fell in love, yet this love crippled him because now he had to choose between love and the gang.

Vito Gerardo wasn't a man of God, although he wanted to be.

I sighed, pushing away those thoughts. I couldn't afford to be anyone but Vito Gerardo who was the leader of BT. I glanced over at a disheveled and nervous Jill. She was visibly shaken, but she was trying not to be. I hated the man I had to be with her, but the only excuse I had for myself to make the guilt not taste so bitter was that business is business. And business in this industry was conducted by any means necessary.

We pulled into the parking lot of the hospital where Jill and I stepped out. Logan would circle around until he spotted us again.

"Can you get us in through a side entrance?" I asked as we made it to the front.

"A side entrance?" She thought for a moment. "Yes, there's one around back. We can go—"

"Hey..." I snatched her by the arm and whirled her towards me. Her eyes were large, and she rapidly blinked back nervous tears. "You better not be trying anything. If we go through the side entrance and we're ambushed, I won't kill you. I'll make sure your mother is tortured and have you listen to her screaming on repeat."

She was trembling now, and even I thought that was a little harsh.

"Let's go," I said.

I held on to her arm as we walked around the back.

"Here," I said, finally letting her go. She took the tissue I'd offered and dabbed her eyes. "If you look too panicked, someone might notice you."

She nodded and took a deep breath before typing in a code. The door unlocked, and I pulled my gun out and buried it in her back.

She stiffened immediately and I whispered, "I don't want to kill you, Jill, but I will if you move without my permission. Now walk."

Stiffly, she walked slowly into the building. I couldn't see her face, but I was praying it wasn't as tense as her body. She looked like a walking brick from behind. As we made our way inside, the hall was empty besides a man pushing a cart of towels.

"Where are we?" I asked.

"This is the employee section. It's normally empty since we're short staffed. We usually have working breaks."

I wanted to keep her talking to get the nerves out of her voice. She sounded like a baby dropped their rattle down her throat. Each word was shaky and spoken slowly.

"How far until the phone?"

"It's just around the corner in the break room."

"Move faster then."

"Jill? Where have you been?" a high-pitched voice rang out behind us, and I grabbed Jill by the waist to pull her in front of me. Without taking my eyes off the giddy woman traveling quickly down the hall towards us, I leaned against Jill.

"Get rid of her," I said in her ear while slipping the gun into her waistband. "If you don't, I'll tell everyone you came in here with a gun." She wanted to gasp but just as the woman came close, I hissed, "Don't react."

"Jill!" The woman whipped open her arms for a hug, but I slung my arm over Jill's shoulder and pulled her back.

"What do you think you're doing?"

The woman shook her stringy blonde hair from her pinched face and looked me over quickly. "Excuse me, but

Jill's never mentioned you before. And I've never seen you around."

"Do you know everyone who walks into this hospital?"

"No." She placed bony hands on stick thin hips. "But Jill's my roommate and I know every guy she hangs out with and none of them match your description."

"Well," I turned to Jill, her eyes were wide, but thankfully she wasn't tearing up, "I bet you're happy you've been away from this annoying roommate of yours. The last few nights have been one of a kind. Haven't they?"

Jill smiled weakly before looking back at her friend.

"He can be crude."

"She loves it." I pulled her closer. "She loves everything about me." I winked at the porcelain-white woman who hadn't blinked at all. Her frozen stare would've chilled me if I wasn't trying to keep my composure.

"Listen, Sammy," Jill said, "I'm really—"

"I've been covering for you all this time." Tears were swelling in Sammy's eyes. "For this?"

"Sammy, I've really got somewhere to be. So, we'll chat later. I promise."

"No." Sammy's voice had darkened, the poor girl looked heartbroken. "We tell each other everything! When did we start keeping secrets?"

"We don't!" Jill snapped.

Sammy and I both looked at her, and then Sammy deflated. All the anger and heartbreak were washed away in two simple words, and now I'd have to kill Sammy and Jill.

"Ok," Sammy whispered.

There was an aching silence that stretched on for what seemed like hours. Finally, Sammy took her eyes off Jill, and they fell on me. Her foot moved, but her eyes never stopped looking at me.

"You're trying to remember everything you can about me," I said, slowly lowering my arm from Jill's shoulder.

"Sammy, run!" Jill screamed.

Ripping the gun from Jill's waist, I fired at Sammy. She hollered and fell to the ground. I whirled around to find Jill running and screaming down the hall. I fired at her, and she crumpled to the floor. I didn't hit her because I needed her. She'd only fallen out of fear. But time was short. Before Jill could get to her feet, my hand was on her collar, and I was dragging her backwards. She was kicking and screaming, and somewhere in the distance I could hear footsteps coming for us.

I slapped a hand over her mouth and dragged her around the corner into the breakroom. Peeking out the door, I spotted two cameras. I fired at them both—which set off an alarm, but I ignored it as I backed into the room and locked us inside. Jill ran to the corner, crying and shaking, but we didn't have time for that. I pulled out my phone and dialed Logan's number.

"Logan," I called over the alarms.

"I'm on my way."

"Southside, back door. But we'll be coming out a window in three minutes."

"Understood."

I hung up the phone, listening to the panicked shouts outside the door. I stayed low to the floor so no one would see me. But then Jill tried to run to the door screaming.

I tackled her, and we hit the floor hard. She took most of the impact, but we had less than three minutes now to call Brandon, and I'd already warned her not to do anything stupid.

"Get up!" I snapped as I pulled her by her shirt. She limped as I dragged her over to the phone. "Call him right now."

"Just kill me!" she screamed frantically.

"Fine!" I raised my gun and shoved it into her head.

She shrieked and dropped to her knees. "Please!"

"Then call him!"

"Ok!" Shakily, Jill reached for the phone on the counter and dialed.

"Tell him to come to the tower if he wants Alex."

She was panic-breathing as she knelt.

Someone came and tried to open the door. Twisting the handle, they called, "Hey! Open up! Someone's dying out here! There's an intruder and we need to evacuate!"

I looked back at Jill; she was cupping the phone around her mouth. "Brandon," she exhaled, "if you want to save Alex, come to the tower."

I fired at the window behind Jill as the pounding ensued at the door.

She screamed out and dropped the phone.

"Let's go!" I shouted, snatching her wrist to drag her out the window

Thirteen

Vito

Jan 12th | 11:49am

"I warned you," I said, taking a sip of orange juice.

"I was afraid!" Jill shrieked.

I slammed my hand on the table so hard, I could feel the heat resonating in my elbow. "I told you I wouldn't kill you. And I'm not going to."

"Please," she begged. Tears and mucus mixed together on her face, making my stomach feel uneasy. "Please, you're not this kind of man. You're not like them." She crawled closer to me. "You're diff—"

I splashed my orange juice in her face and threw the glass to the floor. It shattered, and Logan jumped at the loud noise.

"Don't ever tell me who I am. You don't know me. And it's painfully obvious. Because right now, I have a team of men hunting for your mother. Whatever hospital or home she's staying in, they will find her, and they will torture her until her last breath."

Jill hurled over and screamed at my feet, crying and begging me not to do this. But it was too late. I'd sent the text to Leo the moment I got in the car. The men who'd cleaned up Bridges's body and fully wiped down his house were heading to the location of Jill's mother as I stood there and watched her unravel. Or rather, as I stood there and watched what my own unraveling had done.

"Get her out of here. I want her cleaned up and ready for Brandon in case I need to show him that she's fine." I smirked down at the sobbing woman. "If he even cares about her. And get me the information about Murphy, and anything else from Jill's phone records. I need something on Grizzly."

"Yes, boss." Logan nodded and grabbed Jill by her arm. He led her out of the room as Kat entered.

"What, Kat?" I snapped.

She quirked a brow.

"Sorry," I muttered, "I'm tired."

"I haven't seen you like this in almost seven months. I wonder what brought about the shift in character," she said sarcastically as she crossed the room to me.

"Why are you here?"

"Because you need to bring Iyana home, you're a complete mess without her."

I grunted and turned away, splaying my hands on the table. "You know I'm not usually like this. Even before Iyana."

"And that scares me too," she said softly. Kat knew something was going on, she knew things weren't going right, but she tried to be as compliant as she could.

"What are you actually here for, Kat?"

"I'm here with some of Jill's phone records. Turns out, the tracker information she told you was true. But what she didn't know was that Brandon's location was also being pinged to her. She just doesn't know how to access that information."

"Really?"

"Yes. It seems like everything she said is true. Grizzly is actually after Brandon, and based on Brandon's last location, I don't think Grizzly's found him."

"His last location? Where was it?"

"That warehouse you found Iyana in."

"The warehouse..." I paused, standing up straight and turning to face her. "You think he's hiding from Grizzly?"

"Possibly." Kat shrugged. "The only question is *why*?"

"That may not be one we can answer. Do you have anything from Murphy's place that might help?"

She scrolled through her phone. "Nope. Only important thing from Murphy is that she was on that Maryland case. Aside from the paperwork in Jewels's place, the most I was able to recover is that the original deal that was struck with Grizzly was just a hoax to get more money for JNJ."

"Ok, so Brandon and Jewels were already working with the dealer in Maryland. They were supplying product from the warehouse to the dealer and letting him pose as a supplier to get money out of Grizzly."

"Exactly. But Grizzly still doesn't know that, because Grizzly actually wasn't the one who called in Murphy or killed the dealer." She huffed. "Jewels killed the dealer because of some negotiation. But they framed Gang Grizzly, so now—"

"Grizzly can't do business in Maryland because he can't be trusted. Brandon called in Murphy just like he did with Emilia, and he paid her off with Grizzly's money. But how'd he get Grizzly's money in the first place?"

"My only thought on that is some kind of hookup between Jewels and Grizzly. Apparently, they were together frequently, sometimes even behind Brandon's back."

I raised a brow. "What do you mean?"

"Jewels was in it for herself. That duffle bag wasn't even half the money she had stored away. The guys found it earlier today while you were out."

"You think she's been stealing from Grizzly?"

"And probably the warehouse too. And she was running to meet with Brandon so that he'd never come here and find out. Or she wasn't going to meet Brandon at all. Hardy told me she said she was going to Brandon, but this new information says otherwise."

I leaned against the table, slowly folding my arms across my chest. It was all turning into one big cesspool. Loyalty and trust were everything in this business, and yet, this sort of life is the only one where you can't find them anywhere at all.

"How are you moving forward?" Kat asked.

"What have they uncovered at Bridges's place?"

"Money, contacts, drugs. Nothing connected to Grizzly or Brandon or Jewels yet."

"Bridges didn't have any connection with Grizzly?"

She shrugged again. "I was surprised too. But Bridges was only a middleman in the city. The only way he'd reach somewhere else is a connection through a connection. The main Grizzly connection was Brandon. But Bridges hated Brandon."

"By right. He slept with his first wife."

Kat's eyes widened and then shrank.

"Oh," I sighed, "that was before you got here."

She nodded.

"Well, all in all," I summarized, "Jewels was playing everyone. She killed the dealer in Maryland and framed Grizzly for it. Then she had Brandon call in Murphy so that if the bottom ever fell out, it'd look like Brandon killed the dealer and called in Murphy to clean things up for himself, not for her."

"Yes, and with Grizzly out of the running in Maryland, that leaves the door open for you and the connections you may want to make."

"Find out who Bridges knew in Maryland. I want to set something up for Grizzly."

She was typing down my instructions into her phone when she snapped her head up at me. "Grizzly?"

"Yes. I want to give the king of Jersey a gift. That way, it'll be that much easier to turn him against Brandon."

"Vito..." she reached out for my arm, but I pulled away. Kat has always been overly concerned for me. It's her over-concern that's confusing Hardy. He's taking her gentleness for affection, but Kat's just a caring person.

I heard her phone click closed and her boots thudding as she crossed the floor.

"Kat," I called.

She stopped.

"Thank you."

"Of course, boss."

As she opened the door, the radio on her hip beeped and Leo's voice came over the airwaves. "Kat, Brandon just pulled up."

She immediately whipped her head in my direction.

"Bring him up," I said calmly.

"Let him in," she said into the radio.

"Understood."

The radio went quiet, and Kat and I were left in a staring contest.

"Vito—"

"It's already done. Don't come up here until I call for you."

She nodded and stepped out the room to leave me to my thoughts. The road I was going down was dangerous, and there wasn't really a way out except death or an escape I didn't have. It was unlikely I would ever get out of this life. But I would do anything to secure safety for my wife. At the very least, I was willing to give my own life if it meant I could save Iyana.

I sat at the table, waiting for Brandon. I heard the elevator ding down the hall, and his footsteps came charging towards the door. I pressed a hand into the compartment under the table and a shotgun fell into my lap. Just as the door opened, I raised and charged it. Brandon's eyes were filled with fear and anger when he entered the room and found me there. He resented me, but I didn't even know why because he was the one who'd betrayed *me*.

"I will splatter you all over this wall if I have to."

He panted but said nothing. I smiled and lowered my gun.

"Welcome home, brother."

"Cut the crap!" he shouted. "Where's my wife!? I could kill you for what you've done!"

"What have I done, Brandon?"

"All of this is your fault!" He was shouting, but it wasn't helping me understand his misdirected anger. I still didn't know why I was the one who'd messed everything up, when it was Brandon who'd betrayed me… unless he knew about the bodies in Grizzly's garbage.

"Brandon, calm down," I said, raising a hand. I needed to gage him, to see what he knew. Setting the gun on the table, I stood and slipped my hands into my pockets. "We're brothers, we don't have to resort to violence. Besides, I only invited you here because of Alex, not to settle the score."

"Where is she?" he growled. He seemed distant despite his focused expression. I knew he was trying to remember all the secret places in the tower she could be hidden.

I sighed, still trying to gage him. "Tell me what you know about Gio, Emilia, and Gio Jr.'s death first."

He flinched. "I … I don't know." His eyes searched the floor before he shook his head and snapped his vision back to me. "Quit screwing with me and give me my wife!"

I left the bodies on the night of Gio's accident. If he'd been at Grizzly's when the bodies showed up, then he would know about Jewels. But his focus on Alex meant he had no idea about the bodies.

I exhaled slowly.

"You know…" I took a slow walk across the room to him. "I had no idea you were married. I mean, you hooked up with Jewels all the time, so I couldn't believe you were in a committed relationship." I looked up as I made it across the room to him. "But what do you know about commitment or loyalty?"

He snatched me by my shirt and dragged me close to his face. He was tired, *visibly* tired, up close. Fine lines were now deep grooves and valleys in his face, and his eyes were so puffy, it looked like a medical problem. But that was good because his exhaustion meant he'd be irrational. He'll believe whatever I tell him.

"You're going to kill the only person in this entire tower who knows where your wife is? She'll die if I do."

He studied me, his eyes tried to find the truth or the lie. But I was smiling up at him, not giving any hints away. All he could do was shove me back.

"What other reason would I bring you back here?"

"Is this a game to you?" he grunted.

"No, but it was to you. And that's how you lost her."

He squinted. "What are you talking about?"

"The ping-ponging between your wife and the mistress. Living the double life. She caught wind of your BS because it's not easy to live a lie. You get sloppy." I raised an IncogVito Diamonds card between two fingers and waved it at him. His dark eyes watched it in my hand as I said, "She came to me, wondering about this."

"That's impossible!"

"Why? Because you kept her locked in a castle so that your human punching bag couldn't run away?"

He stiffened.

"Yeah, she talks… a lot."

Everything I'd just said was information Iyana had given me. I'd only spoken briefly to Alex outside of the times I'd yelled at her. And I only spoke to her about little things, like did she want water, or something. But Brandon was visibly shaken, which meant Alex was important to him. And it was bad to let anyone in this business know you had a heart. It was especially bad in this situation because I knew how to twist him until he gave in to what I wanted.

"She wouldn't know to come here." He shook his head. "You're lying!"

"Really? Because I'm sure IncogVito Tower and IncogVito Diamonds probably played no part in all this deep detective work."

"No!" he snapped. "That isn't true."

"You're absolutely right, that wasn't true." I reeled back in laughter, but I quickly recovered as Brandon charged towards me. I jumped out of the way in time, and he crashed to the floor.

"Brandon, you really want to know how I found all this out?" I glared at him. "It's because I saved your wife from Grizzly!"

He was panting heavily on the floor when he snapped his head up to look me dead in the eyes. He was about to burst from fear and shock. "What?"

Got him.

"I found Alex in a hospital waiting room. She came over to me when she heard the staff calling me, 'the Prince of the Apple'. She told me they wouldn't let her see her son. So she asked me to do something."

"What do you mean she was in the hospital, and she couldn't see her son?"

"Wouldn't you like to know?"

I left the foyer and went into my office. I pulled out a folder from my file cabinet and slapped it on the desk just to make Brandon more nervous. He knew I kept records of everything important in there. When I looked up, Brandon had made his way to my office. *One more lie,* I thought, *and he'll be hunting Grizzly for me.* There was guilt swirling in my chest, but I couldn't give in to it. Feeling guilty now was pointless. So much had already happened, I couldn't back away now, even though I wanted to.

"Please, Vee," he whispered. His eyes were glued to the floor as he stood trembling in my doorway. "I need to know what happened."

I didn't say anything for a while. I let his agony reach a boiling point before slowly opening the file on my desk and pretending to read through it. "Your son is in critical condition. Grizzly was after Alex, and I took her to a safehouse. But I couldn't get your son there. He's in a remote hospital I'm keeping an eye on. Because I found out that Jill works there, and I wouldn't want her to pull the plug on him."

"Jill?" Her name was barely audible on his lips as my words stung him.

"Yeah. She's working for Grizzly. He's paying her a pretty penny to keep an eye on BJ. At least that's what she told me."

"And why is she telling you this? You believe her? She a lying—"

"I know. But she told me something that I found was true. She had an inbound call tracker placed on her phone. Every call that came to her was tagged to Grizzly's phone."

He stepped back. "No, something isn't right."

"The men who came for your wife were probably looking for you because of Jill. They almost killed your son, your wife, and your unborn child, Brandon. They beat them brutally. They shot them, and it's a miracle they're still alive."

"And Jill told you all this?"

"Parts. Alex told me most of it. How Grizzly himself and a few cubs came in and attacked her and little BJ."

His eyes darted around the floor before he shook his head. "I don't understand. Where's Jill now?"

Calmly I closed the folder and sighed. "Jill got away. She apparently knew Jewels, and the two ran off."

"Jewels? She's not here?"

"No. No one's here but me right now."

"And Iyana?" He swallowed loudly.

"She's with Alex. They're safe. There's a war, Brandon."

"This isn't making any sense. He said he didn't kill them…"

"Who said that?" I stepped around the desk. "Brandon," I called, "brother. This is bigger than what happened. I can't help you if you don't tell me what you know."

"How can I trust you after everything?"

"Because I'm the only one who knows where Alex is and has a good idea where Jewels and Jill might be. I'm the only one who can save your son."

He swallowed and nodded.

"Why is Grizzly after you?"

"Because I screwed up some deals. I've cost him a lot of money."

I sighed and turned back toward my desk. "Alright. You can't be seen here then. I'll get in contact with you."

"Hold on." He stepped forward, tears rolled down his cheeks. "What about Alex and BJ? Where are they? When can I see them?"

"When it's safe. I'm not putting Iyana in danger for you. You took her from me once, I won't let you have her twice."

He studied me for a long moment. "At least tell me where they are, Vito. I need *something*."

"You need to leave them. You know better than I do that a search party leaves a heavy scent of blood, one that'll be very easy to pick up on. Then you'll have nothing, not even your life."

"You expect me to trust you? You could be lying!"

"All you have is *me*, Brandon! Who can you run to? You've backed yourself into a corner and the only person who is willing to help you is the same brother you betrayed!" I shook my head, my anger finally mounting its peak.

I'd never let myself feel anything about Brandon, and even now, I shouldn't be angry because he betrayed me since, technically, I am betraying him now. But I couldn't help myself.

With him silent and at my mercy, I took the time to snap at him again. "You screwed with everyone," I said quietly. "You tried to reduce BT to a pile of rubble. And for what? You turned on your own brother. You turned on *me*, Brandon. Even after all that stuff with Jewels—"

"You've never let me forget it!"

"Because *you* wouldn't let me! You flaunted your relationship with her around this tower and expected me to be alright!? It took months to get over it, and months to get over her keeping *your* son. And months to just be me. Then…" I swallowed, regaining my composure. "Just as things with Iyana and I began to work out, you betrayed us and turned this tower into a madhouse. Thankfully, you didn't take Iyana, and she and I were able to fix BT."

He was staring at his feet now, clenched jaw, and tears flowing. He was a big man, but Brandon had suddenly shrunken right in front of me, and it felt good to finally be taller than him.

I took a deep breath. "You can't trust anyone in this business. You know that. But you find someone outside the business you can trust, and you do everything you can to protect them. I guess for you, it's Alex. For me, it's Iyana, even though she's right here with me, it still seems like she's an outsider. So, I'm going to do something for you." I leaned against the desk, folding my arms over my chest. "Come back to the tower in seven days. Kat will have a location for you to go to. When you get there, there'll be a phone with Alex's number in it. Call her."

His eyes widened and he nearly crumpled before me. "Call her? How will she know it's me?"

"The phone you'll get in a week will need your SIM card."

His trembling jaw hardened as he nodded. He stood there an extra minute and finally turned and left. When I heard the door of my loft close, I finally exhaled. Everything I'd told him was all a lie. BJ was dead, Jewels was dead, Jill was somewhere in the tower, and Alex wasn't brutally beaten. Whenever the truth comes out, which it certainly would, I'd need to be ready.

Fourteen

Vito

Jan 14th | 3:16am

"Vito," Leo called as he came over to me. We'd been in Bridges's house all night searching for clues and information but had come up short. I wanted to pray for a break, but I was so deep in the things I'd done, I didn't think it was right to ask God for anything.

"Look what I found." Large hands passed me two sheets of paper.

"What am I looking at?" It was digits and letters, some kind of coding.

"It's a backtrack of the location of the inbound calls from Jill's phone. I was looking into it yesterday because something seemed off about an unusual pattern here and here." He pointed with his pen. It was actually a pen he'd found in Bridges's house but since he wasn't using it anymore, I told the men they could take whatever they wanted.

Bridges's death still hadn't hit the streets. I'd been prolonging it since he was known for disappearing to visit his real family somewhere across state lines. The team and I had only been visiting his place in the dead of night on the same path, so the snow wouldn't tell that someone had come by.

"So, what is it?" I asked.

"That pattern shows up every time a location is sent, but so does this one." He pointed to another string of code. "It means there are two locations."

"Yeah, Jill's and Brandon's."

He shook his head. "This pattern is Grizzly's location. We can use it to figure out exactly what location Grizzly had been receiving these pings. Each time a location was sent, his location was sent back to Jill."

I thought for a second. "Does that mean if someone calls Jill right now, the location will go to his phone and his location will ping back to hers?"

He nodded.

I smiled. "Leo, you're a genius."

"I know. You should give me a pay raise."

"For what?" I laughed. "Kat does most of the work. And you live in my tower. What do you need money for?"

"For the brothel and other strip clubs."

I shrugged. "Fine. Take one of Bridges's watches then. Sell it or something."

He rolled his eyes. "You're so cheap."

"You're about to be dead."

"Who'd figure this out then?"

"Kat or someone. You're not that valuable." I pushed past him, and he sighed over my shoulder.

"I'll get right on this, boss."

I waved a hand as I moved into another room where I found Kat hovering over a bunch of documents. There was a string and pushpins on a board like she'd been following some detective case. As I got closer, I nearly gasped at the name in the center, **the Abletons.**

"That's right," she said, standing beside me now. "Bridges will close the gap between us and the Abletons."

"He knew I was looking for them and never said a word."

"Business is business, boss. You know that."

I ticked my brow and sighed. "You're right. So what do you have?"

She went over to the board and began pointing at things. "These are transaction locations of the Abletons. Apparently, they were at a show on Broadway when you went to their place. They'd gotten those tickets from Bridges."

"But why a theatre?"

She shrugged. "Would you really think two old drug dealers were going to the theatre?"

I chuckled. "I guess not."

"The tickets must've been worth something because those same tickets ended up being sold and the people who sat in those seats were not the Abletons. I had a friend on the force check on that night, and a few others." She walked to the piles of documents on the floor and scanned them until she grabbed a pack of papers and extended them to me.

"What's this?" I asked.

"The seating arrangement and the ticket holders."

"Why is this important?"

"Because those seats Bridges bought were really good seats. Very close, very posh. But that section is for season ticket holders."

"So, Bridges liked theatre." I shrugged.

"Bridges bought season tickets and resold them."

"Why does that matter?"

She smirked. "Because of whom he's selling to. That entire section is owned by Bridges. Which means he's selling tickets to people like the Abletons."

I nodded. "People in need of an alibi."

"Exactly."

"So, I'm assuming you've caught up with some of these people?"

"I have." She walked over and pointed to a picture on the board. "This guy worked with Bridges. I caught up with him and he was able to tell me something about the Abletons." She smiled. "Do you remember when I said Bridges wouldn't have any Jersey connections because he hated Brandon?"

I nodded. "That was just a few days ago."

"Well, I was wrong. I came back here and looked over some of this stuff, and I looked back over Tee's info, the guy who knows Bridges." She tapped his photo on the board, and then turned the board over. In the middle was the name **Tee** and from his bubble were lines pointing in all directions—which I assumed were different leads all from just one person.

"You're kidding me."

She shook her head. "Tee told me the Abletons were fishers and they floated money up the Raritan River sometimes."

"Is that how they got all their money out of New York before we found them?"

"Yep. And the Raritan River hits Lake Solitude in Jersey. Which," she pointed, "is where Tee said there's a small gang swelling near that Lake Solitude area."

"That's why Grizzly wanted them so badly. Not just to take down BT, but to take down that rising gang. So, the Abletons are working with this rival gang in Jersey, then?"

She nodded. "Yes. And I sent two men up the river last night when I put it all together. Once we get a glimpse of them, we'll send you to Jersey to get the Abletons and strike a deal with Grizzly."

I looked at her for a while, her shimmering blue eyes, her tight bun and pants suit. Kat was a dedicated member of BT, but she was almost too dedicated. It interfered with her work because if Kat didn't think I was making the right move, she'd take things into her own hands, like she has now.

"You didn't want Grizzly striking a deal in Maryland, so you did all this just to make sure I went down a different avenue."

She took a breath. "Vito, I just think—"

"What's in Maryland?"

She shook her head. "Vito, please."

"Just tell me, Kat, and I'll leave it at that."

Her eyes fell to the floor, and when she didn't speak, I understood.

"When did Iyana tell you about BT falling apart?"

"She didn't have to."

I dropped my head.

"We knew this wasn't going to last forever, we just weren't expecting it so soon."

"So you're making preparations? You've decided you want to be somewhere that isn't ruled by a gang."

"I'm making a new life for myself," Kat explained. "I'm getting out of here by any means necessary. I don't owe BT anything."

"But you owe *me*!" I snapped.

"Not anymore," she snapped back.

We stood there staring at each other, my chest heaving as I tried to understand why Kat would ever want to walk away. She just blinked at me. Perfectly calm. Perfectly poised.

After a moment, Kat handed me a piece of paper. On it was a drawing of a map with symbols and directions and explanations. I snatched it from her and stared down at it.

"Tee said he went fishing with Mr. Ableton. They have a shed which is most likely a safe right along the coast of the Raritan River."

"When will you be gone?"

When she shied away, I nodded and folded the paper. "Here," I handed it back to her. "Consider it severance."

With trembling hands, she took the paper back, and she wanted to speak again but the words wouldn't come. I gazed at her, and I didn't know what to feel. I was relieved that she was going to find her freedom before it was too late, but I was hurt and angry that she would leave BT… that Kat would leave *me*. I'd taken her in and took care of her, and now she was leaving me. Would everyone leave me eventually? Even Iyana?

"Mr. Gerardo?" a voice over my shoulder pulled me from my thoughts. I turned to find a small shapely woman with glasses and wild curls standing in the doorway.

"Who's this?" I asked Kat.

"She was the tech girl for Bridges. She saw everything on cams, but our men found her before she could escape."

"How'd you get her to stay and keep quiet?"

"She has a brother. I paid for his boarding school so she could quit her night shifts at The Club."

I nodded.

"Well, Vito, I'll leave you to Denali." Kat nodded as she stepped by me, but I caught her wrist.

"Kat," I whispered, my voice hoarse.

"She knows a lot more than me. You'll be better off. Besides," she shrugged, and the movement made a twisted look take over her features, "Leo really likes her."

"Please," I whispered, feeling pitiful and stupid. Kat was everything to BT, how could I entrust the Pack to someone else?

"It's been fun, Vee. Will you tell Iyana for me?"

"What about Hardy?"

"It's better this way."

I nodded. "Goodbye, Kat."

"Goodbye, Vito."

She turned to the door and gave a friendly nod to Denali. The young girl had a sullen expression on her face as Kat passed her by.

"One more thing." She stopped at the door, and I took a short breath and pulled my focus to her. "Thank you, for everything."

And with that, Kat disappeared into the night.

Fifteen
Iyana
Jan 14th | 2:36pm

Dafni locked herself away for three days. I thought Tobias would scold me for telling her the truth, but he was actually relieved that he didn't have to. He told me he wouldn't have known where to start, and he wasn't worried about her shutting herself in their bedroom. When she emerged, the two of them went out and hadn't returned yet. Tobias left me in charge, but it didn't matter, all any of us had been doing since we'd arrived was mope.

"Hardy," I called from the bottom of the stairs.

"What?" he called back.

"Alex and I are going to the store, do you want to come?"

"No. Just bring me back food."

"Aren't you supposed to be my guard?"

He didn't respond. I sighed and turned to Alex. "It's just us."

She shrugged. I'd been trying to do more with Alex since I felt so bad for her. Her entire world just came crashing down on her and it was partially my fault. I'd been angry and selfish and bombarded her with the truth. Although, from the way things happened, the truth was going to come out anyway.

Her house was wrecked by Grizzly, and her son was killed by him. I never got the full story from her, just bits and pieces, but I never pushed for it. I figured it was too hard to relive and I didn't want to intrude... but that's actually a lie. I've been wrapped up in my own head. Losing my mother, and not even knowing what's happening with my father, being apart from Vito. It's all so...

I sighed.

If I'm honest, I didn't want to think about what was happening right in front of me. I was apart from my husband, and I had no idea where my father was. If I could just see him or at least know that he's alright, it wouldn't be so overwhelming. But I never let myself entertain the thought of seeing my father again. When I return to New York, I have to be over my mother's death, and I can't let my father be a distraction. When I return, I have to figure a way to bring Vito back to God and get out of BT.

I sighed again.

"Are you alright?" Alex asked softly. She was gentle, like she'd always been. Except the time she came barging into my room demanding the truth. She didn't have to wake me, but I understood her impatience.

"Yeah, I just—" a door slammed upstairs and thumping echoed as Hardy made his way down the hall and down the stairs to us. "You didn't have to come," I said as I folded my arms.

"Yeah, well, I'm here now." Brown hands were stuffed into his baggy sweats as he raised his shoulders dramatically. "Can we go?"

"Why are you so cranky?" Alex snapped.

Hardy and I both stared at her, and then Hardy stepped forward into her face.

"*Hardy*," I called.

"I'm hungry," he said into her face, "and I'm tired."

"Tired of what?"

He sucked his teeth and brushed by her. "Let's just go."

"No." Alex demanded. Hardy stopped in the doorway and slumped his shoulders.

"No? Why?"

"Because there's never enough communication! No one ever talks about anything, and everything is left unsolved or undone! I can't take this anymore!" She shoved by me and ran up the stairs. Her pregnant belly made it a slow trot, so I could've stopped her. But neither Hardy nor I moved. We just watched her take her time making it up the stairs and into her room before slamming the door.

"She's hormonal," Hardy said. "Let's just go."

"I think she's right, Hardy. All of us are dealing with things but none of us are talking about it."

"What am I supposed to say? What is this, some rehabilitation center? We're all too messed up to talk about it. So, it's easier to just let it go, and move on. That's what happens when you're part of a gang."

"What happened to you?" I said weakly. His dark eyes locked on mine and there was a storm raging in the darkness. "There was a time when you wanted to talk to me about what was going on with you and now you're shutting the world out. This isn't like you, Hardy."

"None of this is like any of us! We were all thrown into this world, and then forced to suck it up whenever something horrible happened—which was *all* the time! So I'm sorry that I might've matured a little and don't need a shoulder to cry on anymore."

"You haven't matured in the slightest bit." I shoved past him and out the door.

It was raining outside, but I didn't care. I just needed to get away. Away from Hardy. Away from Alex. Away from everything. I stomped across the sidewalk, hugging myself as the cool January rain fell over me. The dreary sky cried for me, for all of us. All we'd been through and all the pain we tried to fight on our own, we just weren't able to. And now, we needed to address all the hurt because it was staring right at us. Without the daily work at BT to distract us, and for Alex, the daily life of a housewife, we were forced to face our realities.

"Iyana!" I whirled around to find Hardy jogging down the street after me.

"What do you want?" I asked.

He was panting and extended an umbrella to me. "Vito would kill me if anything happened to you."

Slowly, I took the umbrella. I was already soaked, and so was he, so the umbrella made no real difference. In the rain, I could see all of Hardy. His dark eyes and kiddish demeanor were masked behind a young man who was forced to grow up, but he'd raised himself, so he didn't do too well. His face was finally maturing, his jaw was squaring, and his body had changed. He wasn't slender like he used to be. He was strong and lean, and his wet shirt complimented his figure. Broad shoulders, a strong chest that heaved as he looked down at me.

"You were right," he said as a drop of water fell from his soaking curls down his cheek. "We've kept too much pent up, and now none of us knows what to do. I have no idea what to do without Jewels. I... I even..."

"What?" I touched his hand.

"I tried talking to God, but I didn't hear anything." He heaved and dropped to his knees. "I loved Jewels! I loved her so much! How could I do this to her!?"

"Hardy..." I knelt and embraced him. He was sobbing on the ground, begging God to hear him. It was heartbreaking, but I knew that He would hear Hardy. "When I was lost and hurt, and I didn't know what to do, Jesus met me right where I was. He hears you, Hardy, and He's going to meet you right where you are."

"Why won't He respond? Why does He leave me to the silence? I can't take it."

"The silence isn't to torture you, it's to keep you listening for His voice. You'll hear it. And when you do, it'll change you."

"Are you… are you sure?"

"Yes." I hugged him a little tighter as the rain continued to fall. People walked around us as we knelt there, as Hardy sobbed, and as I trembled from the cold.

Sixteen

Hardy

Jan 15th | 2:14pm

"Just let her rest for now. She should be fine by tomorrow," Alex said as she stepped out of Iyana's room. She'd gotten sick from being in the rain with me yesterday.

"Thanks a lot, I didn't really know what to do."

"Mmm." She turned to leave but I grabbed her arm.

Alex immediately flinched away, her big, panicked eyes were glued to mine.

"I'm sorry," I said, slowly letting her go. "I wasn't going to hurt you. I just wanted to talk."

She took a shaky breath and stepped back, caressing her arm. For the first time, I actually looked at Alex. She was beautiful. Full lips and round eyes, soft cheekbones hidden beneath the baby fat on her face.

"What," she started, "what did you want, Hardy?"

"I just wanted to say I'm sorry about yesterday. I really snapped, and I shouldn't have."

She pushed a dark curl out of her face and gave me a half smile. "It's alright. Everyone's been at their emotional wits end."

"I thought this trip was supposed to help, but," I shrugged, glancing away from her, "it's only made things worse."

She giggled, and the girlish noise struck me so suddenly, I had to clear my throat.

"Whose idea was it to send three broken people to an empty house?" she said.

I leaned forward and whispered, "I was thinking the same thing."

She laughed again, her cheeks lifted and her eyes closed. She looked pretty when she laughed, different from the sullen woman who'd been walking around here since we'd arrived.

"Well," she said, "I guess I'd better—"

"Are you busy right now?"

She blinked. "Not really, but I—"

"Do you want to get some food with me? I can drive."

She raised a brow. "Do you actually have a license?"

I dug into my pocket and pulled out my wallet. "It's fake, but I've never gotten caught before. I've been pulled over three times and never once had a problem."

"I'll drive," she said, shaking her head.

"But you're pregnant, like really…" I stared at her chest. I was supposed to look at her stomach, but her chest was just there, as swollen as her belly. Her rack was bigger than Iyana's. I gulped and shifted my weight, trying to pull my gaze but I couldn't stop staring.

"I'm pregnant. Not impaired," she deadpanned, gaining my attention. "I can still drive. I've been doing it all this time."

"Right." I gulped. "But I'd feel safer if I drove."

"Fine, but if we get pulled over, I'm faking that I'm in labor so I can get out of this."

I reared my head back and laughed as we walked down the stairs to the foyer. I hadn't actually laughed since Jewels died. It felt so exhilarating. It felt good to feel something other than the knot in my stomach all the time.

I could forget, I thought as I walked to the car with Alex. *I could forget it all. I don't have to hold on to her. I can start over. I want to start over...*

The traffic here was similar to the crowded traffic in New York. We were nearly stopped now because of an accident further up. There'd been lights and sirens wailing for the past fifteen minutes we'd been inching by, and we hadn't muttered a word since we got in the car. We hadn't even picked a place to eat, we just got in and I took off. It was silent, and we were left to think. No doubt she was thinking about losing her son while I was wrestling with forgetting Jewels, wondering about God, and hoping Iyana was alright.

"Hardy?"

"Yeah?"

"What's your story?"

I clenched my jaw. I hadn't verbalized much of what I'd been going through, but none of us had. I wanted help, but I also didn't want to dump my own problems on her.

"Sorry, I shouldn't have asked."

"No." I exhaled deeply, inching the car through the slow traffic. "I'll tell you but once you know, you'll be locked in this car with me."

She shifted. "Should I be scared?"

"Nah," I chuckled, "but I am. I'm scared because of what I felt when I…" the thought of speaking it out loud almost made me vomit, but I took another deep breath and said, "I killed the woman I loved."

She didn't react. She sat there looking straight ahead. "You're in a gang. People die."

"That doesn't make it right."

"It'll never be right to take a life with no cause, but what am I supposed to say to you, Hardy? If I tell you that I'm afraid of you, you'll be upset. If I comfort you, you'll think I approve of what you've done."

We were at a full stop now, and I dropped my head to the steering wheel. "That's why I'm so confused. Because when I killed her, it was the most freeing feeling I'd ever experienced. But when she was gone, it felt like a hole had been carved out of me. A very jagged and dull knife carved out the space she took in my chest."

"You didn't love her."

I sat up and blinked at her. "What?"

"Love is perfect, or so I've been told. Nothing bad or harmful can come out of love. You were obsessed, not in love."

"You don't know what you're talking about!"

"I *do*," she snapped. "Because I was in the same predicament."

Silence fell over us.

"He was abusive," Alex muttered. "Sexually, physically, emotionally. But I craved him, like I was a wild animal. And when he laid still on the ice, I felt relieved and afraid."

"You killed him?"

She shook her head. "Brandon was still breathing, and I heard one of the men say they were taking him back with them. But I hit him over the head, and I don't know if I wanted to kill him or not. The scariest thing is that I don't know if I *still* want to kill him or not."

"Are you angry at him?"

"I think so. I'm angry that he cheated on me, and I'm angry that I took care of his mistress's son while my body was barely strong enough to carry my own child."

Silence settled again, and now there was a mess of truth and emotions in the car. I slammed my hand on the buttons and rolled down all the windows. Shifting gears, I whipped out of traffic and drove along the shoulder of the expressway.

"What are you doing!?" Alex screamed.

"I can't take it!" I sped off to the first exit. Horns honked at us, and the sirens seemed louder, but no one followed us. I zipped through the red light and drove until I found a dead end and whipped down the street.

Slamming on breaks, Alex screamed as she fell forward and then jerked back into her seat.

"What in the—"

I turned in my chair, the seatbelt bruising my neck, and covered her mouth with my own. She was flailing initially, but when I didn't pull away, her hands stopped beating against my chest. Her arms wrapped around my neck, and she pulled me closer, deepening the kiss.

Alex wouldn't let me pull away for air, which made the feeling of ecstasy running through my body meet a new surge. She clawed at my back, silently begging for more, but our kiss became salty, and when I pulled away, I realized she was crying.

"Alex," I panted, "I'm sorry. You're married. I shouldn't have done that. I wasn't trying to force you, I was just—"

"I wanted you too." She looked up from her lap. "I still want you."

"Alex, we can't. You're married."

She grabbed the ring on her finger and tugged on it until it sprang free. Tossing it out the window, she turned back to me and said, "I'm not married anymore. I never really was."

"I don't have any protection and I don't know if you can," I looked down at her belly, but when my eyes met hers again, there was a blaze in them.

"I don't want protection; I don't want anything to hold us back."

She unbuckled her seatbelt and pushed me back against my door. I swallowed as she was suddenly more sensuous than before. She wasn't the sullen wife of Brandon anymore. She was a vicious and pregnant self-declared ex-wife who was about to rob me of my car virginity.

She pulled her jacket down her shoulders and I watched intently as she began to undress. But before she could even get out of her shirt, sirens wailed behind us as a police vehicle whipped down the street.

She swore loudly, and I released a breath I didn't know I was holding. I'd been saving my first car sex experience for Kat, but she'd been so stiff, and I think she was actually a real Christian, like Iyana, so I wasn't sure when that would happen. I was supposed to be on a 'Jesus Journey' myself, but the moment came with Alex, and I was ready to soak all my problems into her drowning sea.

"Excuse me," the officer called through our open windows.

"Yes, officer?" I asked, looking up at the badly tanned woman.

"You want to tell me why you drove the shoulder?"

"Well, you see—"

"I'm going to need you to step out of the car. Both of you."

"Wait, a second," Alex called.

"It's alright," I said to her, "we'll just get out and see what she wants."

I stepped out first, and the officer sized me up. When Alex came around, she blinked.

"Oh goodness, you're pregnant. Why didn't you say so? False alarm?"

Alex nodded quickly. "We're so close, the cramps come but then they stop completely. We pulled over because the driving was making me sick."

"I remember when that happened to me with my first child. We had so many false alarms. But no matter what, if there's no water, it's probably just a cramp. That's my word of advice."

"Thank you so much, officer."

She smiled and nodded. "You kids be careful. And don't be so reckless with your pretty wife. She's pregnant. One wrong bump and something really bad could've happened." I had no time to react or explain, not that I even could after that.

I nodded as the officer turned and waved as she got back in her car and turned around.

"That was really close," I said.

When Alex didn't reply, I turned to look at her. She was just standing there staring at the ground.

"Alex, you alright?"

"We were about to have sex…"

"We still can if you want to." I swallowed, hoping I didn't sound so desperate. But Alex didn't reply.

I cleared my throat. "We should probably head home. It's for the best."

"I hadn't felt like that in years. You only kissed me, and it shattered me." She placed a hand to her mouth, and I almost drooled at her soft pink lips. "No one's ever kissed me like that before."

"Oh, I didn't mean to overstep my boundaries." I tried to sound like a gentleman, even though I still wanted to lose my car virginity to her. But for the sake of my *Jesus Journey*, and because of her vulnerability, I had to bite the bullet this time and let this chance go.

"I still have this feeling in my chest. This desire..."

I reached out and touched her. Her eyes shot to mine, and she looked nervous.

"Let me take you home, Alex. You're vulnerable, and I don't want to do something that won't mean anything or mean too much in this moment."

"But when I'm better," she said softly.

"When you're better." I leaned forward and kissed her forehead. I didn't know if Alex meant anything she was saying, or if it was just the hormones. I didn't even believe everything *I* was saying. I was still fighting myself about Jewels and trying to figure out who God was. It was better to wait until our heads were in a better place, and our hearts too.

Seventeen
Brandon
Jan 19th | 4:14pm

We'd been hiding in an abandoned building in Queens since Grizzly found us at my house. But with that tip from Vito, I took the battery out of my phone and kept the SIM card for today.

I hadn't told Brooke what Vito had said about BJ and Alex, because I didn't know if I could believe it. I'd given Brooke pieces of the conversation, like things about Jewels and Jill running off, but nothing about his brother potentially beating my son and wife. I don't want to believe that BJ is in some private facility, but I won't know until tonight when I call Alex. If Vito keeps his word, then I'll trust what he said, and I'll be forced to tell Brooke that Dahodda's apology before we left was because he lied. I was hoping it all wasn't true.

I sat on a ripped couch as Brooke counted out the bit of money we had left. If everything went well tonight, we'd have more money and could get out of this dump. There was a guy that walked the street every night looking for his daughter. We planned to jump him and take everything he had and sell it. It was Brooke's plan. He said that he and Dahodda survived the streets this way. Robbing and thugging before they joined Grizzly and JNJ.

"How long do you think that phone call will take?" Brooke asked as he scooped the money back into a sack.

"I don't know. There's a lot to talk about."

"Well, make it fast," he said. "If we leave now, we can be at the tower by five and we have no idea how far away the drive will be. And we're getting low on gas."

"I can't miss this chance."

"Then ask your guy for some money since you're suddenly back on good terms."

"What are you insinuating?" I asked.

Brooke shrugged. "I just think it's weird that this guy has all the answers all of a sudden. And he's not asking for anything? Didn't you work for the guy?"

"Yeah, but something seemed true about what he was saying."

"Or you're just feeling so guilty for what you've done and he's playing you."

"Aye, what's your problem, Brooke?" I erupted from the couch, and he stood from the table at the same time. Unfazed.

"My problem is that you're putting us in danger! What if Vito's lying!? Has that ever crossed your mind?"

"And what if your brother was lying!? Has that ever crossed *your* mind?"

He stared at me for a moment, his brows lowering in anger. "What are you talking about? What did Vito say?"

"Just forget it," I said as I made my way to the door.

"You can't just say that and walk away!"

"Are you coming, or no? Because I can do this on my own and be back here for tonight."

He sniffled and grabbed the pouch of money. Shoving it into his bag, he pushed by me and headed for the car.

We pulled up to the tower and I hopped out and went inside. The men in suits nodded as I walked down the corridor to the front desk, but no one was there. I stood there, glancing around, wondering if this was all a trap. I couldn't walk out there with my tail tucked. Brooke would make a fool of me. I gritted my teeth, cursing Vito and BT under my breath when I heard an elevator ding around the corner.

The Prince of the City appeared in lime green sweats, and his sweat jacket was zipped all the way up, with a baseball cap, and slides. Vito looked like his usual self, but that was what was so dangerous about him. He could lie without his heart racing. He could kill without flinching. He could love without feeling anything. You never really knew what was going on in his head, no matter what expression was on his face. And what made it worse was that Vito never wore anything out of the ordinary. He always looked calm and approachable. He had a handsome face and a friendly smile, he wore track suits and looked comfortable all the time. He was an excellent fit for his title as Prince. But the civilians didn't know how cruel their prince could be. How heartless and cold. But everyone in the gang world knew.

We all knew that Vito could flip his switch within the blink of an eye, and no one wanted that. So we stayed on his good side, or in my case, never let him know you were against him until the very end. However, Vee made it easy to trust him. He only flipped his switch when he felt disrespected. He never once acted to show dominance.

Vee was always kind and joking, and sometimes serious when he needed to be. You could trust him; he kept his word. You could talk to him, he was approachable. You could bring him your problems, he was helpful and always planning something. You could even get over on him a little and he didn't care. But one wrong move could turn the prince into the one who sits in the furnace of Hades.

"I thought you said Kat would have a location for me."

"Do you see her anywhere?" He glanced around and shrugged. "You can't make do with me?"

I didn't respond. I watched him move to the front and look over the desk until his eyes fell on whatever he was searching for. He jotted something down and placed the strip of paper on the countertop.

"Be there in five minutes. It's just up the street. Someone's going to spill trash. Take the brown paper bag and go."

Without another word, he turned to leave but I called, "Wait, Vee, why are you doing this? What's the real motive here?"

His eyes lazily washed over me. "Honestly, I want you to see for yourself just what you left the Pack for."

He left me standing there at the desk, and for once I understood Vito. Most days, even when I worked for him, I didn't understand him. But vengeance, I *can* understand. Anger and resentment, it made sense, almost too much sense.

I read the address over as I barged out the front doors and down the steps.

"Where's the place?" Brooke asked as I got in the car.

"Up the street. At the second light turn right, and I'll jump out there."

"Where do I wait for you?"

"Find a lot nearby. Come back to the drop off point in thirty minutes."

"That's a long time," he said as he pulled onto the street.

"I need to know something, and I need to make sure my wife is alright."

"And Jewels? What are you going to do about her?"

I couldn't speak. Alex had been the only one on my mind since Vito told me she was safe. I was so happy that she'd made it, even though it was all her fault. If she'd just listened and helped me clean the car, I would've been awake to protect her and BJ. But Jewels… running off just didn't seem like her. Especially not with Jill. But she wasn't at the tower, and she hadn't been in contact with me, and I can't call Jill.

If Jill was working with Grizzly, then there's a possibility that Jewels was too. But I doubted that. Jewels had always been mine—she wouldn't turn on me. Which meant there was a reason she's with Jill... *Maybe she's trying to lead me to her?*

"We're here," Brooke said, interrupting my thoughts.

"Right. Circle back here in thirty minutes."

"Hey," he called as I stepped onto the sidewalk. "Be careful."

I nodded and headed inside the small café.

I scanned the area inside, looking for any kind of brown bag. There were women on roller skates carrying big trays of food to tables. Couples sitting close and people smiling. They had no idea what was happening in the underground world. I walked deeper inside and tried not to look suspicious. Everyone was eating, and there was a pink and powder blue jukebox in the corner playing noisy tunes.

"Whoa!" An older man fell into me, and I tripped forward. Whirling around, I went to snap at the old man, but I stopped when I saw the brown bag sitting on the floor beside his food sprawled all around.

"Let me help you, sir." I leaned down and grabbed the bag first, then placed everything else back on his tray.

He looked up at me and gave me a knowing smile before one of the waitresses came over and knelt beside us. I nodded at him as the waitress whined, "I can throw this out and get you something else right away. Are you alright, sir?"

"I'll get rid of it," I said, standing quickly before getting an answer from the two of them. I raced to the garbage and dropped everything inside—even the tray by accident—and ran off to the bathroom.

I burst inside and pushed past a worker using the urinal to get to a stall. It smelled like death in there, but I didn't care. Unraveling the bag, I pulled out the cellphone. It was a sleek black flip phone, with one contact inside…

"Alex," I whispered.

Eighteen
Alex
Jan 19th | 4:15pm

"Hardy," I giggled, "stop it." He kissed my belly even more which tickled like crazy. Brandon had never done that. He was sexual when he wanted to be, but he was never affectionate or intimate. Not the way Hardy has been.

We didn't have sex and not just because I'm *technically* still married. When we returned home, Hardy and I couldn't speak to each other. I was embarrassed and he was too. But then Iyana got better and wanted us all to have dinner together, which was totally fine until Hardy started playing footsies with me under the table. I don't think Iyana caught on to us, but when she went to bed, Hardy crept into my room and lay in bed with me. All he wanted to do was talk. So, I listened.

He poured his heart out to me. He told me he missed his mother more than anything, and he told me somehow that treacherous woman, Jewels, had filled the void left behind by his mother. He also mentioned a woman named Kat and how he wasn't sure what was happening between them, and he wasn't sure he wanted to know.

Hardy was unique and interesting. He'd had quite an adventurous life, which made mine seem pitiful in comparison when it was my turn to talk. But Hardy was more mature than his goofy grin made him seem. He listened and asked questions. He made me feel important, like I wasn't talking to a wall. And when I cried, he comforted me. Maybe that was just kindness. Simple manners. The bare minimum of respect for being a human being, but Brandon didn't have any of that, and this was new for me.

Since our car ride, we haven't been the same. We've been sneaking off to each other's room like hormonal teenagers. Even though I'm seven years older than Hardy, I can't stop my heart from racing whenever I'm around him. And even though I know this was exciting because we didn't want to deal with the grief, I didn't want it to stop.

This has been the most fun I've had in such a long time. I just wished BJ could've met Hardy. He would've loved him. But BJ was gone now. He'd slipped through my fingers, and he'd saved my life. He took a bullet for me, and when I told Hardy that, his response was that I owed BJ my own life. The only way to repay a life for a life is to live a good one, at least that's his plan to get over Jewels.

Hardy pulled away from my bare belly and pressed his hands into the pillows beside my hips as he leaned over and kissed me. He always kissed me so passionately, and I wondered where he'd learned it from. I would take a guess and say Jewels because she'd taught Brandon some things. I just didn't know at the time where he'd gotten some of those ideas from. He'd come home eager to try new things that tortured me in bed, but even when I begged him to stop, he wouldn't.

Everyone was used to having sex, but no one was used to making love. The art had been forgotten, or so I thought. Hardy's kisses were a reminder that love once existed between Brandon and me. But I knew this wasn't love. What Hardy and I felt was just lust and desire. We wanted to feel something other than the pain, we wanted to forget reality, but we couldn't. I'd lost my son, he'd killed a woman. How could we ever forget those things?

But every time he kissed me, every time he touched me or was around me, there was a stirring in my chest I couldn't describe. A new possibility to start over and forget my past surfaced when I was with him. I loved the way it felt, the way my heart fluttered when he smiled, or leapt when he kissed me. When did my heart become so desperate and fragile? It was broken and I didn't know if Hardy had intentions of actually fixing it or if he just wanted a distraction.

"Hardy," I whispered as I gasped between kisses.

"What's wrong?" he said quietly as his lips traced my neck.

"This is wrong, Hardy."

He stopped abruptly and slowly pulled away to look at me. "What do you mean this is wrong?"

"We're having fun, but I'm still married, and I just lost my son. I shouldn't be doing this."

"Why not?"

"Because this isn't real," I said. "We just need a distraction, but this isn't right."

"Why isn't this real?"

I blinked up at him and sighed heavily. "You're too young to understand the difference between lust and love."

"No," he sat back, "I know the difference between a throbbing in my pants and a thumping in my chest. But what I don't know is why you're so afraid to feel either of those things."

"Because my son is dead!" I shouted.

"But *you're* not! Your life didn't stop! You have to keep going. Why are you punishing yourself so hard? You won't even let yourself feel anything, and I know you feel something with me."

"I don't feel anything," I turned my head and tried not to let any tears swell.

"That's not true." His voice was softer now, the key to unlocking the fragile door to my shattered heart.

I was afraid to let him inside to look around and see the darkness. The emptiness. I had only shared a little bit of my past with him. I wanted to share more than just the things on the surface, but it wasn't right… How could it be?

"I'm…" I hiccupped, but the words wouldn't come. The truth was that I was afraid, and I felt like it was wrong to turn on BJ and on Brandon. Brandon was kind too, despite the edge he always had, but what if Hardy changed into Brandon?

I was afraid of being foolish. Afraid of being deceived again. It was all too soon. And how could I just happily walk away with my life when BJ had lost his? It wasn't right. It wasn't fair.

"Starting over can be scary for everyone. All the ghosts of the past dance like the shadows of a flickering flame. But if you step into the light, you'll find they weren't even ghosts." He stood from the bed and headed for the door.

"Hardy wait," I whispered. "What are they?"

He turned and looked over his shoulder, a small smile tugging on his lips. "The darkness you can't remember." He opened the door and stepped out.

"I was just coming to get Alex and then you for an early dinner, so we can watch movies tonight," Iyana said outside the door. "What were you doing in there?"

"I heard her crying and came to check on her." He paused and looked over his shoulder into the room. When his eyes met mine, the urge to call him back almost ripped from my lips, but I covered my mouth instead and let the tears fall.

"Alex won't be well for a while." He returned his focus to Iyana. "I'm not hungry. I'm just going to bed." He left without looking back, and I hunched over and began to sob quietly.

"What is going on?" Iyana said as she closed the door gently.

I shook my head, unable to speak.

"You've got to tell me something because I don't feel like prying it out of Hardy."

"I had to let him go," my voice was shaky and I hated the weakness in it.

"Let him go? Go where?"

"We've been seeing each other."

"What? You two have been sleeping together right next door to me!" She erupted from the bed, but I shushed her and waved for her to sit back down.

"No," I insisted. "We've just been spending the last few days together. But we've kissed and he's been talking, and I've been talking and it's wrong."

"Well yeah you can't kiss him because you're married, Alex."

"I know, and I hate myself for wanting him to kiss me."

"Alex, Hardy is only twenty years old."

I sniffled. "I know."

Iyana sighed and covered her face with her hands. "I don't know what this boy has that's making grown women buckle, but you've got to be stronger than this. Hardy's a child."

"I'm only twenty-seven, Iyana, I'm not in my thirties like Brandon."

She went silent. "Oh. Well, that's still a seven-year difference."

"I know," I said glumly, "but he makes me feel good."

Iyana sighed again and leaned forward, dropping her elbows to her knees. "Hardy is a good kid. He's cute and kind, but he's looking for a mommy. He's looking for guidance. He's looking for God. It's a very confusing time for him. So if you're going to be in his life, be there. But you don't get to ping pong him."

"I know. But I feel like it's wrong. I feel like I shouldn't be allowed to be happy without BJ. And I know I can't dishonor my marriage, but everything in me wants to feel the things I feel with Hardy."

She sat for a moment, looking straight ahead at nothing. Her brown eyes blinked slowly as she thought over what to say. I knew she would scold me, tell me I was an idiot for wanting to be with a younger man. She'd tell me to look down at my baby bump and remember everything I've been through. But that's what I needed to hear. I needed to refocus and get my head on straight.

"It's alright to be happy, and it's alright to fall in love again. I can't encourage an affair, or divorce because I don't believe either of those are right. But I will tell you that I know how you feel. I wasn't sure if it was alright to love Vito when my mother was in a coma, and my father was going through the ringer." She raised her head and turned to me. "But you cannot stop living because of the loss. My mother is gone now, and my father is being dangled by a string. But I can't stop living, Alex. I have to keep going."

"Is it really okay?"

"Way back in the Garden of Eden, God promised that the seed of the woman would crush the serpent's head. I don't know what you believe, but I will tell you … between the Garden of Eden and the birth of Christ, there were plenty of mistakes and death. But if everyone had stopped living every time they experienced a loss, the Savior would not have come."

I didn't know much about God, I'd been to church when I was younger, but I never took it seriously. However, I remembered Eden, I remembered the fall of man, and the rescuing plan of God through Christ. So maybe I was being rescued through all of this. Rescued from the life I was living before. Starting a new life.

When a rose is picked, it begins to wither. And before it's placed in an arrangement, the thorns are clipped. But that rose has a new life, a new purpose in that floral arrangement. Its beauty is beheld in that arrangement, but eventually, it will die. However, what's left behind is the bush where another cycle begins. A new rose cannot bud without the picking of a matured one. Our lives are meant to be picked, withered, and clipped, so that we can start over.

But starting over doesn't have to be hard.

Adjusting on the bed beside Iyana, I asked, "There were also new beginnings in the story of Christ, right?"

She nodded.

"And I can start over with Christ, right?"

"Yes, of course."

"And I heard it said once before that you can die to your old life, and start a new one in Christ? Is this possible for me?"

She smiled and grabbed my hands. "New life is given to those who believe and seek God for it. If you truly want to start over with Christ, you can."

"He'll help me figure this out? I'll know what to do about Hardy?"

"God will give you the wisdom."

"Then I want Him. Please," my voice cracked, and Iyana reached out and wiped my tears.

"You have to want Him for Him, not for Hardy."

I shook my head. "I see how you've bounced back after losing your mother. I want that. I want peace and joy."

"Then repeat after me."

Iyana led me through a prayer that ended with me confessing my sins and accepting Jesus as my Lord and Savior. It was a beautiful feeling of release. She left me to myself to calm down and told me she'd leave me a plate of food in the kitchen. But I wasn't hungry. I wanted to stay in bed and think. Before I moved from the bed to wipe my eyes, my phone blared into the silence. Jumping from the loud ringing, I exhaled and grabbed the phone.

"Brandon?" I gasped as I stared at the screen. It rang a while longer before I could get myself to answer.

"Hello?"

"Alex? Baby! Oh my goodness!" Brandon's voice clamored into my ear for the first time since the beginning of the month. I hadn't heard or seen him since I knocked him out.

I tried to think of something to say, but nothing came. I sat still on the bed, afraid that if I moved or even thought something, he'd hear it.

"Baby? Say something please, I need to hear your voice. Where are you? Are you safe?"

"Where are you?" I asked shakily.

"I'm running around, still trying to make things happen, still trying to protect you."

"I'm safe, Brandon."

"How's BJ? Can you put him on the phone?"

"Brandon…" I stood slowly from the bed and walked across the room. Tears were burning my eyes and my throat felt like I'd swallowed a golf ball.

"What… what happened?" Brandon asked.

I sniffled and dropped to my knees. Brandon and I had been through a lot, but he was still my husband, and BJ was still our son, and breaking the news to him was never something I'd actually planned for. That was partially because I didn't know if I'd ever get the chance, but it was also because of Hardy.

I hadn't truly mourned BJ. I hadn't truly reflected on his passing. But that was because of circumstances paired with Hardy. It was like he was purposely distracting me from BJ and Brandon, but I welcomed it so desperately, it was almost embarrassing.

"There were men who came inside the house, and…" I trailed off, afraid to say it aloud, but Brandon took over and said, "You don't have to say the rest. I'm going to get these guys, and when I do, I'm coming for you, Alex. I'm going to come and find you and we're going to get away from the city." His words seemed to be weighted in truth.

Brandon was my husband, and he'd done everything wrong, but he loved me. We had a daughter on the way, and I couldn't give up my family for someone I barely knew. I wanted my family back, despite how hard it would be without BJ. However, after all of this, I believed Brandon and I would be strong enough to endure the loss. I could introduce him to Christ, and we could do things differently. Our marriage could be better this time around.

"Alex, you still there?"

"Yes, I'm still here."

"I miss you so much."

A small smile tugged at my lips. "I miss you too."

Before Brandon called, I was actually considering leaving him. But as I listened to him now, as I heard his voice and the desperation in it, I realized I wanted to be by his side. I wanted to be his wife again.

"Brandon," I whispered.

"Yes, baby?"

"I want us to start over."

"We can do whatever you want, Lex. I just want to be with you."

"Me too." I squeezed the phone.

"Lex, tell me where you are so I can at least know where to find you."

I wanted this to be real. I wanted us to truly start over, but in the back of my head, I couldn't stop thinking about what Iyana had told me. I couldn't stop replaying our conversation about the truth. How Brandon's been protecting himself.

How do I know if he really means it now?

"Lex?"

If you keep thinking that everything I'm telling you is just an accusation, they'll never leave you alone because you'll keep walking into their traps. You'll always be fooled by the men in these gangs, by your own husband.

I'm afraid of being fooled again.

"Lex? Are you still there?"

I'm afraid of him.

"Baby, say something."

I won't be fooled again.

"Hello? I can hear you breathing, Lex."

I love him...

"Just say something. Anything."

But I cannot be afraid anymore.

"ALEX!"

"Who is Jewels?" I snapped.

The deafening silence made me feel numb.

Please, I begged within, *just tell the truth.*

"Alex, I don't know what Grizzly told you, but I don't know anyone named Jewels. He's just trying to turn us against each other. Baby, I've always loved you, you know that."

I closed my eyes and took a breath.

"Why would you lie to me?"

"Alex, I'm not lying," he snapped. There was a slow growing rage in his voice, the kind that always bubbled over and left me with a new bruise or a black eye.

"Yes," I trembled. "Yes, you are."

He swore loudly. "I am not lying! What'd he say, huh?"

"Why are you so sure that it was Grizzly and not Jewels herself?" I sniffled.

"Because Jewels would never do that to me!"

I held the phone against my ear, imagining the look on my husband's face. The way he curdled over in defeat because he'd gone too far. He'd do that sometimes when he'd punch me or beat me until I was motionless. The beatings weren't as bad once I became pregnant. But he'd also been away more, so all he wanted to do when he came home was release his stress or sleep.

There were still arguments, still punches and slapping. Blood was still spilled.

"Alex," his voice was the weakest I'd ever heard it. He'd told me all I needed to know; all I'd *wanted* to know.

I raised my chin and wiped my tears. "I've got to go now."

"Lex, please wait. It's not what you think."

"For too long I've let you tell me what to think. I've got to think on my own now, Brandon."

"What are you saying? Lex? Don't do this…"

I exhaled slowly as I felt the weight of the world closing in on me. It was crushing me, shoving me face first into the dirt. Crushing my lungs, choking me from within. I hated the feeling. I hated myself for being fooled for so long. But I couldn't do it any longer.

"Goodbye, Brandon," I said as strongly as I could.

"Alex, please! Wait—"

Before he could plead any further, I hung up.

Nineteen
Brandon
Jan 19th | 5:36pm

"ALEX!" I screamed into the phone, but the tone was dead, and she was gone. I squeezed the phone so hard in my hand I thought I could crush it. Who'd told her about Jewels and me? Was it Vito? Was it Grizzly? Why would Vito tell her about Jewels and then let me call her? Was this his revenge? That was too simple for Vito. It had to be Grizzly.

"Hey!" a man called outside my stall. "I'm gonna use the floor if you don't come out of there!" I kicked open the door, making him scream and hit the floor.

"What's your problem!?"

I whirled around so quick, I lost my balance and fell into the stall. Recovering, I snatched the man by his shirt and punched him in the face. He yelped, but it wasn't enough. I was angry, and before I knew it, everything was a blur, and I was hammering on the man with everything I had.

"Hey, get off of him! You'll kill him!" Someone tried to pull me off the man, but I turned away and slammed the guy pulling on me into the wall. When I returned my focus back to the man beneath me, he was lying still. I clenched my fist and raised it above my head, panting heavily as I stared at the lifeless man. I'd beaten him with my own hands. No guns, no knives, just my bare knuckles.

Slowly, I stood to my feet.

"Did you kill him?" the other man was asking as he got off the floor.

"No." I shook my head. "I didn't do that."

"I'm calling the police!"

"No!" I grabbed him before he could rush out and we struggled until I wrapped one arm around his neck and gripped my forearm as I choked him.

He was kicking and trying to screech, but I needed him quiet so no one would come in here. His pale skin began to redden as he kicked and scratched at me. I twisted and turned, trying to avoid his flailing. But eventually he stopped moving, and his body fell limp in my arms. Panting, I dragged him into the big stall and laid him over the toilet. I placed the other man I'd beaten in another stall. He'd already soiled his pants and the feces made the entire bathroom smell.

Pulling myself together, I stepped out the bathroom and headed straight for the exit. It was freezing outside, the cold nearly took my breath away as I pushed through the doors, but I had to search for Brooke. He hadn't come back around, and I was beginning to feel nervous that someone had caught me.

I took a casual stroll as the city began to fall asleep. I could hear my heart pounding. I could feel sweat trickling down my neck. My hands trembled in my pockets as I searched desperately for Brooke. Before my nerves broke, I started walking down the street just to get away. I kept my head down and walked slowly. I heard the bell from the restaurant clang.

"There he is!"

I glanced over my shoulder and two men were pointing at me. Without even thinking, I took off, racing down the street as they yelled for others to stop me. The cold air burned as I sucked it in. I pumped my arms hard and forced my legs to break through the cold as they tore into a sprint. My heavy boots sloshed into the ice and snow mixture but, thankfully, I didn't fall. People jumped and moved out of the way as I raced across the street, dodging cars, and taking turns without a plan.

I couldn't run forever, but I could at least find somewhere to hide. Just as my breathing became erratic, I heard a car blowing its horn behind me. I glanced over my shoulder and recognized the car as Brooke's. The men chasing me were a few paces behind, giving me enough time to slip into the car.

"Drive! Drive!" I screamed.

"I'm trying!" Brooke whipped the car into traffic. Cars honked loudly at us as he swerved through a red light and turned down an alleyway.

"What are you running from?" He was still yelling even though we were far enough away from the danger.

"There was a problem in the bathroom. Me and a guy got into it."

"What? Brandon you can't be drawing attention to us!"

"I know!"

"Then act like it!" He slammed on the brakes, throwing us forward and backward.

"What is wrong with you?" I snapped.

"I just…" he took a breath and leaned on the steering wheel. "I just don't want to get caught, alright?"

"I know," I said flatly. "We won't get caught if we keep moving. Let's get close to the tower. We can dump the car somewhere and go back to Vee."

"Are you listening!?" he yelled. "I don't want to get caught! Vito is not our friend, and he is not the answer! Wake up, Brandon, or you'll get us killed."

"Vito can help us right now! He's our best shot at survival."

He shook his head and snatched the car out of park. "Well, you're not driving."

"Brooke, don't be an idiot! Turn around so we can get back to the tower."

"No," he said.

"Brooke."

"No!"

"Brooke!" I leaned over and grabbed the steering wheel. I needed to go back to the tower. I needed to know if Vito told Alex anything. I needed to know where she was. The car swerved as I pulled on the steering wheel.

"Stop it!" Brooke screamed. "Let go!"

"Turn around!" I punched Brooke in the head and yanked the steering wheel. We began to spin out of control as we fought for control of the car.

"Take your foot off the gas!" I screamed. But before I knew it, we hit a lamp and spun down into a ditch on the outskirts of Manhattan.

I coughed and opened my eyes. We were upside down. Every move was torturous and slow. I unbuckled my seatbelt and fell into the ceiling of the car.

"Brooke," I whispered. "Brooke?"

He groaned and jerked awake. Blood was dripping from his face, and he didn't look good. I didn't know what was wrong with me yet, but I knew we needed to get out of the cold before we died. Since my window was busted out, I was able to orient myself and crawl out of it. My leg ached as I rolled over in the cold, panting on the rocks. For the first time, I listened to the river. We were right by it now, and I could hear it rushing at full force.

"Hello?" a woman's voice called out. "Is anyone out there?"

"Help!" I managed to call. "Please! Help me!"

"I'm coming! Stay right there!"

I lay on the cold ice and stared up at the dark sky. Winter always made the days shorter in the city, and the cold seemed to be bitter tonight. But the coolness was numbing the pain I felt all over. It was helping with the aching.

"Help…" there was a forced and raspy whisper coming from Brooke. He was still in the car, strapped in and bleeding out. I turned my attention back to the night. There was nothing I could do for him, and nothing that would be done for him. It was his fault we were in this predicament, his fault that he was trapped in the car. There was no reason to save him anyway, he looked pretty injured.

"I'm coming!" the woman shouted. I could hear her getting closer until she was hovering over me.

"Goodness! Are you alright!? I need to get you inside or you'll freeze out here." She leaned down and tried to help me up.

"On the count of three," she said as she adjusted me on her shoulders. "One… two… three!" She stood abruptly and we stumbled as I cried out. Something was wrong with my leg, but it wasn't broken. We struggled to the house, grunting and groaning until she got me inside.

The place was small, but it was still a house and there weren't too many of those in the city. Whoever this woman was, she had to have a little money to have a house, which could be good *and* bad for me.

As she sat me down on the small beige couch, she dropped to her knees. "I'm going to call the police," she said through short breaths.

"No!" I yelled. "Please don't. I've already had a run-in with them tonight, I can't do it again."

"But you're injured, and your car is down—"

"I'll be fine. I'll get my car in the morning. Just give me the couch tonight and I'll be gone by the morning. Please." Brown eyes looked away from me and down at my leg. "Let me at least clean this up."

I nodded but said nothing else. When she left for the kitchen, I glanced around the small space, looking for exits or weapons. There wasn't much to see; a living room, a cramped dining room, and there was a hall that ran further back to what I assumed would be a staircase. The woman reappeared without her jacket. She was wearing sweatpants and an oversized shirt, carrying a silver tin of supplies.

"Ok, I'm going to cut your pants."

Shakily, she cut around the gash in my leg. It was bruising and swollen, and even I knew that meant something was wrong.

"What happened?" she asked as she tried to stop the bleeding. She wasn't looking at me, her eyes were focused, and her hands were steady.

"I lost control of the wheel."

"Were you were running from something?"

"Yeah," I said curtly.

She dug through the box and found a small bottle of liquid. Tearing the cap off, she poured it all over my leg. I groaned at the pain.

"This gash is deep, and bruising is indicative of at least a fracture. You should go to the hospital in the morning. For now, I'm going to add a splint to your leg, here and here." She pointed to two spots around the injury. "It's going to hurt but I'll add a little padding to ease the discomfort. Unfortunately, that's all I can do for you."

"Why?" I breathed for a moment. "Why are you helping me when I said I was running from the cops?"

She stopped unrolling her bandage and looked up at me. Buttery yellow skin and mini braids that hung just above her slender shoulders, she reminded me of Alex with her look of innocence.

"You're injured." She chewed her lower lip as she looked me over. "I've worked on criminals before. My job is to see that a patient is ready for the next day. Whether the next day is their trial or their first day behind bars, I just have to get them there." Her voice betrayed her innocence. She sounded like a mature woman, but she didn't look like one. I didn't know what to say, but I also didn't know what kind of answer to even expect.

Not all people are bad, that's the only explanation for this, I thought.

"I'll get the splint on, and then you'll want to rest. The best I can give you is ibuprofen for the pain."

I nodded.

"It's going to hurt a lot, so just bear with me."

"What's your name?" I asked as she stood.

"Dr. City, but please, call me Vali."

— **BT** —

I woke through the night in a sweat. My leg was aching, I was hungry, and I was exhausted. My body felt like it'd been through the shredder twice, but I needed to get moving.

Gripping the slick suede couch, I sat up with a grunt. I took shallow breaths as I prepped myself to stand. I had to make it outside to the car. I was afraid that if I left Brooke out there, he would scream for help, or Vali would get curious.

Slowly, I stood, and when I tried to limp, there was a ringing pain in my leg so treacherous, I crashed to the floor, dragging everything down with me. The small folding table holding supplies, the lamp nearby.

"Brandon?" I lay there, just breathing as I stared up in the darkness at nothing. I heard Vali coming down the stairs and then a light clicked on. She gasped. "Brandon, what are you doing? You're supposed to be sleeping."

"I can't sleep," I said as I tried to sit up. "I have to go."

"No." She ran over to me. "You need to rest."

"I can't rest!" I shouted as I shoved her away.

She stumbled backwards before falling to the floor. Baggy clothes and a tight frown, Vali moved to her feet quickly and came over to me. "You're in my house," she seethed, "you're not going to fight me!" She reached down so quickly, when she snatched me to her face by my shirt, my neck snapped from the force. I didn't know if I should be surprised by her strength or by her change in personality.

"Let go of me!" I shouted after regaining myself. I grabbed her arm and twisted it. She screamed and let my shirt go. Holding her by the arm, I slung her across the room. As she hit the floor, I took the time to try to get to my feet. But I was struck on my back before I could even get one of my feet under me.

I hollered and collapsed onto the floor again. Another swack made me cringe.

"Stop!" I screamed. "Please! Stop!"

Vali froze, panting hard. It wasn't until I rolled over that I realized she was holding a bat.

"I'm sorry, ok? Please," I begged.

"You'd better not try anything if I lower this bat."

I shook my head, and she lowered the bat but kept it aimed at me. "You'd better start telling the truth. Why were you trying to leave? Who are you really running from?"

"The police, I swear. I just needed to get outside because I didn't want to leave my friend out there."

"What?" She took a step back, and all her features were suddenly pinched together.

"He lost control of the car, and when I woke up," I paused, "he was already dead."

"Why didn't you say something sooner? I could've done CPR on him!" She dropped the bat and rushed for the kitchen.

"He's already dead. It's below zero out there, and it's been hours."

I heard her shuffling stop.

"You let him die. What is wrong with you?"

"I need to get rid of the car, and the body." I said as she came back into the living room.

"You want me to be an accessory to murder? No. You're going to have to leave." She walked out and came back with my coat and threw it at me. "Get out of my house! I didn't leave Jersey for this." She nearly doubled over in tears as she covered her face.

I struggled to get my jacket on, but before I could get to my feet, the doorbell rang. She stared at me for a second. Wiping her tears, she turned off the light.

"Don't say a word."

She left me lying there as she walked through the dark house to her front door. She opened it. "Why are you here in the middle of the night?"

"Why are you awake?" The voice was familiar. So familiar I gagged in fear and tried to hold in the sudden urge to vomit.

"You promised you'd leave me out of your mess."

"You promised to *stay* out of it."

"Dad, you need to leave. I can't help you, and you're not going to ruin my career."

It was silent for a moment and then the voice asked, "Have you seen him? People said they saw him running around here not too long ago. A strange nine-one-one call came in a few hours ago. They said a woman dragged a body from a car on the Hudson River Bay. Only one person I know capable of that over here."

"Well, keep searching, Daddy. You shouldn't even be over here."

"And you shouldn't lie to me."

I squeezed my eyes shut as sweat was dripping into them. If this exchange was what I thought it was, then I'd be in serious trouble.

"Anything else?"

"If you're lying, you know it'll cost me. Which means it'll cost you."

"I'm not one of your cubs. I'm not scared of you, Daddy." She chuckled. "Or should I say, *Grizzly*."

I sucked in so hard, I almost coughed. I clamped a hand over my mouth and held in the cough that was scratching at my throat.

"You should be scared. I only go easy on you because you're my daughter."

"I don't care. Anything else?"

There was a momentary pause before Grizzly said in his raspy voice, "Goodnight, Vali."

"Goodnight, Grizzly."

When she closed the door, I turned over and vomited. I was at the mercy of Grizzly's daughter, which explained why she was so strong and tough.

The lights turned on, and when I looked up, she was standing there with her arms folded. There was no longer a look of innocence on her face. She now had resemblance to Grizzly, and she looked just as intimidating as he did.

"Clean your mess up. If you want to stay safe, you'd better make yourself at home."

Twenty
Iyana
Jan 21st | 6:13am

I went jogging this morning. I just needed to clear my head. I'd been jogging since we arrived in LA, except when I'd gotten sick from being in the rain with Hardy. I never jogged before so I didn't know just how helpful it could be. Forcing my legs to keep going past the burn so I couldn't feel a thing. Trying to control my breathing. Jogging with no real destination in mind, I just went for it. It was freeing and it opened my mind.

Today I stopped by a hotel a few miles away from the Gerardos' home. I've gotten faster and I've built up some pretty good endurance. I was hoping that once we returned in a little over a week, I'd start doing a morning run around the tower. But I knew that was impossible with the war brewing. When I returned, I'd need to get Vito out and everyone else that I could. I'd also need to find somewhere safe to go. It'd been pressing on me, as well as worries over Vito and my father.

Vito could take care of himself, but my father, I had no idea what he'd do when he found out mom had passed. When I found out Brandon was the one keeping my mother induced and had pulled the plug on her, I went into rage mode. But every night I've been here, I've prayed harder and longer than ever before. I've forced myself to believe in the plans of God. I've forced myself not to blame Vito for not helping my mother sooner. I've forced myself not to feel sad, and that's how I started running.

I wiped the sweat from my forehead as I stepped into the hotel. It wasn't hot, but it was a little muggy and the free water sitting out looked so appetizing, I couldn't resist it. I took a cup from the table and filled it up before slugging it down. All at once, I had a brain freeze, and I squeezed my eyes shut so hard I was seeing stars.

"Ma'am? Are you alright?" One of the receptionists was by my side now, guiding me to the lounge area to sit.

"Do you want me to call someone?"

I waved her off. "No, I appreciate it. But it was just a brain freeze. That cold water was a little much."

"You sure?" She adjusted her glasses and I nodded.

"Yes, I'm fine."

"I can have someone assist you to your room if you'd like. You were looking dazed when you walked in, and then you looked pained after drinking that water, I just wanted to make sure you're alright."

"Thank you, but I'm seriously fine." I tried not to let the worry show on my face that I didn't have a room here. It never even crossed my mind that I needed a room to drink the water. I shook my head, getting to my feet. "Thank you for your kindness, but I want to finish my workout now."

"Are you sure you're alright? You don't need to call anyone, let them know that you're running?"

"No, I'm fine." I paused and blinked at the woman as an idea formed in my head. "Actually, I would like to call someone."

"Of course. You can use a phone at the front—"

"Do you have somewhere private I can make a phone call? I just would feel more comfortable that way."

She almost didn't buy it, but I slapped a hand to my head and winced and she nodded.

"Ok, come with me."

I followed her to the employee lounge. There was a black phone in the kitchenette area of the lounge.

"You can use this one."

"Thank you so much."

"Of course."

When she was out of sight, I picked up the phone and listened to the dial tone. Slowly, I typed in the number and listened to the phone ring.

Come on, I thought, *pick up.*

"Hello?"

I gasped.

"Hello?" the voice called again.

"Daddy?"

"Iyana?"

"It's me, Dad." I covered my mouth as tears sprang free. It was the stupidest idea to call him right now in the middle of a war, but at least everyone would think I was at this hotel, and not with the Gerardos if the call was ever traced.

"Iyana," he breathed, and I could hear him moving around. "How are you?"

"Dad, I'm so sorry," I whispered. "I'm so sorry I blamed you. I blamed you and left you to deal with everything on your own."

"No, Iyana, I'm the one who is sorry. I should've told you a long time ago, but I was in too deep. I couldn't tell you. I never thought you'd end up on the other side of the law to find out."

I chuckled as I wiped at my tears. "It's not like I wanted to be here. Now I'm stuck."

"Me too."

Silence.

"Iyana, there's something I need to tell you."

I took a deep breath. "Mom's death is my fault."

"What? How'd you know about that?"

"There's a lot more going on than you think, Dad. There's a war coming and it's going to get ugly."

"Iyana, hold on. I'm still stuck on how you knew about your mother."

My dad was always slow to understand, but the clattering heels of the receptionist were ringing out down the hall, and I didn't need her hearing this conversation.

"I can't tell you everything, but Brandon is just as much a part of this war as I am now. If they can't get me, they'll try to come for you."

"Who will? Who's coming for you? Tell me."

I shook my head and pressed a palm to my forehead. "Promise me that if Brandon comes for you, you'll get out of there."

Her steps were closer now and my nerves were meeting their wits' end.

"Alright," he said slowly, "but where would I go?"

"Go south. As far as you can. Don't sell anything, don't do anything out of the ordinary. Buy a car with cash and leave at night. Take whatever you can carry and—"

The door to the lounge opened and I clutched the phone. "Dad, I've got to go. I love you so much. Please be careful."

"Iyana, wait a minute."

I hung up the phone and turned around as the woman rounded the corner.

"You all set?"

I nodded. "Thanks." I pushed past her and rushed out of the room and down the hall to the first exit.

When I made it home, I was greeted by Dafni and Tobias. They were sitting at the table, drinking lemonade and talking like the happiest people in the world. Tobias was smiling for once, and it was odd. He still looked like rogue Santa, but on a good day, I guess. And Dafni was glowing. Her honey skin was smooth like Vito's…

My mind froze as I stood in the archway. I'd thought of Vito in passing only. We'd spent the last six months together, and I had fought him on leaving. Had sobbed as he'd held me in his arms. But now that we've been separated, I've barely thought about him. There'd been so much going on, I hadn't even wondered about him except to worry that he hadn't died at least. But I should be more honest with myself…

I didn't want to wonder about Vito.

I wasn't afraid he'd be out with other women. I wasn't afraid that he'd forget me. I was afraid that Vito would move on with the business without me. I was afraid that when I returned, BT wouldn't need me. I wouldn't be the leader of the Pack anymore, I'd just be Vito's wife, and he wouldn't need me either. There was nothing wrong with BT growing, but I'd spent so much time building it up, I'd feel slighted if it was getting on its feet without me. But the world keeps spinning, even when you stop moving. I just hoped that Vito's world hadn't spun much while I was away.

"Iyana? Are you alright?" Dafni was standing now.

"I'm sorry." I forced a smile. "I didn't know you guys were home. You surprised me is all." It was a lie that only Dafni bought. Tobias only raised a brow at my response, but Dafni whirled around to say something and his face changed in a flash. He was smiling and nodding at her. Their mouths were moving but I wasn't listening. There'd been so much going on, even being here away from BT, there were still problems to deal with.

"I think I'm going to lie down," I said abruptly.

Dafni and Tobias both looked surprised. "You don't want to go—"

A loud crash sounded from upstairs, followed by a piercing cry.

"Alex!" Hardy cried. I could hear him racing down the hall. My eyes fell back on Dafni and Tobias who were standing from the table now.

"Come on!" I yelled to them. We moved at once and raced to the stairs. When we reached the top, I ran into Alex's room to find Hardy helping her to her feet. There was glass on the floor, and the chair to her desk was tipped over.

"What happened?" I asked.

"Get the glass!" Dafni shouted to Tobias. He nodded and moved around the room.

"I felt dizzy, and I hit the floor before I knew it. Sorry," Alex muttered.

"Dizzy? Why are you feeling dizzy?" Hardy asked.

"I'm pregnant, Hardy." She looked up at him, this was the first time the two of them had spoken since their argument the other night.

Hardy nodded like he understood, but I knew he didn't.

I moved to grab Alex's hands as I asked, "Are you sure you're alright?"

"I'll get you some water," Dafni chimed in before she turned and headed out the room.

"I'm alright. These dizzy spells have been happening a lot more lately. This one just scared me."

"I think we should share rooms," I said. "It'll be better. That way I can keep an eye on you."

"No." She shook her head slowly. "I'm alright, I promise. I just…" She stopped talking and made a strange face. It morphed from thankful, to confused, to embarrassed in three seconds flat before she shoved Hardy aside and went for the bathroom.

"Alex!" he shouted. But she slammed the bathroom door in his face.

"Alex, are you alright?" I asked outside the door.

"I can't stop peeing! It just happened all of a sudden." Her words forced me to look down at the trail of water from where Alex had fallen that led across the room to the bathroom where she'd just locked herself inside. When I looked back up, Dafni was standing behind us with a water bottle.

"Oh my goodness," Dafni said, "her water just broke."

Twenty-One
Vito
Jan 21st | 5:19pm

My men were able to find the Abletons and their safe. They've been keeping a twenty-four-hour surveillance on them. I decided to leave the safe to Kat, but I'd pass the Abletons on to Grizzly. If he's chasing them and Brandon's chasing Grizzly, then that adds seconds to the steadily ticking clock. Murphy and Bridges's bodies were still sitting in my freezer. I was waiting for an opening to set up their deaths, but if I waited too long, I'd have to dump them myself and I wouldn't be able to use them as pieces in the puzzle.

"Well, well, Grizzly, this a lovely place you've got," I said as I strolled into his cove.

He sat in front of a fireplace that only glowed with light, there were no actual flames, no heat coming from the place, but it did offer an ambiance to the cove. Grizzly sat at a massive desk made of strong oakwood, with little to nothing on it. Two cubs stood by his side. I'd never really seen any of Grizzly's men, but the two here looked young. One was dark skinned with cornrows, and the other was brown skinned with a crew cut. They had patches of fur on their shoulders and on their arm bracers, resembling their cub rank. I'd learned all about Grizzly and his cubs after he came and told me I had a rat.

Cubs were only allowed a little fur to wear. As the cubs matured, they were given more fur, until they were adult bears and full-blown guards doing dirty work for Grizzly. Grizzly wore a long brown fur coat, while those just below him wore short brown and black fur coats. They were more organized than they seemed and, frankly, I liked the fur theme.

"What are you doing here?" Grizzly asked in a low grumble. He looked surprised, and he should be, because not a single one of his men out front made it back here to tell him I was here. I had to find my way back here myself. Adding six to my body count.

"I came to tell you that the little pet rat you'd kept for me came scampering back home a few nights ago. I know where he's hiding if that interests you."

His eyes narrowed as he folded leathery dark hands atop his desk. He was trying to remain calm and in control, but I loved watching him unravel the way he watched me about six months ago. "I'm not interested in him."

"Pride *always* comes before a fall." I shrugged, but I was only able to play it cool because Brandon wasn't my only card. He was my gauge. After finding Grizzly's den through Leo's backtracking, I decided I'd visit him and see where he stood in this war. Thankfully, from the string of dead bodies I left outside his door, it didn't seem like Grizzly had enough men to carry out a full attack. But that was only his lobby where Grizzly was known for using his cubs as pawns, so I'm sure he had better assets deeper in the den. Either way, I wanted to prepare for the worst, so I took the liberty of buying myself time for preparations by bringing him the Abletons. If he didn't take Brandon as bait, I'd swing the Abletons his way, but not before mentioning Maryland to see just how sensitive he was about it.

I took a step towards his desk, and both cubs reached for their weapons.

"Grizzly, your cubs are getting active."

"No one approaches without my permission."

I waved a hand and walked forward.

"Aye!" one of them shouted.

"This ain't New York, prince, you've gotta be careful." Grizzly grinned.

I chuckled. "Don't make me turn Jersey into Maryland and kick you out of your own place, Grizzly."

His eyes widened and he glanced around. "Who told you?"

"*Never sit too high*, isn't that what you told me when I had a rat problem? And then you proceeded to sit highly." I sucked my teeth and walked up to his desk. Splaying my fingers across the rough top, I smirked at him. "Yeah, I came to tell you that your rat is a talker. Talked so much, I found out about

Maryland, and a few other things I'm sure you'd prefer me not to know."

I was confident now because I could walk away just with the rat on the table, but that wouldn't be enough to keep Grizzly busy with the Abletons and not the dead bodies. Right now, Grizzly didn't have a clue where the bodies had come from, so throwing a rat in the midst would shake him even if he didn't budge. It would cause a frenzy in his ranks, and he wouldn't know who to trust, and who's been slipping off, telling secrets, and setting him up.

But that would only go so far before the truth seeped out. Before things stopped adding up and people started talking. I was screwing myself into a stripped hole, it would never really work out. But it was too late now. The lies just got deeper, they got more serious. I needed to cover more things up, needed to make it look like BT was operating without a hitch. But that just wasn't the case.

The Pack was technically flat broke. We're accruing debt by the millions every week from the forest fire and buyers wanting in on the ice rink and on Malawi. Both of which no longer exist. The ice rink was going to be legit, but I was going to use half the money from Malawi to build it up. I invested in diamonds, but I'm cashing in on all my investments starting this week to put towards my future with Iyana, and hopefully give out some severance packages to my closest guys. Right now, the Pack was floating along because we still had people buying our regular weed and products. But that money wouldn't cover how much we actually owed.

The sampling parties had been a success. Logan was in charge of them, and he was getting people to actually sign agreements that I approached them about days after the agreed payment date. If we actually had product, and BT wasn't in debt, I'd run my roots deep into the heart of the Great American Melting Pot. From coast to coast, I could've expanded BT, but instead, it was crumbling all around me.

"You're the scum of the earth," Grizzly said forcefully.

I raised a brow. "Yikes, I came here to share information with you, yet you're calling me scum? I'm the only one who actually knows who the rat is."

"Tell me who he is!"

I sighed as I looked over the tired old man. Wide eyed and spittle flying, I moved back from his desk before I said, "I'll tell you one thing. Rats always have a reason. Sometimes it's not food, it's the convenience of the food. They…" I paused as I remembered Emilia's and Gio's advice when I had a rat problem. "They never stray far. You always look closer, rather than further."

I chuckled as my eyes dropped to his desk. "Someone told me that. They told me that rats can be lured out, you just have to find what keeps them coming back." I looked up, pushing away the grim feelings that were clouding my mind. "But you took the people who meant the most to me, and now I have no one."

"That had nothing to do with me." Grizzly was concerned now, and even though I knew the truth, I needed him at my mercy. Crossing jurisdictions was one thing, but crossing them and killing the family of the one who ruled there was a crime even in our world. He looked like he wanted to say something else, but he didn't know what I knew, particularly about the dead bodies.

"You didn't send someone out to kill my family on the night of my wedding as a message? You didn't kidnap one of my men?"

"No." He stood from his desk, big broad shoulders covered in his usual brown fur. "Now I've told you the truth. You need to leave."

"You crossed the line when you let Brandon kill my family and two people from the Pack, and I will never let you forget it. Came all the way here to tell you that." I rapped my knuckles on his desk and grinned up at him before turning to leave.

"I didn't—"

"Oh! One more thing, Grizzly," I cut him off. "One of your rats is that cub right there. He led me right to your rival gang, the ones living off the Abletons."

"Hold on!" he snapped. "Him? He's the rat?" He was pointing at the cub with dark skin and braids. I nodded and, without hesitation, Grizzly pulled a gun from the desk and shot the boy three times. The cub's face never even registered what happened. He dropped to his knees with a pleading look on his face before falling forward.

"Actually," I said, staring at the body, "now I'm not too sure if he was the rat. Two of them came together. They looked alike." I shrugged.

Grizzly went to raise his gun at me, but the other cub grabbed him.

"No, boss! That'd be a debt we can't pay off!"

"You should listen, Grizzly, because I've got one more thing to offer."

The old man was grunting and pushing against the young cub. I pulled out a piece of paper and tossed it on the floor as I backed out.

"It's the location of the Abletons. If you don't get to them in the next twenty…" I stopped and looked at my watch, "sorry, *nineteen* hours, I'm going to get what I'm owed from them and I'm going to make plans with that little gang. Just giving you a fair warning."

Grizzly shouted something I couldn't understand, but the cub was fighting him relentlessly, preventing him from firing the gun. I stepped out of the room and jogged down the hall until I reached outside where Logan was waiting in the car for me.

"How'd it go?" Logan asked as I slid into my seat.

"It went well, I think." I opted not to mention the dead bodies or anything else unimportant. Killing Grizzly's cubs was the least of my worries since he now knew that I thought he was the one responsible for the car crash. And technically, until proven otherwise, he *was* responsible. And I got to determine the worth and value of my family that'd been killed, so I could've killed more cubs than that for repayment.

"You think?" Logan's voice pulled my thoughts back to him. His brow was quirked in the rearview mirror, but he kept his eyes on the road as he pulled into traffic.

"Well, he got a little pissy, but I would too if I had a rat."

"I told you not to go the rat route."

"He would assume it anyway. No one would think we've been in Bridges's house putting things together."

Logan shrugged. "I hope you're right."

"Logan," I called, looking out the window.

"Yeah, Vee?"

"Is this what you want to do forever?"

"Drive you around?" He shrugged. "It's not a bad gig."

"I mean be in a gang."

He didn't speak for a moment. "Where's this coming from?"

I leaned over in the seat and opened the box beside me. It was full of binders and leather-bound books with pages made of money. I had a large portion of the money from the clinic put into these books so that I could send them off to Iyana without suspicion. I was going to put the rest of the money in a safety deposit box, and what I couldn't put away, I would ship overseas to a personal friend of my father who handles international banking.

"Just answer the question."

"I don't know. I never thought about it honestly." He swallowed. "I mostly just take it day by day."

"So, if I handed you ten million dollars, what would you do?"

"I'd get hookers of course, and then—"

"No. Logan, you have to think beyond sex and drugs and alcohol." I tsked him. "Never mind." I sank my face into my hands. I'd done a lousy job of helping him see what was important. All I'd done was let Logan have fun because that was my way of thanking him for his loyalty. It was all I had to offer in this dark life.

"Boss? Can I speak?"

"Go ahead," I said behind my hands.

"I'd give it back."

I raised my head to see him through the mirror, but he was looking straight ahead with an absent expression on his face.

"I'd give it all back, and just ask you to take me with you. I wouldn't know how to spend that kind of money." He chuckled, more out of embarrassment than humor. "So, if you were giving me money to walk away, I'd give it back in exchange for staying with you. You, BT, Iyana, and Hardy, you guys are all I have. All I've ever really had. I wouldn't give that up."

Twenty-Two
Hardy
Jan 29th | 12:31am

Alex was in labor for over forty-eight hours. It was her first baby, and the baby had come suddenly and early. It also didn't help that Alex's body was weak, and the contractions weren't strong enough to push her daughter along. She'd gotten an epidural, but that seemed to make her even weaker. She wasn't pushing, she was sweating and sleeping. She even passed out because the medicine was too strong, and when it wore off, the pain was too much.

It was hard to watch, it was hard to sit beside her and hold her hand. Every time her body went limp, and her hand fell from mine, it was like I was losing her.

I'd decided that what I felt for Alex was just lust, like she said. But when she asked me to stay with her in the hospital room, I couldn't help but feel differently. I don't know if it was love that I felt, but there was something steadily blossoming in my chest. I knew it was real. I knew it wasn't lust. Not anymore. Because I'd finally stopped thinking about Jewels. And when Alex passed out, I wasn't afraid of losing yet another person... I was just afraid of losing *her*.

Somehow, Alex had become important to me. She stirred my heart, but I was afraid that I was wrong. I was afraid that I was the only one who felt this.

Sitting beside her bed, I listened to her heart monitor. I'd been spending most of my days there, in the small chair by her bedside. She got sick right after her daughter arrived; she came down with a cold. The doctor said it was normal because her body was under so much stress.

Dafni had been visiting the baby, along with Iyana and Tobias. I didn't really want to visit little Ava, so I stayed with Alex. She came back to consciousness here and there, but she mostly slept. I didn't mind. I needed the silence to think. To pray.

I'd been asking God to help me, to answer me. He hadn't said anything, but when Iyana lent me her Bible the other day, there was a bookmark in a passage.

It was the story of a strong man named Samson. Apparently, when I tried to research 'Lehi', it turned out that Samson's story with Delilah was very well known. I scrolled for hours, reading different interpretations of his story until I finally read it for myself. But I never made it to his romance with Delilah because something stopped me.

After Samson burned down the wheat fields of the Philistines and was taken before them, he defeated a thousand of them with a jawbone from a donkey. But that wasn't what mesmerized me, it wasn't what pushed me to believe in God. It was the next passage.

All this time, all the fighting between Samson and the Philistines was over a woman he wasn't even supposed to be with. But when he defeated the thousand Philistines, he asked God for a drink, and God answered him, and I believed. Samson had done wrong by marrying the Philistine woman, yet God was merciful to him and did not let him thirst. If God had been merciful to Samson, then I believed He would be merciful to me. And when I asked Iyana about it, she told me that Jesus died so that mercy and grace could be extended to me.

I didn't know that if I believed in Jesus and asked for forgiveness, God would hear me. He would show me mercy the way He showed Samson mercy, and I realized there was hope for me.

Alex groaned into consciousness, pulling me from my thoughts of Samson. She took a deep breath, and in the darkness, I could hear her shifting in the bed.

"Alex? Are you alright?"

"Hardy?" her voice was hoarse and tired.

"I'm here," I said, moving closer to her.

With hesitation, I felt for her hand in the dark. It was by her side, limp like she'd been passed out for a while. When I touched her hand, I paused and shied away, but she reached out and grabbed it. Her fingers began to tangle with mine, and she whispered, "You're still here."

"I didn't want to leave you."

She was silent.

"You won't be discharged until after we leave, but Dafni and Tobias will look after you."

"This is it." She adjusted in the bed, pulling her hand from mine to sit up. She clicked on a small lamp, and the glowing yellow light seemed to shine brightly in the darkness of the room.

I squinted at the flash of light, blinking away the cloudy darkness to see Alex sitting on the bed, tired and sad.

"You're going back to New York," she said softly.

"The plan was for all of us to go back." I shrugged as I pulled my chair closer.

"I can't go back now."

"I know."

"So you stayed to tell me goodbye?"

I clenched my jaw and shot my eyes to the floor. "I … I don't know why I stayed."

"Don't go back to New York."

I snapped my head up to see her. She was sitting up straight, unafraid and not cowering away. She was solid in what she said, and I didn't have to wonder what she meant by it.

"You want me to stay with you?"

"Yes."

I swallowed nervously. I didn't think that was what she was going to say when she woke up. I thought there was going to be a repeated argument about our relationship, and I'd go back to New York focusing on Kat.

"But what about Brandon? And I'm not a father. I'm just—"

Alex reached out and touched my hand. "I'm not asking you to fall in love with me and become Ava's father. I'm asking you to stay."

"Alex, I don't want to stay if I can't be with you."

She nodded. "I know. But we don't have to rush into a relationship. We are still two very broken people, Hardy. We need to heal, but I think if we do it together, we can make things work."

I sat back in my chair and studied her. Her eyes were shying away from mine now. She was looking at the bed, hands folded neatly in her lap. Alex had always been a beautiful woman. Ever since I first really saw her, I couldn't stop looking at her. Brandon had always gotten the best pick of everything. *Am I stuck being second to him?* I shook my head.

"Alex, my job is in New York. I have to go back. I can't stay here wondering if things will ever work out between us once we're done being broken. I can't make myself stumble over someone else's uncertain feelings."

She nodded again, and I could see tears forming in her eyes. I couldn't let her keep me at bay because she was afraid of losing me *and* afraid of keeping me. She needed to choose, but I wasn't going to stick around to find out if and when she ever made up her mind. I'd done that with Jewels, and it hurt every day, watching her flirt and talk with other men. Knowing she was sleeping with Brandon and Logan. I couldn't do it again. I *wouldn't* do it again.

"So, is this goodbye?"

"I wish it wasn't," I said as I stood, "but I can't let my heart be dangled in front of you until you're ready."

She opened her mouth to speak, but she didn't say anything. Tears streamed down her cheeks, and I could feel my heart aching the worst it had since I'd arrived here. To be honest, I really wanted to stay with Alex. I wanted to be by her side, but I was too fragile to be hurt again. I was too desperate to think straight. If she wouldn't say yes now, I didn't know if she ever would, and I wouldn't spend my life wondering.

Her silent tears turned into soft whimpering, and I leaned over and turned out the lamp. Pressing my lips to her forehead, she trembled beneath me, crying into her hands.

"Goodbye, Alex," I whispered into her hair before pulling away and leaving her room.

Twenty-Three
Iyana
Jan 29th | 4:14pm

I packed up my suitcase and left two outfits out. Returning home to Vito was exciting. But, how far into the war was BT? How much had happened without me? Does BT even still need me? Does Vito need me? I tried not to think about it as I zipped my duffle bag closed.

We were returning on the thirty-first without Alex, and I wasn't sure if that was alright. I had no way to tell Vito, but it didn't matter that much anyway. Alex would've been a liability, leaving her here with Dafni and Tobias was best for her.

A knock came to my door, and I called, "Come in."

"Ana." Hardy was standing in my doorway holding a box under his arm.

"What is that?"

"It's for you from Vito. There's actually a couple of them downstairs, but this box has a number one on it, and the others have corresponding numerical order."

I paused for two reasons. The first was because I'd received a package from Vito, my husband whom I hadn't spoken to in an entire month and expected to waltz back into his life like I'd never left. But number two, Hardy had just said something was done in 'corresponding numerical order' and while that wasn't a big deal, it made me remember that behind his big eyes and happy smile, his childish teenage behavior, Hardy wasn't like the rest of the members of the gang.

"Thanks, Hardy," I said as I took the box. "I'll open this one and then come down to look at the others."

He nodded and turned on his heels to leave. I sighed as I closed the door. Hardy had matured but, unfortunately, pain had to be his teacher. He'd killed a person, a woman I'd known, and that had changed him. It was easy to see how different he was because of this, and that kept me from feeling hesitant around him. Which would've been a little shallow, considering my husband's introduction to my life was him putting a bullet in one of his men's heads without batting a lash. Not to mention, giving the order to kill three floors of people.

I sat on the bed, dragging an ink pen down the tape and ripping the box open. Inside was a letter sitting atop a book. The cover read, *Cross Academy*. It was my favorite book that I discovered while being in the tower. Hardy bought it for me when I sent him to the store one evening. He told me there was a big display of it and since it was Christian fiction, he thought I would enjoy it. He was right. Eventually, Vito found out and he bought me the second book in the series, *The Howler's Cry*, and it topped the first one. But, looking at the book here in the box, I didn't know why he would send me a second copy of the book, unless it was a signed copy, but then he could've given that to me at home.

I set the letter down and grabbed the book, but it felt odd in my hand. Not like any book I'd ever held. With one peek inside, I dropped the book on the floor and gasped.

"What?" I whispered as I leaned forward and grabbed the book again. When I opened it, all the pages were made of folded hundred-dollar bills. There were no words, no story, just pages of hundreds. But the pages weren't like paper either. They were laminated with a seal on the top. If I tore the seal, the money would come out, and if I pulled at its perforation, the entire page of money would be released.

"What is this?" I flipped through the pages of the book a little longer before reaching for the letter on the bed. When I turned it over, I sucked in a small bubble of air. It read, *Iyana*, and for the first time, I saw Vito's handwriting. It was almost girly, which made me laugh. Thin strokes, with a loose hand; I never imagined Vito's handwriting would look like this.

Pulling the letter out, I opened it and began.

Dear Iyana,

This is so weird. I haven't written anything down in years. I've probably jotted something down here or there, but writing a document, writing a letter, I haven't done that in a while.

We spent an entire month apart; I can't wait to see you. But the truth is, I don't want you to see me, or who I've become. I realized while you were gone, that I was nothing. Nothing but a façade.

I rose to the top of New York because I pretended to be a nice guy. I won everyone's heart because I wasn't brutal. But the sad truth is that I was brutal… I am brutal.

People trusted me and loved me because they didn't want to deal with me when I wasn't pleased. I'm not one to display dominance, but I am one to make a habit of being respected. I wanted to be different, and I swore I was. But, honestly, I'm not any different from Grizzly. He's brutal and will kill for no reason. I won't kill for stupid reasons, but I will kill to keep myself on top. I will do whatever I need to for the Pack, and now, for ***you.***

Being a nice guy is natural for me, and that's why so many people wanted to work with me. They knew that as long as I was happy, the Pack's resources were open to whoever needed them. I made a brotherhood out of the gangs of New York. I let the brotherhood spill into the civilian markets, government, and affairs just to prove that I was a nice guy. And I did it all smiling. But, really, I was just doing things for myself, to keep the Pack at the top of the pyramid.

For the longest, I believed that the pyramid must stand, until I realized that because of you, the pyramid must fall.

I've done things I'm not proud of, Iyana.

I wish you would stay in California. I know you won't want to, so I've sent you some literature to hopefully convince you. Boxes one through five are yours. You can decide what to do with them. If you decide not to return to New York, I will accept that. But only if you stay in California where it's safe. Box six is for my parents, and boxes seven and eight are for Hardy and Alex, respectively.

I'm not a good man, Iyana. But for you, I really tried to be. I love you so much, and if you never return to me, I will still love you because of who you've shown me I could be.

Inside the envelope, I left something for you. You showed me that God hadn't given up on me. You showed me that I could be loved. You showed me how to love, and I am forever indebted to you for that.

May your faith keep you strong, and if we ever meet again, I hope to be a better man. You deserve the world, and more. If I had the universe to give, I'm certain it wouldn't be enough.

I love you.
Cortez Ortega.

"That's not true," I whispered as tears rolled down my cheeks. "You are a good man, Vito, I swear." I hiccupped as I clutched the paper to my chest and fell over. I wept into the carpet, begging God to show Vito that he's good, but God's only response was one sentence: **Remember why I called you.**

Slowly, I sat up, wiping my eyes. I reached for the envelope and found the cross I'd given him when we went on our first date. It almost summoned new tears, but I swallowed the lump in the back of my throat and got to my feet.

"Hardy!" I called as I rushed out of my room.

"What?" he called back as he stumbled out of his own.

"Go down and bring all the boxes to my room."

"For what?" he asked, though he was already passing my room to the staircase.

"Because I need to look at everything."

"Fine," he called back.

After two trips, Hardy had brought two big boxes with smaller boxes in them into my bedroom. The first box had the boxes for me in it, and the second box had the ones for Hardy, Alex, and Vito's parents inside.

"Here, Hardy, this is for you, and this is for Alex."

His hand flinched at Alex's box, and slowly I lowered it back to my lap.

"Did something happen?"

He shook his head. "What are these boxes?"

"Hardy."

His eyes lifted to mine, and there was a tight smile on his lips. I wanted to know the truth, but he was doing his best not to let whatever happened between the two of them bother him. It was enough we'd be leaving without her with no return date. This was going to be it for them, if there even was a 'them.'

"The boxes," I cleared my throat, "are full of books. Open yours."

He nodded, and I could see the relief washing over him, glad that I'd changed the subject. Slowly, he cut open his box, and he pulled out a book. There were three in total inside his box. I watched him as his fluffy lashes blinked slowly while opening one of the books.

He froze.

"What is this?" Hardy looked up at me.

I said, "I think it's some kind of parting gift. I think Vito's trying to make us stay here."

"What? Why?"

I shrugged. "He wrote me a letter saying that he wanted me to stay in California."

"The war," his words were soft and as absent as his eyes.

"Yeah, I think something bad has happened. There's even a box for Dafni and Tobias."

Hardy thumbed his brow for a second and then shrugged. "I don't get it. What could've happened that he wouldn't want us to return?"

"I don't know. But we're going back."

"What about the books?"

I thought for a moment. "We leave them here."

Twenty-Four
Brandon
Jan 30th | 11:11am

The first night I was here, Vali got rid of my car and the body inside. I don't know how, and she never said, but it all happened after I passed out on her couch. She admitted to giving me some kind of concoction because when she came to bring me inside right after the accident, she thought she saw another body in the car. When she went back, she recognized Brooke. He'd been snatched off the streets with his brother and she'd never heard from them again. She recalled a story of how Brooke and Dahodda tried to rob her, and she'd been trying to get them clean and off the streets. Brooke was always much weaker than his brother, and he usually gave in to whatever Hodda wanted. Brooke never wanted the streets, but Dahodda did, so he followed his brother. Little did she know, I was the one who pulled them off the streets.

"I can't stay here forever. Grizzly will figure out that I'm here," I said as I forked peas from my plate. Vali was a trauma surgeon working in the emergency room. She spent most days at work, with a few days off randomly. When she was gone, I was here resting. It's been the most stressful and relaxing week or so since Vito found out I betrayed him. But I was so uncomfortable, knowing that Vali was Grizzly's daughter, Grizzly was still hunting for me, and my leg had only gotten a little better. The pain was still almost too much to walk on, but I knew I'd just have to endure the pain.

"Trust me, Grizzly is a pain, but he probably won't be back for a while. My dad doesn't like this city very much. So he stays away."

"Yeah, but your father hates me now."

"I don't pity you."

"I wasn't asking for pity," I snapped.

She set her fork down and crossed her arms. Big curls were loose from the mini braids she often wore around the house. "If you're that scared, why haven't you left yet?"

"I don't have anywhere to go. I told you that."

Vali made me tell her everything about my involvement with her father but, thankfully, I was able to spare her the details about BT.

"Well, then, you should stop worrying. If my dad comes back, which he won't, I'll ward him off again. I'm not a complete idiot. I know my father. If he comes sniffing again then it'll be time to leave. Until then, we're fine."

"We?" I raised a brow, and she looked confused, as if I had said something odd. "Vali, we're not a team. This isn't a new episode of Bonnie and Clyde."

"That was a movie—not a show with episodes—and they were real people. And I know we're not Bonnie and Clyde. But do you really think my father is going to let me walk after keeping you here? I'm in for it now." She shrugged, and I could see how much this actually bothered her. She had the same fearful look Iyana had after first being taken. The way Iyana tried to be strong even though she knew her life was over. Because in all actuality, once you're in, the only way out is death. Vali had realized this, and despite her effort to pretend it didn't bother her, I could look at her and tell she was shaken.

"Why would you risk everything for someone you didn't know?"

"Because I couldn't just let you die. That's wrong."

"But why did you lie?"

She rolled her eyes. "As if my father was going to let you live. I didn't mean to insert myself into this. The moment I saved you, I was screwed. And when I saw Brooke there, still and silent…" She closed her eyes. "I knew something was terribly wrong, and I knew my life was over."

"That's why you got rid of the body and the car. You were buying yourself time."

"Yeah," she said flatly.

"How did you get rid of it?"

"I left Jersey because I wanted to focus on my studies, not be part of my father's gang. But that didn't mean I lost connections with a few friends in Jersey and made connections in the Apple." She stood and grabbed her plate. "I'm working overtime. I won't be back for a few days. Just lay low."

I nodded as I watched her toss her plate into the garbage and head to her bedroom. I sighed and placed my hands over my head. I was ruining Vali's life. Just like I'd ruined Jewels's life, and … I sat up abruptly.

"Alex," I whispered to myself. I moved from the table, limping by the garbage and shoving my plate inside before reaching the couch. Vali had managed to grab me some clothes from her job out of the lost and found, and I dug through the pile and found my phone. The screen was cracked, and it was nearly dead, but I could manage to make a single phone call. I tapped her name and held the phone to my ear.

"Pick up, Alex, please."

It only rang.

When the automated voicemail began, I hung up and tried again. This time, it went straight to voicemail. I wanted to cry, to throw the phone across the room, but I only laid back on the couch and closed my eyes to get some sleep.

By morning, Vali was gone. She'd left for work, and it was just me again. I'd explored a little here and there when I first arrived, but my leg was in such bad condition, I mostly remained on the couch. Today, I would move around. I wanted to find a charger for my phone, and I needed to give Vito a call. If push comes to shove, I was hoping to leave Vali with Vee.

I limped through the house, opening drawers, digging through bags. I wanted to know what she'd done with Brooke since she'd known him, and I wanted to find her Jersey connections. If she knew anyone I knew, I could possibly get out of here. I needed to get away from Vali if I could, and hopefully, I wouldn't need to take her to Vito. We're not friends, but Vito's loyalty is his best quality.

I dragged myself up the stairs to her bedroom and limped around. There were papers all over the floor and the whole place was a mess. Moving around the twin bed, I was surprised at how modestly she lived considering she was a surgeon *and* Grizzly was her father. Gang Grizzly wasn't loaded the way BT was, but they lived good lives.

Limping back across the room, the floors creaked beneath me. I spotted her closet on my way out. There were bags and a big sack of laundry in front of it that I lugged out of the way. When I pulled it open, there was nothing but a gold key hanging from a rope. I snatched it and the lightbulb above me broke.

I covered my head, protecting myself from the shattering glass when I heard an engine roaring outside. Then another. And two more. Gripping my leg, I limped quickly to the window and peeked out. There were four black trucks parked in front of the house. The door opened to one of the trucks and Grizzly stepped out. Other cubs and guards began to dismount from the trucks, but before I could even make it back across the room, Grizzly was shouting, "Break the door off the hinges! I want every room checked!"

I glanced around, looking for a place to hide. There was a loud thud that came from the front door, it sounded like someone had kicked it. I limped forward, but the floor creaked, and I needed to be hidden in the next five seconds before the door opened. Throwing things out of the way, I fell into the closet on the broken glass. I grunted in pain just as I heard the door crash open, and I grabbed the closet door, pulling it shut as quietly as I could.

"I know he's here. Find him," Grizzly said.

I wanted to kill Grizzly for what he'd done to Alex, but now wasn't my chance, and I didn't know when I'd ever get one. But I couldn't think about that. I was trying not to panic as I heard the men rushing through the house. They sounded like your worst nightmare, pounding at the door of your mind. Trying to seize your thoughts so that your only focus was fear.

Goosebumps rose along my body, sweat dripped down my forehead, my stomach flipped, my breath was short. There was only a matter of time until someone came in here. If I could manage to get the jump on them and get the bedroom door closed again, I could make it out the window.

I closed my eyes, clutching the key in my hand that I'd pulled from Vali's closet. Thick boots that seemed to crush the floor came closer to the room, stopping right outside the bedroom door.

I was afraid, and I hated that. I'd always put myself in a position to be the hunter not the hunted, but now, everything was falling apart. I could die in the next moment, but I didn't want to. I still needed to find Alex, smooth things out with Jewels, and get revenge on Jill. I needed to see BJ and I wanted to see my daughter—if she was here yet. I didn't want Alex to give birth without me, but I knew the due date was coming up soon.

I covered my mouth as I listened to the door creaking open. Someone entered slowly and stopped to look around. He began throwing things, completely ransacking the place. He opened drawers, he dug through them. There was a dragging noise, I assumed it was him moving the bed, because the next sound was the mattress hitting the floor. I tried to steady my breathing as he moved around Vali's small room.

When the torture was over, the thumping boots carried him back to the door, and I tried to sit as still as possible. I couldn't even feel my leg throbbing anymore. I was in shock, swallowed by fear, hoping that whoever was out there wouldn't notice the closet, but when his feet stopped short of the door, I knew he'd found me.

Each step he took back to the closet was like a punch to the gut. Each one was harder than the last. And even though I tried to prepare myself for what was coming, I couldn't possibly be ready to die.

The fear swelling in my chest made me want to vomit. But if he opened the door while I was vomiting, then he'd catch me in a vulnerable state—so I held it in. The man grabbed the handle to the closet, and I took a quick breath. Quickly, he snatched it open, and I stiffened on the floor. Blinking up in my sweat and fear, I let my eyes drag along the figure. His boots had spikes, indicating that he wasn't a cub… anymore.

When my eyes met his, I recognized the young boy as Dahodda. He just stared at me, in his short fur coat and brass knuckles. He'd moved pretty high up the ranks; he'd gotten everything he wanted, while his brother died a cold and miserable death. Brooke died hoping that Dahodda would eventually come find us. But he wasn't being held captive, he'd done exactly what Brooke had feared ... he'd decided to stay.

Slowly, Dahodda closed the closet door without a word. I listened as he walked and called,

"All clear, boss. Each room's been swept. He's not here."

Grizzly swore. "She must've gotten him out of here. Let's move. I know one of her hideouts."

"Understood," Dahodda said. "Boys, let's move," he called in the same breath. He wasn't even one of them anymore... Dahodda was me. He'd taken my spot as Grizzly's new righthand. Technically, I never even had that spot. Grizzly would never let me be part of the gang.

When the house fell quiet, I couldn't move. I think I would've sat there until Vali returned if I hadn't suddenly felt the urge to vomit.

Shooting forward to hands and knees, I puked all over the closet floor. Wiping the sweat from my face, I gathered myself and limped out the closet with my hand to my mouth, in case I vomited again. I got to the window, but there was no one outside. Everyone was gone again.

I couldn't wait for Vali. I needed to leave while I had the chance. I moved from the window to the door, and tripped over a bag, sending me soaring to the floor. I slammed down on my bad leg and hollered out. With trembling hands, I slowly reached for my leg. It was throbbing, and I could hardly breathe from the pain. But I had to move.

I fought to sit up from the floor, noticing a bag tangled around my foot. I took slow breaths and turned the bag over to find there was a lock on the zipper. Shakily, I used the key from the closet and unlocked it.

Inside was money, a gun, and two rounds of ammunition.

Without another thought, I slung the bag over my shoulder and got to my feet. I found my way down the stairs and shoved food and water into the bag before taking off.

Twenty-Five
Iyana
Feb 1st | 1:53pm

The glistening black tower was as mesmerizing as it had always been. New York was as it had always been. BT was as it had always been, at least I assumed so when Hardy and I arrived at the tower. I was excited and nervous to be home, but something felt off. Although everything looked the same, somehow there seemed to be some kind of shadow clawing through the tower. As we walked inside, Challa took off down the hall. Leo was the only one at the desk; the men dressed in suits sitting around all nodded as I walked inside.

"Welcome home," Leo said as we approached the desk.

"It's been a while," I said. I couldn't help but give in to the smile tugging at my lips.

"We really missed you, Iyana. You have no idea."

I squinted. "What do you mean?"

"You should see Logan before Vito." His smile had faded, and he looked concerned now, which made the anxiety I was already feeling about seeing Vito increase.

"Why?" I glanced around. "Where's Kat?"

Leo only gave me a stiff smile which made me drop my bags and race for the elevator.

"Iyana, wait!" Hardy called as he ran after me. The elevator dinged and I stepped inside with Challa. Hardy ran in behind me and grabbed my arm. "Iyana, calm down. You don't know Vito as well as you think."

I pulled into myself. "He's my husband—"

"He's been my boss longer than he's been your husband," he said forcefully. "I've seen Vito when the lights go out."

I didn't want to believe it. "No." I shook my head. "You don't know what you're talking about." I snatched my arm from him and pressed the button for our floor. We rode in silence and when the elevator opened, I could hardly wait to get out.

Without hesitation I opened the door and stepped inside. Logan was sitting on the couch, holding a drink in his hand as T'Challa ran inside and began turning circles in excitement.

"Where's Vito?" I demanded.

"Calm down." He took a sip of his drink. "You don't need to see him right now."

"Excuse me?"

His dark eyes focused on mine. "He was the worst I'd ever seen him while you were gone." Logan shrugged. "But he did what needed to be done." He seemed to fear him and praise him, but my heart only ached for Vito.

Setting my purse down in the dark and cold apartment, I headed for the bedroom.

"He doesn't want to be bothered!" Logan called over my shoulder, but I didn't stop moving until I made it to the bedroom.

This wasn't what I was expecting to return home to. Vito is a gang leader, but he's not the lifeless man this apartment speaks to.

When I stepped inside the bedroom it was quiet and empty, dark and gloomy. But there was steam rolling inside from the cracked bathroom door. Slowly, I began to undress. I left my boots at the door. Unbuttoning my shirt, I dropped it to the floor. My skirt came next, and I left a trail of clothes behind as I opened the door and stepped into a steamy bathroom. The heat was nearly suffocating, the water was rushing loudly in the shower.

I stood there staring at the man surrounded by fog through the glass shower. His hands were pressed against the wall, and water ran over his head and down his back. This was not the man I left. This was not the man I married. This was a fractured lonely version of him. Despite the heat in the room, there was a chill working its way up my spine.

Each step towards the shower brought me closer to a man who was the furthest from me he'd ever been. *Will I be able to reach him? No ... God, will You reach him? Help me, Father...* the prayer was stirring in my heart as I opened the shower. Heat of an intense anger, or something deeper… the heat of guilt was overtaking me as I closed myself in with him.

Being naked in front of someone other than your husband is shameful. And the man who stood before me was not the same as my husband. But I knew Cortez was still in this shell and I wouldn't hide from him. I wouldn't run and fear him. I would stand with him. I would bear myself to him as he stood with shame and regret.

Nudity brought wholeness into a marriage. It linked two wandering souls to each other, it allowed two bodies to communicate until they could agree and become one. There was no shame or embarrassment in the marriage. And what happened to one person in the marriage happened to the other.

I took a breath of steam into my lungs and placed a small hand on the center of his bruised and scarred back. Each one detailing another horrific event, each one symbolic of his will to live, each one a reminder that he was human and could feel things besides anger.

Discomfort and relief are knit together as one and cannot come without the other. And every scrape and bruise would always serve to remind Vito that he was not just the leader of BT. He is Cortez Ortega, my husband. And this discomfort and pain would not last; relief and joy would come.

When my hand touched his back, he didn't react. Not until I whispered, "Cortez."

He glanced to the side, looking over his shoulder, but not at me. He didn't want me to see him like this. He didn't want to be like this, and it was ever so present the moment he pushed off the wall and stood up straight. He was a lean man, but in this moment, he looked like the strongest man I'd ever known. There was an intensity that swirled around him as he turned to finally face me.

"Cortez," I whispered again as he stared down at me. The shower water rushed over his shoulders as he stood there. His eyes were a brewing storm while simultaneously holding a void look in them. The same emptiness was there the very first day I'd met him. When I had feared him. But I found that Vito didn't want to be feared. He wanted to make sure BT was secure, and that darkened him, voided him.

"This is not you, Cortez."

He didn't speak.

"There is a light in your chest." I stepped closer to him, and he didn't move. But there was a flicker of emotion in his eyes when I moved. Raising my hand, I pressed it to his chest, but the next moment he grabbed it without warning, and I jumped.

"You should be afraid of me," he warned.

"You don't mean that," I said. There was a thick layer of fog in the shower now, but it didn't smother me the way it had before. Vito was still clutching my arm tightly, glaring at me weakly and glumly, despite his efforts to look angry.

"You are my husband, Cortez, and I love you. You are not the leader of BT." I paused and lifted my chin a little higher. "I am."

The words must've snapped something free in him because he let my arm go. He stepped back further into the pouring water, and for the first time since I've been here, Cortez heaved a deep breath. There was a sudden change to his demeanor, like there was a realization that brought relief and recognition that he wasn't in this alone.

I said, "There's a light in your chest that you don't have to hide anymore. You are free, Cortez."

"How can I be free with the mess I've made?" His voice was weak, and his eyes were filling with tears. "I killed people, lied, and hurt so many people in the last four weeks, let alone in my entire life."

"But you still believe. You still believe Jesus is the Christ, that He is the Son of the Living God. You still believe, and all it takes is faith to please God, and a mustard seed to move a mountain. You have everything you need inside you." I reached out and took his hand. "And you have me."

"But then that dumps everything onto your shoulders, and I can't do that." He tried to pull his hand from mine, but I clutched it so tightly he flinched and looked up at me. The water had soaked my hair, and both of us were being washed in the heat of the shower.

"We are as one, so when you are free, that means I am free."

"But what about BT?"

"Let it fall, stop trying to hold it up. The longer you hold on, the darker you will become. And I won't let you be consumed."

"Iyana—"

"No," I cut him off and dropped his hand. I stepped closer, so there was no space between us, and looked up at him. He had softened. His face wasn't hard, and his eyes that were brewing in stormy emotions before were now spilling tears from the storm clouds within.

"I won't lose you," I said firmly.

"Don't let me go," he whispered as he leaned down. He pressed his head to mine, and he closed his eyes. "Please don't let me go."

"I won't," I said.

His lips found mine, stirring a rush of heat that didn't come from our surroundings. It was coming from within me, from within *him*. As we shared this moment in the shower, there was a release of ecstasy, and the binding of a new commitment, a new vow. To never leave, to never be separated, to be the anchor we need to hold each other down. It was a new promise I would never break, and one Vito wouldn't either.

When our worlds collided, there was fear. But when our worlds began to flood into each other's, we found that our water was the same, and so was our source. We found that the water that could flood his world was the same water that could flood mine, and when our worlds were sinking, whose water was it that we could pinpoint to blame?

Marriage united us, despite the calamity that brought us together. And as the ship of BT sinks, we will sink with it, so that when we re-emerge, we will be completely new. Completely redeemed. Completely as one.

Vito was weighted with emotion as his body clung to mine. There was a controlled fire within him that poured into me. The fire called to me, and I answered. The heat swarmed me, and I was consumed. The pleasure engulfed me, and I gave in to it. He held me close. His hands were my protectors, and my body was his cavity. I was rejuvenated with him, and he was renewed with me. We bathed in each other's affection until we drowned. There was a newness born in that moment. Vito and I would cherish it forever.

I lay in bed, panting. Vito was beside me breathing deeply as well.

"Tell me what happened," I said in our silence.

"Our fields burned."

I closed my eyes and folded my hands over myself as I lay there. Vito would need time to tell me everything, but I didn't want to react, no matter how bad it got.

"That was just the catalyst," I replied.

"People still wanted to buy, so I held sampling parties. But they got suspicious when a close contact of mine went missing, so I stopped having sampling parties."

I swallowed. "You were letting people sample products they couldn't buy?"

"I was letting people get high off the small amount of product I had, and then taking their money as a down payment for products they couldn't buy."

"But why?"

He shifted. "The plan was to try to get an import of something, but it was too expensive, and too dangerous, so instead, I decided to get you out of BT."

"What?"

"I… I found Brandon."

"Vito, what happened? Why is Brandon involved?" I sat up and looked over at him. He was lying with his hand behind his head, looking up at the ceiling. He looked exhausted and drained. He was empty, but somehow there was a sign of life in his eyes now.

"Things got out of hand, and I made decisions that sank BT. We have to run now."

"Why?"

He turned to me. "Because I've only been able to buy us time. We set Grizzly up, Iyana. That will only last so long. He'll eventually find out it was us and come for us. By then, the hope was that we'd have an even stronger defense, but that was only possible—"

"By making connections with the Malawi."

"Yeah."

"And when that went out the window, you did what needed to be done," I echoed the words of Logan as I realized what he meant. "How is Brandon involved?" I asked after a brief moment of silence.

"I made Jill call him and tell him I had Alex. He came to the tower, and I told him that Grizzly had hurt Alex and BJ, and that BJ was in critical condition."

"You lied? Why?"

"Because I was going to use his death to pit him completely against Grizzly. And I told Grizzly that Brandon was the one who left those bodies in his cans."

I gasped. "You are using the death of a *child*!"

"I know!" he yelled back. "But what was I supposed to do? If those two are chasing each other, then we have time to figure everything else out."

I sank my head into my hand and took a deep breath. "I can't believe this."

"Iyana, I'm so sorry. I wasn't thinking straight. I just jumped at whatever opportunity I had and tried to make the most of it."

"Vito, you sank our ship. What are we supposed to do?"

He sat up out the bed and clasped his hands around his knees. "Kat found the Abletons, and I gave their location to Grizzly. We'll have some time to figure things out. Did you get the boxes I sent?"

"Yes," I said, adjusting the blankets around me. "I can't believe this. We're screwed, Vee. The moment the two of them find out we're at the center of all this, and the rest of the world finds out you're selling ghost tickets to the Malawi show, IncogVito Tower won't be standing anymore."

"Which is why I need your help."

I shook my head, pulling my eyes from the blanket. Vito looked desperate, but he was trying to stay in control.

"Help with what?"

"Brandon's phone has a tracker on it. If we can—"

"Why are you tracking Brandon's phone?"

"To make sure Grizzly doesn't find him. If Grizzly finds him and makes him talk before killing him, they'll turn on us. I'm just trying to keep them separated, but Brandon's phone has been off. I can't track him anymore."

"So send some men to find him."

"If Grizzly finds out we're looking for Brandon too, he'll know something's up."

"Ok, hold on." I waved my hand around. "How did Brandon's phone get a tracker on it?"

"I had Leo put one on a phone I gave him."

"You *gave* him a phone?"

He opened his mouth and then closed it, then he let go of a long sigh and said, "I let him call Alex."

"What? Vito, you put our lives in danger! Your parents, Hardy and me, even Alex! What is wrong with you?"

"Oh, is it any more dangerous than what you put yourself in?"

I squinted. His jaw was screwed shut and he looked so menacing. I wanted to scream at him, but I was genuinely confused.

"What are you talking about?"

"You think I don't have your dad's house tapped? I told you I'd take care of your mother. So I had a few men tap your father's lines to listen in on his conversations for leads, I just never gave the order to *stop* listening in. So I heard that phone call you made to him."

"What else have you done behind my back?" I was outraged that he'd heard everything, but mostly because I was embarrassed. Vito and I didn't spend every living moment together. He'd done things without me plenty of times, but learning things so late made me feel so small in the grand scheme of things. It was like I wasn't even part of BT, or what was left of it ... Or this marriage sometimes.

"That's not behind your back. It's called protecting you," he snapped.

I pulled the blanket from off the bed and wrapped myself in it as I stood.

"Where are you going?" Vito demanded.

"Away from you! Here I thought you were this broken man! You're ridiculous, Vito, and you love it."

"*You* love it!" he screamed back at me.

I whirled around to find him marching around the bed with his shorts on now. "No, I don't!" I argued. "I'm afraid of you, Vito! You make these decisions and do these things—"

"You're afraid?" He frowned and looked me over quickly as if he was searching for a stench in the room. "Iyana, we just had the best sex of our lives. You're not scared of me." He chuckled as he stepped forward and leaned over me. A smug smile captured his lips as he purred, "You love every inch of me."

I raised my hand to slap him, but he caught it and lowered it. Trembling, I fell into his chest and began to sob. "I'm scared, Vito! What are we supposed to do?" My biggest worry was that BT would move on without me while I was gone. But my biggest worry *now* was how much time we had until the doors of BT were beaten down.

Vito pulled me close, wrapping his arms around me. "We're going to figure it out. I promise."

Twenty-Six
Vito
Feb 2nd | 10:00 am

Eventually, Iyana stopped crying yesterday. That day almost went exactly as I thought it would. The only part I was not expecting was the sex. I thought she'd be too angry or upset but, thankfully, she didn't find out all that'd happened until after we'd finished.

I felt so guilty, even after telling her the truth. Part of the guilt came from the shame of my inability to make rational decisions while she was gone. But the other part of the guilt came from Iyana's kindness. Iyana was always sweet and gentle, and today, she got out of bed and got dressed just like this day was no different than any other. She even wore the skimpy clothes I liked, and she didn't treat me any differently after learning the truth.

It was hard, watching her eat breakfast, hold my hand, smile at me. She told me she missed me but couldn't get herself to think of me while she'd been gone. I wasn't offended. I'd been so terrible while she was gone, it was good she didn't try to think of me. However, the only thing that made all this worse was that Iyana had bounced back like yesterday never happened and it reminded me of how quickly God forgives.

Even when we're wrong, He forgives us. I hated being forgiven because it felt like I owed something every time I was forgiven. But in actuality, it's the truth. Having Iyana around me turned the light back on, and I was able to feel the warmth she'd always brought because of her faith. The light exposes the dark, and it showed me that I will always be indebted to God because He forgives me, even in my deepest sin.

"Vee," she snapped, "are you listening?"

I nodded. Her polished nails glistened against my desk as she leaned over it. We were discussing a plan that was supposed to happen tonight, but I couldn't stop drifting.

"You're distracted." She folded her arms.

"I'm sorry. You said the plan was for me to go see Grizzly tonight and tell him about Bridges. Got it."

"No." She slowly dropped her arms and said meekly, "I'm going to see Grizzly about Bridges."

"What?"

"I'm the leader of—"

"You're a *figurehead*." I stood abruptly. "You're not going to see Grizzly."

"Yes, I am. You can't just tell me no. I'm going and that's final." She crossed her arms again like a brat and flopped down into her chair.

I grunted. "Fine, then we're both going."

"No thanks, I can go on my own."

"Please," I threw a hand at her, "you wouldn't last five minutes in his cove."

She leaned back and cackled. "Is that how scared you were when you went to see him? Five minutes in and you were shaking in your winter boots."

I snorted and laughed, and she continued to laugh too. "Fine." I exhaled. "But you have to take Hardy. I can't let you go to our rivals, who we're technically still at war with, without any protection. I don't trust Grizzly. Right now, we're in a standstill until the body fiasco is fixed, but he's unpredictable."

She shrugged. "Alright, I'll take Hardy."

I raised a brow. "That was easy. You like Hardy or something?"

She rolled her eyes. "Hardy means well, that's all."

"Well how well does he mean?"

"What kind of question is that?"

"You're smiling about another man in my office. In *my* tower."

"Vito, you run a brothel from *our* tower. I don't want to hear it."

I chewed my response and sat back at my desk. She was unfazed as she went back to looking over a binder in her hand.

"Vito? Iyana? You guys in here?"

"Speak of the devil," I taunted.

Iyana rolled her eyes. "Come in, Hardy."

When he stepped inside, for some reason he looked different. Like he got a little taller, a little stronger. Like puberty had actually hit him and he got his first chest hair three days ago. I looked back at Iyana, and noticed for the first time that she was thinner than when she'd left. Both of them had gone through changes, physically and emotionally. I didn't care about Hardy's changes, and since Iyana hadn't changed too much, there wasn't much to be concerned over.

"What's going on, Hardy?" I asked as he closed the door behind himself.

"Has anyone seen Kat? I can't find her at all."

I hadn't told either of them about Kat yet. I managed to tell Iyana a few more things yesterday, like about Bridges, and I told her about the Maryland stuff. I also told her about how I fooled Grizzly into thinking there was a rat in his ranks, but for some reason, Kat just never came up.

"Why don't you take a seat," I said with a sigh.

"Where is she?" Iyana was squinting at me now and I could feel the nerves rising in my chest.

"Kat left," I said flatly.

"Where'd she go?"

"Where do you think?" I snapped at Hardy. "She's not at the grocery store buying steak for your next dinner party. She left."

"What dinner party?" Iyana asked.

"How'd you know we'd have dinner sometimes?" Hardy was squinting now.

"Yeah?" Iyana asked with a slow nod.

"Neither of you are paying attention to what I'm saying. Kat left BT. She's gone. She didn't want to stay. She told me to tell you bye, Iyana, and that it was better to leave things this way with you, Hardy." I paused. "Oh, and Kat's taken ingredients from me for one of your dinners."

"She left," Hardy said slowly. "But, why?" His boyishness had returned, and his eyes had turned into big marbles blinking at me.

I glanced over at Iyana who was covering her mouth, and exhaled loudly. "Listen I—"

Knock. Knock. Knock.

"What?" I called.

"It's me, Leo, got a second?"

"Make it fast," I said.

He opened the door and stood in the doorway. "I just came to report that we let Jill's mother go. Unfortunately, she wasn't fit to be on her own and ended up wandering into traffic..." his voice trailed off as he caught the looks on our faces, but he didn't need to finish the rest. We could read between the lines.

Jill's mother was dead.

I rubbed my face roughly as Iyana spoke up, "Why did you have Jill's mom?"

"Well, we've still got Jill locked in one of the bedrooms of the tower. She messed up some work while you were gone so I had to find her mom just to scare her." I sighed. "I told her I was going to torture and kill her mother, but that'd only been a threat at the time. I never thought the old woman would actually end up dead."

Neither Hardy nor Iyana spoke. They were both still distraught about Kat's decision to leave, but also surprised that Jill was still in the tower.

Leo shifted in the doorway. "What should I tell Jill about her mother?"

"Anything," I replied. "She won't believe us either way."

"True," Leo said, jotting something down on his notepad. The radio on his hip rang and he tapped it. "What is it, Denali?"

"I'm sending up a woman named Bug. She said she knows Boss."

"Bug?" I frowned.

"No." Leo's face morphed from boredom to fear in an instant and he turned so quickly to leave I thought he'd spun out of control. "When did you let her in?" he said in the hall.

"What's happening?" Iyana asked as I moved from the desk.

"Stay here. Bug is from the Bronx, she's a notorious gang leader over there. It's a small gang, but the bit of business they handle is not done so kindly."

And there was only one reason a rival gang leader would show up at my tower unannounced…

I jogged out the room behind Leo. He was walking quickly to the door, speaking forcefully into his radio. "All men standby! We've got a bug in the tower."

"What are you going to do?"

"She's probably somewhere in the tower hiding out," Leo said, turning to face me. "We've got to flush her out."

I nodded. I was secretly proud of Leo. He'd always played secondary to Kat, but he knew his stuff and had been holding the tower down in Kat's absence.

"Just stay here," he said as he turned for the door.

"When you find her, let her kill Denali before squashing her."

He laughed as he grabbed the door handle. "I certainly will." Pulling the door open, a shot went off and I immediately dropped to the floor.

"Leo!" I screamed as I pulled my gun out.

I scrambled to my feet and ran to the front door where Leo lay on his back, a bullet lodged in his head. Stepping over his body, I passed into the hall, but no one was there so I moved back and snatched the radio off Leo's body.

"Man down! Man down!" I yelled into the device. "The bug is still loose! Find her!" I tossed the radio behind me and grabbed Leo's arms to drag him inside.

"Boss! What happened!?" Hardy was beside me now, pulling Leo with me.

"Bug came from the Bronx, she shot Leo probably thinking she—" gunshots went off from the hall into my apartment.

"Get down!" Hardy tackled me to the floor, and we crawled into the sunken living room for protection. The lights flickered and I could hear things crashing all over. "I'm fine! Go to Iyana! Make sure she's okay!" I yelled over the gunfire.

"Understood!" Hardy scrambled and ran low as he disappeared around the corner. I loaded my gun as Bug's voice cried out, "I want my bricks, Vito!"

I invited Bug to one of the sample parties and she paid a hefty price to secure some Malawi. I told everyone it'd be a few weeks for imports because of the winter weather, but people were beginning to get antsy, especially with Bridges suddenly missing.

The sound of a shotgun went off, and a man in a mask flew by the door. Two more shots went off, and then there was screaming followed by silence.

"Boss?"

"Logan!?" I slowly crawled out of the living room, aiming my gun, but Logan rounded the corner holding his shotgun, and I relaxed.

"I heard the gunshots and came running." His hair was wet, and he had a towel wrapped around his waist.

"Were you in the shower?"

"Yeah. When I got out, I heard all the firing and came up."

I exhaled and he extended a hand to help me up.

"I'm going to check on Iyana."

Running around the corner, I grabbed the door and tried to open it, but there was something against it. "Hardy, it's me."

"Oh sorry, boss," he called from the other side. I heard him grunting as he moved whatever was blocking the door. "Ok!" he called, and I pushed open the door.

"Vito!" Iyana cried as she leapt into my arms. "I was so scared."

"It's happening," I said into her hair.

"What's happening? Because we've never been attacked before, not at the tower," Hardy exclaimed. I looked over at Logan, but he glanced away. After our conversation about what he'd do with millions of dollars, Logan finally figured out that something was up. I didn't need to say much, he just made it very clear that he was ready to go whenever I was.

"We're in a little mess," Iyana spoke before I could. She pulled away from me and turned to Hardy who was looking wide eyed around the room.

"This isn't a little mess, Iyana," he said carefully.

"You're right, it's not. And I'll need you to help clean it up."

"Not until you tell me the truth."

She nodded. "We'll take a ride tonight, and I'll tell you everything."

"Great," Logan stepped forward, "now that you two have figured that out, what are we going to do about Bug?"

"We're going to see her tonight." I pushed past the crowd and went to my desk. I shoved all the papers off of it to the map of the city sealed beneath the glass on my desk.

"And do what?" Iyana asked.

"We're going to return the message she came to deliver."

"Why? We do owe her, just let it go," Iyana said.

"And let some garbage gang from the crevices of the Bronx show us up?" Logan shook his head as he slung his shotgun over his shoulder. "I don't think so."

"This isn't up to you." Iyana stepped to him.

"Hold on," I said, trying to spare my wife and brother. "Iyana, we have to retaliate, we can't let this go."

"Yes, we can."

"You could've been killed!"

"But I wasn't! I'm right here! Thanks to Logan, Bug got scared and ran off. The situation is over. But if we don't stop meeting violence with violence, this cycle will never end."

"It's a cycle that isn't meant to be broken." Logan pushed past her and left the office.

"I know what you mean," I said, and Iyana refocused on me.

Hardy stood silently, watching between Iyana and me, trying to find where his loyalty should lie. But it was an easy choice, because Iyana and I were a team, and I had to remember that. It wasn't my word against hers, or hers against mine. When I married her, I gave her power over BT, and I needed to respect that. But Iyana also had to understand that there were things that needed to be done in ways she didn't always agree with.

"Attacking Bug would only give Grizzly another ally, and alert everyone to our hoax. But if we don't retaliate, it'll look like Bug was right and we cannot afford that right now."

"So, what's the plan?" Hardy finally spoke.

"Logan and I are going to the Bronx. We'll send a message, but it'll be authoritative."

"What does that mean?" Iyana was less tense now as confusion morphed her features.

"It means we won't kill anyone because we don't have to. But we'll show Bug that we have the capabilities to wipe her out. She needs to be reminded that her gang, and all the small gangs of New York, thrive off the back of BT. They're at our mercy, and they only survive because I allow it." I took a breath to let it all sink in and then I added, "Besides, if we don't stop this pest problem, other small gangs we've ignored may think this is their chance."

Iyana sighed and nodded. "I understand."

"Good, because I need to get a move on, and so do you." I came around the desk and kissed her head. "Hardy, she's your responsibility until I get back. Got it?"

"Understood."

"Ana," I pulled her by the hands away from Hardy to the opposite end of the room. She was giving me a half smile, and her upturned eyes looked worried. "You'll be fine tonight. Just be confident, and don't do anything risky. I want to sleep with you tonight." She quirked a brow, and I shook my head. "I mean, I want you home tonight. I want to sleep *beside* you."

"We just got back together, and now we're separating again." She exhaled. "Just promise me no one will get hurt."

"I can't promise that. But I can promise if someone gets hurt, it won't be on purpose. I'm not looking to kill anyone, Iyana. I'm just sending a message."

She studied me quietly before taking a deep breath and pushing away the fear and sullen look in her eyes. "Alright. I'll see you tonight."

BT

Logan and I left the tower with a group of men without letting Iyana know. Logan told Hardy, but Iyana was still on edge about tonight's plans, so I slipped away when she got into the shower. We rode through the boroughs, silently watching the people passing by, sitting restlessly through the stretching traffic. It was a horrifyingly long ride to the Bronx, but we got stuck in rush hour traffic. The only good thing was that it didn't matter when we showed up, as long as we did.

One of the greatest attractions in NYC and in the Bronx specifically, was the Bronx Zoo. Tonight, we planned to set off an explosion in the zoo, and in three more locations throughout the borough just to remind Bug to stay under the rock she'd crawled from. She took a life, and I had every intention of taking hers, but, because I'm determined to be a man of God, and now that Iyana's back, I've decided to show her mercy.

I'd initially felt bad for wanting to meet violence with violence, but I know that I have to send a message, I know that if I don't retaliate, things will get worse much quicker than if I do. It isn't an excuse, but I'm grateful that for the first time in a month I can't ignore my inner turmoil.

Iyana was right; violence met with violence won't do much, and I was frustrated because I knew she was right. But I was also frustrated because it had never crossed my mind that it was wrong. That was the way life was here, and there was no getting around that. And even though I felt bad, I knew I'd still do what needed to be done to save Iyana. But I also learned that it was alright that Iyana recognized the wrong in attacking another gang. She was my wife, and if no one else could help me, I knew she could. Even if I didn't like what she had to say.

Before I became the head of BT, I was part of a singles Bible study class. They were teaching us about how to prepare for marriage, and one of the ways to prepare is to know your role, as a man and as a woman. Men needed to know their role as a husband, but they also needed to know the role of their wife, and that it had nothing to do with being a slave or a servant to them.

In turn, women needed to know their role and the role of their husband. I learned that wives were submissive to their husbands the way we submit to God, through reverence and obedience. And husbands, we were to also submit as servants to our wives as Christ submitted to death, and to God for His bride, the Church. In that way, each of us is making a sacrifice and letting a part of ourselves go. But the part that's missing is made up for by the wife or husband.

It was the same way with Christ. He had to give up His life in order to receive His wife. We have to give up our life to receive salvation. And when we are weak, God's strength is perfect. When God wants praise, our life devotion to Him brings Him glory. Therefore, it is a marriage, one that is eternal between Christ and the Church. Each serving the other in a continual journey, each is respected, and each is loved. So, where I lacked knowledge, Iyana provided that. Where I lacked faith, Iyana compensated. And where she lacked strength, I was there. Where she lacked protection, I surrounded her. But it all came from our own submission to God. And now that I'm refocused, I can be a good husband to Iyana, and eventually, a real man of God.

As we pulled up to the zoo, I sighed, but there was no turning back now.

"Alright," I said as we got out of the car, "I want the smaller bombs in the Asian Plaza and the Dancing Crane Plaza. In the fountain, I want a big explosion."

"What about Bug Carousel, boss?" one of the men asked.

I smirked. "I want to double up on the big explosion. We've gotta send the right message, that she's not the only one who'll be hurt, but she will be crushed."

"Aren't we breaking the civilian code by messing with the zoo?" Logan asked as he unloaded the trunk.

"No," I said firmly. "That's why we're here after hours. Not a single person will be hurt."

He nodded and continued to place ammunition and weapons in his duffle bag. He and two other men were heading by foot up the street to set off explosions in the surrounding area.

"After tonight, boys, everyone will get the message. Not just Bug."

"Yes, boss," they all said together.

It was bittersweet, looking at my men standing together, ready to work. This may be our last chance to prolong an attack from the outside, but sooner or later, these same faces will be lifeless bodies who died for no other reason than to save me.

I climbed into the front seat of the truck to leave them. They would all find their way back to the tower on their own, that would help make things look less suspicious.

"You all better make it back tonight."

"Yes, boss," they said.

"Alright, get moving."

I pulled my door shut, and buckled myself in. The ride home would be a long one.

Twenty-Seven
Hardy
Feb 2nd | 6:00pm

"I can't believe he just left me," Iyana snapped in the back of the car.

"He didn't want to make you nervous," I said, waving a car to turn in front of me.

"Oh please. You're on his side now?"

"Iyana, there aren't any sides to this." I rolled my eyes.

"Yes, there are, Hardy!" Her voice cracked, drawing my attention to the rearview mirror. She dabbed her cheeks as tears began to fall. "I'm so scared," she whispered.

"I know," I said. The car rattled as we passed over a pothole.

"I have to lie and convince Grizzly that Bridges's death was his gang's fault. I have to lie, and I just scolded Vito for being violent. But I'm no better. Now I'm here, afraid I'll mess up the lie, and I just can't—"

"Didn't Rahab lie?"

She looked up at me, and I could see her reflection in the mirror. She was shocked.

"God hates liars."

"But she was King David's great grandmother, wasn't she?"

"Yes, but that didn't make it right."

"But she was used by God to save His people."

"Yes, I know," she said flatly. "But I just don't want to lie."

"Then don't."

"What?"

"Don't lie." I shrugged. "If the point of all this is just to put more space between BT and it's enemies by making it look like we're investigating, then there's no reason to lie, since technically we *are* still doing an investigation of Bridges's house and belongings."

I swallowed because Iyana was giving me a sour look in the mirror. Flicking my eyes back to the road, I said, "Just tell him you know who did it, and you want to check his gun against a ballistic report."

"What if he doesn't believe me?" She wasn't crying anymore. She adjusted in her seat and was squinting out the window, waiting for me to answer.

"If he doesn't believe you, then threaten to go public with touchy details that can incriminate him. The truth is, we know who did it, and we need time to make a good impression on the city since we owe a lot of people. But Bridges had a lot of enemies, Grizzly's gang was an enemy because of Brandon."

"Why Brandon?"

"It's a long story." I sighed. "Anyways, the point is that we have enough evidence to point the finger at anyone. We've got fingerprints and DNA, but no eyewitnesses. Any story could be told."

She was silent for a moment. "Jewels always said you were incredibly smart, and very intelligent. Thank you."

I squeezed the steering wheel. "It's not me. I think it's God. Finding a way not to sin, only God would help you do that, right?"

"Yes."

I didn't say anything else and neither did Iyana. I know she just wanted to compliment me, but Jewels's name still sent a shudder through my body because of all that came with it.

Jewels brought back the fact that I'd killed a person, killed a person I swore I'd loved, and her name summoned memories of Kat. Memories of how thankful I was to have met her, and now she was gone before I ever got to apologize for being an idiot. Jewels also brought back Brandon, my enemy.

I tried not to let hatred stir in my heart for him because I'm not supposed to hate, I'm supposed to love even my enemies. Brandon makes it so difficult to forgive him, let alone love him, but I try every day. However, connected to Jewels, Kat, and Brandon, is the one person who has changed me forever…

Alex.

The brief time I shared with her was so rich and warm. She was beautiful and attractive, even with her baby bump. But who she was, that fragile, kind woman, my heart ached for her. I adored her. I liked her. Maybe it was love at first sight, maybe it wasn't, but I didn't want to think about her.

If I let myself think about her for too long, my mind would become foggy with our memories which could be overwhelming. But because of her, I found myself talking to God more. Begging Him to protect her and Ava. Asking Him to keep Alex out of my mind. I wanted to be with her, but I needed to work on myself. I needed to *fix* myself first.

"Hardy? Are you alright?"

"Yeah?" I glanced up while waiting at the red light. "Why?"

"You got quiet after I mentioned Jewels. I shouldn't have said that."

"I've got to get over her, over what I did to her."

"For your sake or Alex's?"

I took a breath. "For mine."

"I'm proud of you, Hardy." She reached forward and grabbed my hand. "I'm really proud of you."

I chuckled and closed my hand around hers. "We're not dying tonight, Iyana, so stop being mushy." I let go of her hand and grabbed the steering wheel. Holding her hand, hearing those words, it all made my heart stir in a comforting way.

I slowed as I pulled up to Grizzly's place. It looked like an abandoned building instead of an actual place of living, like the way IncogVito looked. The building was rectangular and caged. It was the makings of something out of an apocalyptic film. Broken windows with curtains hanging out, an old black door, and across the nearly corroded bricks was the name 'Gang Grizzly' spray painted in green letters. I never got a good look at it when Kat and I dumped the bodies—I'd never realized how horrible it looked.

"Vito didn't tell us it was this kind of place," Iyana said.

"Yeah."

She tried to steady herself by closing her eyes and whispering a prayer. "Let's just get this over with."

"How do we get in unannounced?"

"Vito said to just walk in and tell them I have a meeting with Grizzly."

I nodded. With no real directions from Vito, we didn't know what we were getting into. Opening the center council, I grabbed two handguns and slipped them into their holsters under my arms. I pulled my jacket on and stepped out the car so I could help Iyana out into the thick snow. The place hadn't been shoveled at all; I got through the snow just fine, but Iyana was short, so I had to help her get over some of the higher banks until we reached the front door.

"Should we knock?" I asked.

"We should, and we should pray." She closed her eyes and mumbled something beside me. In my heart, I pleaded for protection in Jesus' Name. "Ok, let's do this," Iyana said.

Knock. Knock. Knock.

Silence.

Thump. Thump. Thump.

There was a loud racking of the slide of a gun right behind the door. I snatched one of mine out and stepped in front of Iyana. When the door opened, I raised my gun as quickly as the guy standing there.

"Who are you?" he asked aggressively.

"We're here to see Grizzly." I tried to sound tough, but my voice cracked, and I didn't sound like anything but a scared boy. I was always just a boy to everyone. But I didn't want to be a boy anymore. I wanted to be a man. But what did I know? The man in front of me had a tight grip on his gun without an ounce of fear in his eyes, while I did everything I could to keep myself from trembling.

I'd done work before, but never anything this serious. Until recently, all my job entailed was driving Brandon around and then standing in the background while he made business deals or conducted meetings.

This was entirely different.

The man squinted and looked me over, then flicked his gaze over to Iyana. "I don't recognize either of you."

I nervously adjusted my grip on my gun. "I told you we're here to see Grizzly. We don't need to tell you any more than that."

He smirked. "You scared, boy?"

I felt Iyana grabbing my jacket. "No." I cleared my throat. "What do I have to be scared of?"

"You look scared, boy."

The winter chill washed over us, and Iyana whimpered beside me.

"You need to let us in," I said forcefully.

"That wind's making you cold." He leaned back to laugh, but I was tired of being a boy. I was tired of being laughed at and made to think that everything I thought or felt was invalid because I was young. It had been a slow simmering anger, but in that moment, it suddenly boiled over.

I lunged forward and snatched the man by his shirt and yanked him halfway out the door. He yelped, and I shoved him against the door post, pressing my gun to the back of his head.

"Get the gun!" I yelled at Iyana.

She nodded as she grabbed the gun with trembling hands.

"Who is in here letting all my heat out!?" Grizzly stepped into view and stared at me holding one of his men against the wall. He was older than I imagined. The few times I'd seen him in passing, I couldn't make out his features as to whether he was old or young. But his broad shoulders holding a large brown fur cloak that trailed to the floor, and his signature gold teeth made him easily recognizable.

"What are you doing?" he asked.

"We're here to talk."

"Who are you?"

Iyana stepped inside and extended the gun to him. "I'm Mrs. Gerardo, the head of Bellen Tupp."

He stepped back and looked her over. "You're his wife. You're the Princess of the City."

"If my guard lets your man go, will you call the cub off? He's a little trigger happy."

Grizzly snorted. "Alright, you can let him go. Cuba, go find my other men. I don't know why there isn't a single cub out front besides you."

"Hardy…"

I didn't respond right away. Iyana had been speaking with such authority in her voice, I didn't recognize her as the scared woman from the car. But maybe she didn't recognize me either.

"Hardy," she said again, and this time I obeyed, and let the cub go.

He whirled around and stared at me.

"Shoo," I called at him, and he frowned darkly before turning and leaving.

"We need to talk," Iyana said to Grizzly.

"I feel like I know you from somewhere." Grizzly was looking intently at her as he towered over her.

"You asked me on a date once. But as you can tell, I was already taken."

Grizzly mulled it over before the lightbulb clicked on. "You're the girl from that grocery store. You were with him all along, which means—"

"We need to talk."

He grunted and eyed me before looking back at Iyana. "Fine, but make it fast. I don't like liars and cheats."

"Then you'll love what I have to say."

He took the gun from her and waved us on to follow him down the long hall.

We passed through doors made of wood with claw marks carved into them. Inside was the makings of a romantic getaway from the seventies—completely opposite of the raggedy exterior of the building. There were furs all over the floor and couches, blunts between the fingers of women lying half naked all over the room. Incense was burning, and two guards dressed like the one who answered the door stood behind a wide old desk.

"Hodda, take the ladies out, and get on that tracking," Grizzly ordered.

The guard nodded and crossed the room without even giving Iyana and me a sideways glance. I watched silently as the women got up and left out through the back door. When they had gone, all that could be heard was the crackling of Grizzly's fireplace.

"You can approach the cove," he said as he sat at his desk.

Iyana nodded and sat across from him, but I only moved to stand against the wall.

"Almost twice in two weeks, I've seen someone from BT on my doorsteps. New York must be dying."

"Or your gang is," Iyana said with a smile.

Grizzly and I both stared at her, and his once smirking face suddenly dropped to a frown. "You better watch your mouth, girl."

"Let's talk business." Iyana disregarded the statement and dug through her bag. When she pulled the folders out, I could see her hands trembling. She flopped them on his desk and sat back in her seat.

"What is this?"

"Open it."

"Don't give me orders."

"I can either give you orders or give you a death sentence." She leaned forward. "Open the folders."

Grizzly grunted and leaned back in his seat for a moment. He eyed an unblinking Iyana until he nodded. "You're playing mighty tough. Makes me think that good girl act is just a façade."

"I'm whoever I need to be."

"Very good. You'll survive in this business, then." He grabbed the folders and opened the first one. "Tell me something before we get into this, why Vito?"

Iyana looked startled for a second. She regained herself and shrugged nonchalantly. "I wanted big."

"You're in it for the money?"

"For the status. I can have whatever I want in the city just by mentioning my name."

He grinned. "I think I like you, Ms. Iyana. You seem like a better man than your husband, or whatever he is to you."

She only nodded, and I could tell she was beginning to feel nervous. Vito was her husband, and she loved him, but everyone believed their marriage was a sham. Pretending to be distant seemed difficult for Iyana. *How long can she keep this up?*

Thankfully, Grizzly never looked up to see the nerves on her face. He slowly looked through the images in the first folder before swapping for the second and reading the reports.

"Bridges is dead? He's a city guy, right? What's this got to do with me?"

"The report has inconclusive data surrounding the gun. You need to clear your name."

"Why? What reason would anyone believe that I killed Bridges?"

"You or someone who used to work for you. Bridges had a lot of enemies."

Grizzly hung his head, and his voice came out cold and tired, "Including Brandon."

"He's been quite costly since you took in our rat."

"Don't mock me," he seethed as he raised his head.

"Then take this seriously. We can't make it public with who the killer is unless there's a perfect match against the ballistic report. Three different guns are in question."

"If I don't do this, what are you going to do?" Grizzly folded his hands atop the folders and stared darkly at Iyana.

"I have to make sure my city believes in its Prince."

He scoffed. "Why am I surprised? You said you like your status."

"I do. And that should scare you."

"It doesn't."

"Then we're done here." Iyana stood and grabbed her folders.

"Wait," Grizzly said. "Why are you doing this? Why did your husband just give me the Abletons, and now you're here giving me a hand?"

"Because…" she paused to chew her lip. Her eyebrows pinched in worry and her eyes swept the room for an answer. "We are still at war, Grizzly. But we don't need to involve others and we need to stop spilling blood. I don't want to wage war on this place, but I will if you don't cooperate."

"Your man shot mine."

"And what have your men done when we hadn't even retaliated?"

She was referring to the dead bodies Kat and I placed in Grizzly's trash. He took a breath, and said, "February fourth, evening time."

"I'll have someone from the lab there to discuss the process."

"You better not be screwing with me."

"You better show, for your own good."

Without another word, Iyana turned to me with eyes full of fear. She nodded and I grabbed her arm and escorted her out of Grizzly's cove.

Twenty-Eight

Brandon
Feb 3rd | 10:00 am

I groaned as I rolled over. The king-sized bed I found myself in was filled with bodies. I'd spent the night with three different women. It was the most fun I'd had since Grizzly started chasing me. The sex was better than anyone I'd ever had. The drugs were stronger. The liquor was richer. And the smoky haze made the entire room feel like I was dreaming. Every night here was technicolored, and I wasn't tired of it at all.

I stumbled into this house the day after I left Vali's. I couldn't take sleeping in another abandoned car and took my chances here at a crack house. It turned out good. There wasn't much conversation, which was what I wanted. I was tired of explaining myself. I was tired of being chased like I was an animal. I was tired of being treated like someone who'd gone rogue.

We were all rogues here. There wasn't a clean or pure soul in the building, and the dirtier you were, the better the sex was. The scroungier, the better the drugs felt. The wilder, the harder the alcohol hit. It was like living a dream where reality disappeared for good, and all your fantasies came true. These women could handle anything I gave them, and it satisfied me.

Trea, a honey skinned woman with dark hair gasped as she sat up beside me.

"What's wrong?" I said sleepily.

She reached for one of the sleeping women beside us. "I think Abigail is dead."

I rolled over and sat up. My eyes lazily traced Abigail's body, and then I remembered choking her last night. It was something I'd done in a moment of passion, while we were making love—though there was no love involved in the act at all.

The ecstasy had driven me wild. Awakening dark desires I didn't even know I had. One moment we were having normal sex, the next, my hands were around her throat.

I'd wanted to see her struggling beneath me. I thought it would intensify the pleasure. But before I finished, she was lying still and lifeless.

Reality settled its heavy hands onto my shoulders, but I fought the feeling and rolled over. I was in the perfect place, no cops or Grizzly. No one to guilt trip me. Everyone here would just think the drugs killed Abigail, and my conscience needed to believe it too. I didn't want to feel guilty. I didn't want to be responsible because I couldn't control myself. I wanted her to suffer. I wanted *someone* to suffer. *I* was suffering. I hadn't felt anything but grief since I left BT, no matter how badly I forced myself to feel anything else.

"Brandon, do something!" Trea called.

"No. I'm tired."

"Come on! I don't want to lay next to a dead girl."

"Then just kick her out the bed. What am I supposed to do with her?"

"Shh!" someone on the opposite end of the bed called. "It's too early."

What had my life become? Weeks ago, I was living the best life I'd ever had. Now I'm sharing a bed with naked people, doing hard drugs, and literally having insane sex. Wasn't it supposed to be fun? Wasn't it supposed to be fulfilling? Even though I kept telling myself that it was all those things, I knew it wasn't.

The vomiting, the headaches, and erratic heart beating. I hadn't felt my legs since I got here. I hadn't bathed and I'd barely eaten anything. Abigail wasn't even the only person to die in this bed. Some guy named Kent died in the bed from an overdose when I'd first arrived. All we did was drag him outside and come back to the bed. The next morning, he was gone.

Trea climbed over me to sleep on my other side. I didn't want to deal with anything. I wished for death every night. My whole world had been flipped upside down. *What would Alex think? She's too good for me. I shouldn't go back to her.*

I reached forward and tangled my hand into Trea's hair. She didn't speak. Maybe I'd start over with Trea. I can still hustle the streets somewhere out of here. Maybe I'd get away and get a real job, anything would be better than this. I just didn't want to do it alone. I wanted to spend my life with someone who's suffered like me. I'm sure no one ends up in this situation if everything is fine. No one with good in their heart ends up here, and that's what I needed. Someone who's as filthy as I am. Then no one could point the finger.

"Trea," I whispered.

"What?"

"Don't you get tired of this?"

"Tired of what?"

"This life. The drugs. The bodies."

She paused. "Do you?"

"Well, yeah."

"You just got here and you're already tired? You're not taking the right stuff then."

I stared at the back of her head for a second. "Don't you want a family?"

"This is my family."

"No, Trea, your own family. Kids, a dog, a house. We could do it."

She was silent for a moment. "I can't have kids. When my husband found out I couldn't get pregnant, he beat me and put me out. I've been here ever since. Well," she corrected, "I wandered for a while, but eventually I wound up here and stayed."

Slowly, I unraveled my hand from her hair. Everyone had a story, but I didn't need to hear any more of hers. Somehow, she'd undone my entire theory that good people don't end up here. Trea was barren. Not a gang member. Not a killer. Not a criminal. She was just a woman who couldn't have kids and was sent to the streets for it. She'd made the most of it, and now she's stuck here.

I was suddenly aching for Trea, even though we'd barely known each other. I wondered how long she'd been here, but I didn't ask. Instead, I just rolled over and came face to face with Abigail. Her head was turned, so she was looking at me. Empty orbs and vomit on her mouth and down her neck. Her skin had lost its color, and her eyes had lost their twinkle. I wished that things were different. I wished to be better.

Why didn't I stop choking her? What's wrong with me?

My thoughts trailed off when the sound of cars picked up outside. I sat up in bed and glanced around. "Trea? You hear that?"

"Go back to bed," she groaned.

"I'm serious," I said as I shook her.

She sighed and rolled over. "I don't hear anything."

"I swear I heard—"

Thump! Thump! Thump!

"Open up! Police!"

"We're getting raided!" someone shouted in a drunken slur.

I threw the covers back and jetted out of the bed. I grabbed anyone's clothes I could get on and raced through the abandoned building for my bag. I'd left it in the bathroom so the junkies wouldn't get to it. When I got there, thankfully, it was still there. I snatched it and threw it over my shoulder as I rounded the corner for boots. The pounding was still going at the door, but it wasn't a fist anymore. Someone was about to kick the door down.

"Trea!" I screamed. But she was only half dressed and trying to find clothes. The whole room was in a frenzy. I glanced around and found a window. When I peeked out, there was a cop car out there. The place was completely surrounded.

"Trea! We're surrounded! We've gotta get out another way!"

She came racing over to me and grabbed my arm. A woman named Winrey and three other people were crossing the room when the door crashed open, and the police flooded in.

"Get down!" Winrey shouted.

I grabbed Trea's hand and raced for the window. If the cops were inside, then there was a chance none were outside, at least, that's what I was hoping.

When we got to the window, Trea lifted it and Winrey hopped out, then another man. Finally, Trea and I hopped out, but as I hit the ground, gunshots went off inside and outside. Trea screamed beside me, and Winrey hollered out, falling flat on her back in the snow.

"Come on, Trea!" I grabbed her hand and yanked her as I took off.

The police fired at us as we ran into the streets, racing between cars, and tripping into a trash can. They were hot on our tails as we rounded a corner down an alleyway.

"It's a dead end! Let's go before they catch us!" Trea shouted. She was pulling me, turning me around.

Stumbling, I regained my footing and followed behind her. As we rushed back down the alleyway, we were met with a cop. "Hold it right there!" he shouted.

Trea shoved him and we both whisked by. My heart was pounding in my chest as we ran down the street. I shoved a woman with a cane out the way and reached for Trea's hand again.

"Cut through this diner! We can make it out the back!" Trea shouted to me, but her words were smothered by the popping of a gun.

Time suddenly slowed, and Trea's hand slipped from mine as she fell to the ground.

"Trea! Get up!" I screamed as I leaned down and grabbed her. Weakly she held onto me as I got us to our feet and ran for the diner. "Hang in there," I called as we entered.

"Oh my goodness!" a woman screamed while Trea and I made our way through.

People moved out of the way as I dragged Trea to the bathroom. "Trea!" I screamed, tears flooding my eyes. She was taking short erratic breaths as I laid her on the bathroom floor.

"Sir?" A small hand tapped my shoulder.

I whirled around to find a young lady with her hands raised.

"I'm a nurse, I can help."

I nodded and she squeezed by me.

"Please save her," I whispered.

"She needs medical attention right now." The woman turned and shouted, "Someone call an ambulance!"

Trea slowly lifted her hand and touched my face. "It'll be alright, Brandon." She forced a smile as she began to hiccup on her breaths.

"Please don't go," I whined as I cupped her hand against my face. Her body began to tremble, and her hand went limp in mine. "Trea… Trea… please! Quit playing, Trea, get up!" I shoved the nurse out of the way and pulled Trea's body into my chest. "No!" I cried. "No!"

I could hear commotion in the diner, and then voices yelling, "Police! We're looking for two people, a man and a woman!"

I snapped around and stared down the hall.

"They're in the bathrooms!" someone shouted.

I laid Trea down and kissed her forehead before swinging my bag around and pulling my gun out of it. Then I grabbed the nurse by the arm and pulled her to her feet.

"I won't kill you, but I need to get out of here." I pulled her along until I came face to face with a cop halfway down the hall. I pressed the gun to her head. "Let me go or I will blow her head off."

"Calm down!" the cop yelled.

The nurse was crying uncontrollably now as I jammed the gun into her head. "Let me go!" I cocked the gun, and the cop tightened his grip on his own. "Fine," I said flatly.

I shoved the nurse into him and fired the gun four times before rushing off. There were screams and cries, and a man tried to stop me in the doorway. But I didn't have time, I shot him and he fell to floor, screaming. Stepping over him, I raced out the door and down the street.

I'd lost everything. Trea had been my last hope and now she was gone. She was taken from me, just like everything else had been taken from me. I couldn't hold on to anything, not even my own wife. She was taken from me, my son was in the hospital, Jewels was forced to run off, and Jill was a traitor. Nothing had been easy for me.

I slowed my pace and leaned against a building. "Why?" I sniffled. "Why!?"

"Hey! Brandon!"

I whipped around but stopped suddenly when I saw the flash of a bat. My tears slipped into the snow, freezing into snowflakes as the dim morning light began to fade.

—— BT ——

When I opened my eyes, I saw total darkness. I tried to move, and realized I was tied up.

"Get the bag off," a voice ordered.

Before I knew it, light was burning my eyes and I took a breath of fresh air. I was drenched in sweat as I blinked back the light and saw my captor… Grizzly.

"We finally found you," he said with a smirk.

"What do you want with me!?" I shouted. "I could kill you for what you've done to me!"

He raised his hand, and someone came up behind me and slammed a plastic bag over my head. They pulled back on it and I began to squirm for air. I riled against the ropes on my wrists, burning them and cutting them deeply as I fought to breathe.

"Enough," Grizzly said.

At once the bag was ripped off and I lurched forward for air.

"Now, Brandon, I just want to have a conversation with you before I kill you. If you have another outburst, I'll just kill you without talking at all."

"Kill me? After everything you put me through!?"

His big black hand fired across my face, and my vision blurred from the force. The incredible pain scorched my face like a branded horse.

"Do you know how much money you've cost me? Do you know what kind of predicament I'm in now because of you! I had two bodies show up in my garbage and one of them was Jewels! Now it looks like me or you got out of control with one of Vito's most prized possessions and killed her."

"Wait..." I shook my head. "Jewels isn't dead. She's on the run with Jill." In the silence, I raised my head, but Grizzly's twisted expression let me know something wasn't right.

"What are you talking about?"

"Jewels is on the run with Jill."

"Jewels is dead, Brandon." He paused. "You killed her and one of Vito's guys."

I was suddenly winded. I wanted to scream. I wanted to die. I didn't care if Grizzly killed me. Jewels was dead and I was alive. How could this be?

"Jewels isn't dead!" I screamed. "I won't believe it!"

"You dumped their bodies in my garbage the day you ..." he was leaning over me as I wept furiously. "No, that's not right. How could he have dumped the bodies if we had him tied up? Hodda!"

Dahodda stepped forward from the dark corner of the room and glanced over at me.

"What happened the day we brought Brandon in?"

"We went to the house, captured him, and brought him back. When he woke up for questioning, someone came in and said there were bodies left in the garbage. Then Brandon escaped."

I watched the confusion rushing over Grizzly as it rushed over me. My distraught heartbreak was stopped when Dahodda retold how their day went.

"What happened to my son?" I spoke weakly.

Grizzly's eyes were wide, and he was standing as stiff as a board.

"What happened to Bridges, Brandon?" he asked.

"I don't know." I shrugged dramatically. "What happened to my son!?"

"He was killed! He's dead! You knew that already."

My eyes flitted to Dahodda's. He was standing there, unashamed of the lies he'd told.

"But you said you didn't kill them? How is he dead? Vito said he's—"

"Vito?" Grizzly snatched me by my shirt to his face. Me and the chair both were off the floor as he stared darkly into my soul. I swear there was steam rolling off his shoulders. "You've talked to Vito?"

I didn't want to answer, but when Grizzly slammed me back down to the floor, he pulled a gun out and shoved it into my head. "You better answer me!"

"Vito said he had BJ at a facility and Alex was in a safehouse!"

"What else?"

"And he said Jewels and Jill ran away together, and Jill was working for you!"

He pulled the gun from my head and backhanded me with it. The chair wobbled and flipped over, slamming me hard against the floor.

"That piss tail prince has played us! Your wife and son are dead! Jewels is dead! And he told you I was responsible for their deaths and told me you were responsible for Jewels's death and Bridges's death!"

"BJ is dead?" was all I could manage to ask.

Grizzly stood over me. He had a tired look on his face. "Your son died, your wife died, Jewels—"

"Alex is alive. I talked to her days ago. She's alive."

Grizzly looked over his shoulder at Dahodda but said nothing.

"You killed BJ and almost killed Alex," I said to Dahodda.

"You killed my brother," he responded.

"Hey!" Grizzly snapped before the tension could rise any further. "We have a bigger issue right now. Vito is the one who's actually the problem. Hodda, untie him, we need him now."

"For what?" I snapped. "So you can take everything else from me!?"

"No! So you can stop blaming me for the things *your* leader did! You believe every word Vito says, but you have no idea what he's capable of, do you? He played you, Brandon. Made you think I was your enemy. He swears he has Alex somewhere safe, but she's in the tower! Jill's in his tower!"

"You're just saying that!" I screamed.

I didn't want that to be true. Vito wasn't like me. He didn't make plans and swindle people. *Not Vee...*

I almost choked as Dahodda cut me loose. I didn't know who to believe anymore. Was Alex actually in the tower? Had Vito really tried to confuse me?

That couldn't be right because BJ was dead because of Grizzly. But something wasn't making sense about Jewels.

"You know," Grizzly said as I stood, "those bodies, Jewels and Rion, they showed up the same day you arrived here. And when I found you at your home, you were out cold. So if you didn't kill Jewels, and I didn't kill Jewels, and she lived at the tower, who do you think killed her?"

He was right. I didn't kill Jewels, and since their bodies showed up at Grizzly's doorstep while the cove was full, there was no way Gang Grizzly or his cubs and bears were out killing Jewels. They would've had to break into the tower to do that.

Jewels told me at that event that she was on twenty-four-seven security. Knowing Vee, he probably put someone on her security detail, which must've been Rion. But why was he killed? Why would anyone kill either of them?

"That little snake is costing me money. I did everything I could to keep this war bloodless, but he's showed me there's no way that's possible." Grizzly moved to sit behind his desk. He opened his drawer and pulled out long sheets of paper. "We've got one night to make a plan. Are you in or out?"

I glanced at Dahodda, but he wouldn't look at me. I'd killed his brother, but he'd killed my son—if BJ was even dead. I didn't know what to believe. If I fought for Vito, and he'd done all these things, I'd never forgive myself. But fighting against him if he's innocent would be no different for me. I'd turned against him once, and I'd do it again if it meant finding out the truth.

Is BJ actually dead? Are Alex and Jill in the tower? And... why did Vito kill Jewels?

I'd have to stop letting myself get emotional until I learned the truth.

I took a breath and stepped forward. "I'm in."

Twenty-Nine
Iyana
Feb 4ᵗʰ | 10:01am

Vito never gets the paper. I didn't even know people still delivered newspapers, but there was one sitting on the breakfast table with the headline, **'Explosions Set Off in the Bronx Zoo.'** There were a few reports of missing and injured animals. But no casualties just like Vito had promised.

"Ana," Vito called.

I snapped my vision up from the paper to blink at him.

"We said grace and you haven't eaten a thing. We haven't even had a real breakfast since you got back. We've been too busy."

"Sorry," I muttered as I folded the paper and set it on the table.

"You want to talk about last night? Hardy said you did great."

"Vito…" I took a breath, his brown eyes wandered over me before reaching mine. He lowered his fork and sat back in his chair. His smooth skin was radiant as the sun washed over him.

"I'm going to kill Grizzly tonight," I said.

There was a stifling silence that squandered between us until I cleared my throat.

"If I kill him, then we're free, right?"

"Iyana, you don't have to do that."

"Why else would you bring Grizzly to the tower? I'm not stupid. You want to end this war."

"I do." He nodded. "But not by killing Grizzly. I want to burn down his cove. With nowhere to return or meet, his cubs will be disbanded. I'm going to keep him here to release him to a few friends of mine on the force."

"So, you're not going to kill him?"

"No." He chuckled. "I just needed him here for my guys in lockup, but they can't cross jurisdiction or state lines."

"Well…" I scowled. "You should've told me your plan instead of leaving me in the dark."

"I didn't know if things would go well last night."

"You didn't think I could do it?"

"Iyana, it's not—"

"You think I'm weak. Well, I'm not. I can do this on my own." I stood and marched off, but I quickly realized there was nowhere I could go to escape him. I was trapped here, yet again, with nowhere to run or hide.

"Iyana, wait," Vito said as he rushed behind me. He grabbed my arm and turned me back to him. "Why are you upset that I was worried about you?"

"I'm upset because you think I'm not capable! You think I have nothing to offer you, and it shows in the little amount of work you *let* me do. In the small bit of information you *choose* to tell me. And you're not even the leader of BT anymore."

He dropped my arm and stepped back. Sealing his hands in his pockets, he nodded.

"Vito, it's not like that."

"No, I get it. I need to know my place."

"That's not what I meant."

"I'm sorry I haven't included you. Tonight, it's all you. Whenever Grizzly arrives, you call the shots. The guys from lockup won't be able to swing by until late, so if Grizzly's here before nine, just keep him around."

"Vito, come on, I'm sorry," I said, reaching for his hand.

He sighed and gave me a forced smile. "Every time you remind me you're the leader, I remember that I failed all of BT, my father, and you."

"Vee, that's not true." I took his other hand and held them both as he stood there avoiding eye contact. At his core, Vito was a kind man who wanted to be loved and in turn, loved very easily. He was knowledgeable, and he was always thinking. He tried to cover every angle, and avoid hiccups, so it was hard to watch him be sour over his mistakes.

"BT is still standing because of you," I said.

He shook his head. "It's standing because of you, Ana. You came into BT and got the books together, our finances in line, and lowered our debt. I was just coasting along, hoping Brandon would handle everything, and look how that turned out. And every time I have a chance to lead, it's some messy plan that has too many risks."

"Don't be so hard on yourself," I said as I let go of his hands and cupped his face. "Everything I learned at BT, I learned from you."

I felt his arms wrapping around me as he looked down at me. A smirk traced his lips and he said, "I taught you everything about BT, and everything about me." He paused and leaned forward, pressing his lips against my neck. "I taught you everything about you, the parts of you that you didn't know existed." He pushed me against the wall, and his mouth covered mine. I gasped, wrapping my arms around his neck. "I taught you about a pleasure you didn't know existed."

"Teach me again," I whispered.

Lifting me off my feet, his lips found mine as he carried me to the dining table. Plates and food clattered to the floor, and a giggle escaped me. Vito's chuckle was lower than normal. It rippled against my neck as he kissed it again. But the moment was lost when the door opened and Denali, Logan, and Hardy walked in.

By the time evening came around, Vito and I had skipped the day and stayed in bed. We never found out what Logan, Denali, and Hardy wanted, but we didn't really care. As soon as they interrupted, they immediately backed out of the room, issuing a dozen apologies.

Whenever I tried to leave the bed, Vito pulled me back. When I wanted to shower, he did too. When I was tired, the rhythm of his heart rocked me to sleep. I'd never spent a day like this before. I had never been pampered before. It was nice, sleeping beside my husband, eating breakfast for lunch, and enjoying this day with him as the evening came.

"It's time to get up, isn't it?" I asked as we lay beside each other.

"It's time to finally get rid of our biggest problem."

I reached across the sheets and took his hand. "When tonight is over, what are we going to do?"

"We're going to sit down and figure out how to actually get out of here."

"Boss?" Hardy's voice rang out behind the door.

Vito and I glanced at each other.

"Boss! Grizzly's downstairs."

"What?" I said as I sat up quickly.

Vito grabbed my arm and called, "Get him to the thirtieth floor, there's only one room. Keep him there until Iyana shows up."

"You guys better hurry."

Hardy's steps disappeared and I let go of a breath.

"I'm not ready."

"You'll be fine. Take a shower and get dressed. I've got to get the tower in order."

"What do you mean?" I asked as Vito leaned over and kissed my cheek.

"I'll need to get Hardy wired up, and check with Denali and the security team."

"Hardy's going in with me?"

He nodded.

Placing a hand to my chest, I felt a little relief wash over me. There wasn't a need to be scared, but something just felt off. Like, today wouldn't go as planned, like we were missing something or overlooking something. Maybe it's because we have to trust that Grizzly won't try anything, but how can we trust our rival?

BT is ready for anything, I told myself. *I have to trust BT—No—I have to trust* **God***.*

"Iyana," Vito's voice was firm and commanded my attention. "You'll be fine."

I nodded nervously. I wanted him to keep encouraging me, keep my head from drifting, but I needed to be strong. I didn't need to fold right now. Pulling my arm from Vee's grip, I tossed the blankets back and headed for the bathroom.

In the shower, I thought over the plan for tonight. I thought over how tonight would end the war, and open the door for Vito and me to leave BT. With Grizzly gone by our own hand, we'll have access to his contacts—to his entire gang. With that, Vito could assign a new leader to BT, and we could safely step down without being traced.

Our debt would be transferred to the next leader, and we'd be able to get away. But that seemed too easy. Vito had done everything he could to make sure our escape was solid. It'd cost us so much. And now it was just handed to us? I couldn't shake the fear stirring in my chest as I stepped from the steamy shower.

Slowly, I got dressed and ready for the meeting. I knew Hardy wanted me to hurry, but my legs felt like they were tied to the floor. I walked slowly through the apartment with Challa at my side. He'd grown so much and had become such a good companion. He brushed his body against me, trying to comfort me as I walked stiffly to the front door.

Vito had left an earpiece on the table for me, but no instructions. I placed it in my ear and tapped the button. T'Challa trotted beside me down the hall as the earpiece buzzed to life.

"You're finally on," Vito's voice came through the earpiece.

"Where are you?"

"I'm not far from the room you'll be in. Go down to the thirtieth floor."

"I was too scared to go alone, so I took Challa," I said as he walked onto the elevator with me. He sniffed for a moment and then sat beside me.

"You took him with you?"

"I couldn't help it."

"It's fine. I'm stepping away for a moment. Don't go into that room before checking in with me."

"Ok."

I watched the floors change as I rode the elevator. I wished to see Kat once more. I wondered what she would tell me. Probably something good. She'd probably quote a scripture.

The elevator slowed as it reached the floor, and I began quoting the only Bible verse that came to my head.

"The Lord is my shepherd, I shall not want. He maketh me lie down in green pastures, He leadest me beside still waters. He restores my soul. He leads me in paths of righteousness for His name's sake."

I took slow, methodical steps as I reached the door.

"Ye tho I walk through the valley of the shadow of death, I will fear no evil. For thou art with me." I paused and placed a hand to my chest. "For You are with me," I repeated. "Thy rod and thy staff, they comfort me."

I stood at the door. I'd never been to this floor before.

I took one deep breath and whispered, "Thou preparest a table before me in the presence of my enemies. Thou anointest my head with oil, my cup runneth over."

Slowly, I raised a hand and pressed it against the door. "Surely, goodness and mercy shall follow me all the days of my life and I will dwell in the house of the Lord, forever."

"Iyana, you there?" Vito asked.

"I'm here … I'm ready."

"Good. Hardy's already inside. He and Denali kept Grizzly busy. I'll have Denali step out to let you in. She'll take Challa for you."

"I want him to stay with me."

"Alright. I'll send her out."

"Cortez," I called quickly.

"Yeah?" His voice was as lazy as it'd always been. Calm and not shaken.

"I love you."

He grunted. "I love you too."

The door slowly opened and Denali stepped out with a withered smile.

"He's very impatient."

"Thank you, Denali."

She nodded and stepped to the side. She and I had little interaction with each other. But I remembered Logan pleading her case when Vito tried to kill her at the front desk for letting Bug in. She was shaken today, but she was still as charming as I remembered.

"Grizzly," I said as I walked inside.

Hardy was standing off to the side with his hands behind his back. I nodded at him as I passed by to take a seat in the empty white room. The only thing inside was a table and some chairs. Grizzly looked like a stain in the perfectly white room with his dark brown furs and black boots.

"You wasted my time," he snapped as I came to the table. Challa came and sat beside me as Grizzly snarled, "What took so long? Where are the men from the labs?"

"Calm down," I said nervously. "I didn't know you were here."

"Ana, you're doing great," Vito was talking in my ear again, just like the first time I met Grizzly. "Don't let his temper scare you. My guys will be here soon. Just keep him talking."

"And when your little guard here went to tell you, I still waited for over an hour for you!"

"I know, and I'm sorry." I grabbed the folders full of information and opened them. "We can start with—"

"Sorry doesn't cut it. Especially not for cheaters and liars."

I snapped my vision up at him, and he slowly stood from his seat.

"I think I mentioned that I don't like liars and cheaters, yet you stood right in my cove and lied to me."

"I don't know what you're—"

"Shut up!" he screamed. Challa lowered his head and let out a low growl. Grizzly didn't even look his way. His rage was only focused on me now. Hardy could probably sneak out if he wanted and Grizzly wouldn't even know it.

"Hardy, get ready. If he does anything, shoot, but don't kill him," Vito instructed in our earpieces.

I tried to keep myself from jumping at Grizzly's loud voice. Slob was hanging from his mouth, and his eyes had grown cold despite his fiery anger. "You tried to set me up," he snarled. "Tried to use me because your filthy husband is no prince at all." His words were dark and he hissed each one at me.

The thundering in my chest grew wilder, and I knew that every bad feeling I'd had all day was coming down to this moment.

"You're a fool," he spat. "And I'm going to kill you right here."

"Hardy!"

Gunshots exploded and I screamed and dived under the table with Challa. Grizzly hollered as a shot hit him. He dropped to his knees, and when he saw me under the table, he took aim. But the next moment, Hardy tackled him, and his bullet grazed me. The fire that ripped through my flesh made me cry out in agony.

"Ana! Hardy!" Vito was yelling now. "Hardy! Get her out of there!"

"He can't! He's fighting with Grizzly!" I screamed. Hardy was trying to break the gun loose from Grizzly's hand as the two rolled around the room.

Vito yelled, "I'm on my—"

Gunshots started going off all around us, in my earpiece and outside the room.

"We're being ambushed! Ana, get to the garage and wait for me there!" Vito shouted.

"I can't leave Hardy!"

"Just go!" Hardy ordered as he continued to tussle with Grizzly.

"No! I'm not leaving!"

"Ana! Go!" Vito was yelling in my ear, but I ignored him and got to my feet, holding my arm. Gunfire was going on right outside the door, and I could only imagine Denali trying to hold her own out there. IncogVito was under siege which meant, tonight, BT would fall.

My arm was bleeding heavily, but I ignored the pain as I pushed the table over. It crashed onto its side with a loud clattering noise, and I got behind it with Challa for protection.

"*Think*, Ana," I whispered.

Denali would only last so long. Someone might come through the door, and I needed Hardy out of the way. Rubbing my head, I tried to think of something as Challa began to whine beside me.

"Not now, Challa," I said as I pushed him away. He shoved his head back into my lap, and I snapped, "Not—" Then I noticed the gun taped to the bottom of the table behind Challa. I nearly shouted for joy, and thanked God as I reached behind him and pulled the gun free. A shot fired and Hardy shouted. I sat there trembling as the room fell silent.

"Hardy!" I screamed.

"Go, Ana!" His voice was strained.

But there was nowhere to go except through the door we'd entered which was on the other side of the table. I heard shifting, and it grabbed my attention. I knew Grizzly was getting ready to finish Hardy off.

Nervously, I clutched the gun. I didn't want Hardy to die, I didn't want to be the one responsible for his life. I wanted him to live. Hardy was like a brother to me, and I loved him like family.

"Hey, Iyana," Grizzly's voice was exhausted now.

I perked up at the sound of it.

Do something, Ana! God, please!

I shoved my head into the table, pleading up at the ceiling for God to help me. For Him to remember me, to remember Hardy.

"I'm going to kill your little guard. Anything you want to say? I got him good in the side, so it's best to just finish him. And then you."

I stared at the ceiling, and a plan bloomed in my head.

"Hardy," I said flatly, "run."

I fired into the air and took out the lights. Grizzly swore violently, and I heard Hardy shuffling. The only light in the room came from Grizzly's gun firing off. Challa and I raced through the room, and I screamed, "Hardy!"

"Get to the door!" he called back.

"None of you are leaving!" Grizzly shouted as he fired again.

As I crossed the room, I realized that Grizzly couldn't see us, and although I couldn't see him either, I knew where he was. The flames that flickered from every shot all came from the same spot, which meant the person firing the gun was standing still.

When I made it to the door, I felt along the wall and found Hardy sitting against it.

"Let's go!" I shouted.

When the door opened, I knew it would let in the light and reveal our location. I needed to take Grizzly out in the dark.

Slowly, I raised my gun. He'd fired all his shots and I heard his magazine hit the floor.

He's reloading.

I took a shot in the dark, and Grizzly bellowed out a scream.

"Come on!" I said as I grabbed the door and ripped it open.

Hardy tumbled out, and I helped him to his feet as Challa darted from the room. There was gunfire down the hall, but we needed to get moving. Getting under his arm, I pulled Hardy to his feet and whistled for Challa to follow. He groaned loudly, and I desperately pleaded with Hardy to stay quiet.

"Sorry," he whispered as he clutched his side.

We limped down the hall and rounded the corner, but it was a dead end. Just a wall. Challa climbed up and scratched on it with a whimper. The elevator was back the other way towards the shootout. We were stuck.

"Oh, God!" I cried. "What are we supposed to do?"

With a grunt, Hardy pulled his arm from around my shoulders and backed against the wall. He took slow breaths as he cupped his ribs. Blood stained his shirt. He didn't look good at all. And even though there was gunfire and screaming all around us, all I could focus on was Hardy. With a shallow breath, he raised his head. Somehow, he'd managed to produce the boyish grin that swooned the world.

"Ana, don't look so worried. I'm alright."

"No, you're not," I insisted. "You're not alright at all."

"We don't have time for this." He pulled a gun from its holster and racked the slide. "They're going to come around the corner when I do this. Just take this gun and follow the pathway to the stairs. Take them all the way down to the basement. From there, you'll be able to get to the garage."

"No." I shook my head. "I'm not leaving you."

"I'll be fine, Ana. I promise."

"Please, Hardy," I begged.

An explosion went off around the corner and screams bellowed out. I jumped from the loud noise, but Hardy stabled me.

"Ana," he whispered.

When I looked up at him, he leaned down and kissed my forehead. Before I could refuse to leave him again, he shoved the garbage can to the floor and stepped on the tile beneath it. The floor began to vibrate as the tile shifted and opened to a stairway.

"Go!" He shoved me down the hole with Challa, and closed us in.

Challa squealed as he turned over to stand while I slowly tried to recover after being thrown down into this passageway.

"Come on," I whispered as I rolled over and stood.

The stairs led to a floating walkway that Challa and I ran across. I kept the gun low and tried not to think about Hardy or the fact that we were getting invaded. When I reached the top of the stairs, I stared down the long way to the bottom.

"Thirteen flights," I whispered.

Another explosion happened somewhere above me and I prayed that everyone was alright.

Making my way down the stairs, I could hear the gunshots, the explosions, the firing. It was total chaos happening outside of this secret passage.

I tapped my earpiece and tried to connect with someone. "Hello!? Anyone there?"

No answer.

"Hello!?"

There was still no answer, which made the fear in my chest throb harder. I stopped jogging and broke into a sprint down the stairs. I was racing myself to the bottom. I needed to know if Hardy was okay. If Vito was ok. He was on his way to save me when he got ambushed. Did he make it? What if he didn't? How long should I wait if he didn't make it? The nerves forced me to stop and hang over the railing as I gagged. Challa groaned and lay beside me, panting loudly.

"Get off me!" The voice in the distance sounded familiar, almost like Denali.

There was a struggle ahead, shifting and fighting, grunting and screams on the other side of the door. I stared at it, wondering what to do. Challa and I were only three floors from the basement now, almost to the garage. *Vito could be waiting for me down there,* I thought. I stood there for a moment, but I couldn't leave her. I'd already left Hardy. I wouldn't leave Denali too.

"Challa, stay!" I called as I burst through the door.

Denali was engaged in hand-to-hand combat with a man twice her size. But she wasn't afraid, and she was using a book as a weapon. With two hands, she swung the book, giving him a crack across the face before ramming him in the gut with it. He snatched her by the hair and yanked her around, then he slammed her to the ground.

With trembling hands, I extended the gun. I didn't have a clear shot on the man dressed in furs and black boots, the typical Gang Grizzly attire.

I screamed, "Get off her!"

Both of them looked up and I raged forward and tackled the man. We fell to the floor, tumbling until he was on top of me. With three firm punches to the face, I thought he'd broken my jaw. He raised his fist to punch again, but this time I reached forward and clawed him down his face. He screamed curse words and reeled back, giving me the chance to shove him off. But Denali was still there. She was above him now, beating him with her book.

She wrapped her arm around his neck and squeezed tightly. I could see every muscle in her arm flexing. He struggled, hitting her repeatedly on the head, but Denali didn't stop holding him.

Shakily, I reached for the gun in my skirt and realized I must've dropped it. Looking around frantically, I spotted it in the corner of the room. "Denali! The gun! It's behind you!"

Immediately, she let go and the man slumped forward, coughing and heaving. In a matter of seconds, shots were fired, and the man didn't need to catch his breath anymore because he was dead. In the distance, there was more gunfire with Challa barking at the passageway door.

"Mrs. Gerardo," Denali said as she came over and helped me stand. "I have to get you to the garage."

I nodded slowly as I stared at the dead man. "Let's go before they find us."

Pressing her earpiece, she said, "Logan, I've got target one. Target two's location is still unknown."

"Copy that," Logan replied loud enough for me to hear. "I'm bringing around the truck. Bring target one down."

"On my way," Denali said.

Thirty
Vito
Feb 4th | 7:41pm

The smoke and haze of the thirtieth floor burned my eyes as I stepped off the elevator. There was not a single sound, but somewhere below there was still shooting and wailing. BT had been attacked. BT was falling. This was actually the end of the story. This was the end of my career as the head of BT. The Woof Pack was losing its members after everything the Pack had gone through. From the rising of our Beta to that Beta becoming the Alpha. The Woof Pack finally had a good leader in Iyana, just to have it all snatched away. It was bittersweet, knowing that this was the end. But we wouldn't go down without a fight. I wouldn't let BT fall without biting back.

Carefully, I opened the door to the room we'd been holding Grizzly in. When I peeked inside, I saw a figure standing over another. The man on the floor groaned and he wheezed, "Hodda? What are you doing? Help me!"

The voice belonged to Grizzly, but the figure didn't care. He slowly knelt beside the old man, and the next moment, Grizzly was gurgling. I stepped from the room and leaned against the wall. I could hear Grizzly fighting, wanting air, wanting to live, but his killer didn't care.

Tiptoeing down the hall, I stepped over bodies and weapons that lined the floor. It'd been a massacre in this tight hall, and I was certain that no one was alive until I saw a figure sitting against the wall. I shined my flashlight on it, and found the figure was Hardy. He raised his head, sweat drenched his hair, fatigue claimed his body, and death had almost claimed his life.

"Hardy," I whispered as I knelt beside him. "Where's Iyana?"

"She's… in the garage," his voice was weak, and I felt relieved but only for a moment.

"We've got to move. There's a…" I paused as I stared down at his bleeding side. "You're losing a lot of blood."

"Just leave me," he said. "It's alright."

"Iyana would kill me if I left you. C'mon," I said as I fought to lift him to his feet. He was weak, but he tried to be strong. The garbage can near the wall had been moved and the escape was only half closed, I figured he must've sent Iyana down this way.

I opened the hatch and let him go down first. As I made it to the bottom, I grabbed his side again and we made our way down the flights of stairs.

"I kissed Iyana today," Hardy said as we walked.

"Really? You think I won't throw you over this railing for that?"

He chuckled. "Just her forehead. She's like a sister to me, so I wanted to save her."

"I appreciate that."

We walked in silence for a little longer. I was grateful for the quiet. I'd had conversations with many dying men, more than I cared to mention. But the difference between those men and Hardy, was that Hardy wasn't going to die. I had every intention of saving him, and I'd have it no other way. He saved Iyana, and for that I owed him my own life.

"Vee?"

"Hmm?"

"I think I fell in love."

Hardy and I were as close as a boss and employee could be, partially because of Logan. The two of them were good friends, and so often Hardy and I hung around each other. But typically, Hardy spent his days with Iyana, or sulking, so this conversation was feeling a little awkward, especially in our circumstance. However, it was better than listening to the horrific cries of my men dying for me.

"Really?" I said. "Whoever she is, she better not be Iyana."

He tried to laugh but the pain made him choke, and we stopped so he could catch his breath. When we resumed down the stairs he said, "No, it's not Iyana. But I don't know if it's love because it happened so fast."

"You mean like love at first sight?"

"More like first interaction."

"Then I'd say you're more of an adult than you look."

"Why?"

"Because we men know these things early. We know what we're looking for, and who we want to do life with. It's like a sensor or something."

"A sensor?"

"Or something," I said dramatically. "Why are you telling me this?"

"Because I don't know if what I feel is just lust."

"Oh," I said flatly. "You think about having sex with her?"

"Yeah, sometimes."

I cleared my throat.

"All the time," he corrected sheepishly. "But it's not like Jewels. All I wanted to do was prove to Jewels that I was a man. More of a man than Brandon. But with this woman, I don't care about that."

I didn't say anything as we reached the fifth floor. The elevator on this floor would take us right to the garage.

"Well," I said as Hardy caught his breath, "I fell in love with Iyana when I barely knew her. You religious at all?"

He nodded.

"Then I'll give you the only example I know. Have you ever heard of the story of Adam and Eve?"

"Yeah." He was panting as he clutched his side. He leaned over the railing and said, "Give me a second more."

"Fine, then I'll give you the example while we wait. There was a scripture in their story that said there was no suitable companion for Adam, so God made Woman out of Adam's side. And God brought the woman to Adam. When he saw her, he claimed her."

"I don't get it."

"What I'm saying is, wives are actually part of us. When Eve was brought to Adam, he claimed her as his because he recognized her as his own flesh and bone. God always brings our wives to us, and that's why men fall in love instantly. We recognize the part of us that's been missing."

Though he'd been paling and heaving for air, Hardy looked like a light inside had turned on. Like he was suddenly better, or his will to live had returned. He stood there for a second, searching the ground, trying to make sense of what I'd said. But since we'd already wasted time letting him catch his breath, we needed to get moving again.

"Come on, think while we walk."

He didn't say anything else as I lifted his arm. When I opened the door to the fifth floor, it was quiet. I dragged Hardy along and stepped into the hall. Bodies and blood, scorch marks and gun shells were everywhere. I tried to walk carefully around the people. Some I recognized as my own, others were dead in their furs from Gang Grizzly. I never thought BT would be outnumbered by Grizzly. I never thought much of Grizzly at all, but that was my own fault. Because I sat too high and looked too low, and suddenly came tumbling off my white horse.

"Vito! I've been waiting for you."

I froze as I recognized the voice behind me.

"Hardy, get to the elevator," I said. "If I'm not down in the garage in ten minutes, just go without me."

"But—"

"Listen to him, Hardy, because he won't be going anywhere."

Hardy didn't want to go, but he knew he was in no condition to fight. Shakily, he lowered his arm and limped to face the man before us.

"I thought when I saw you again," Hardy said slowly, "I'd hate you. But I don't feel anything but gratitude."

I looked over at Hardy, who was smiling now.

"Because of you," he said, "I found the woman I can spend forever with."

It all clicked. Hardy had fallen in love with Alex.

"What did you say?"

Hardy turned back to me and extended his hand. "I know you'll—"

"Get down!" I shouted as I tackled him to the floor. My shoulder felt like there was a roaring fire engulfing it as I hit the floor with Hardy.

"Vito!"

"Just go!" I shouted.

Rolling off him, I pulled my spare gun from the holster on my leg and fired back at Brandon, providing cover for Hardy. He was wearing the official uniform of Gang Grizzly. Brown furs, big black boots with spikes across the top, and the black uniform. He was one of them now, but I wasn't surprised. This whole thing I set up was just to keep Grizzly and Brandon apart for as long as possible. This was what Brandon wanted, to be accepted. However, he would die today without being the one thing he wanted more than acceptance, the entire reason he'd betrayed me: to become a leader.

When Hardy was gone, and Brandon was reloading, I called into the open, "Hardy's going to marry your wife. You know she doesn't even wear her wedding ring anymore? She took it off for him."

"You can't shake me! I know Alex is in the tower!"

"Really? Well, she should be dead by now then since Grizzly's men came in and shot up every floor."

"Shut up!"

"And Jill? I got rid of her a few weeks ago. Her body is probably rotting right alongside Jewels's in Grizzly's garbage." But that wasn't the truth. Jill was probably dead now from the invasion. She'd been living on the fifteenth floor as a prisoner of BT.

"I said shut up!"

I got to my feet, just to be tackled by Brandon. He was taller than me and stronger than me, but he wasn't faster than me. I'd beaten him once before to be initiated into BT, and I would beat him again.

We were tangled together, throwing punches wildly, drawing blood recklessly. And even though I was angry, even though Brandon had betrayed me, I didn't want to kill him. It wasn't just because I secretly still considered Brandon my brother, and had hoped he would return to BT. But, the more pressing issue was that I didn't want to kill anymore. I didn't want to do things to oppose God anymore. However, I knew the day Brandon betrayed me … that when his end came … it would be by my hand.

The only way to stop a man who's lost everything was to end him.

I tussled with Brandon because I was tussling with my own emotions. I knew once this fight was over, he would be gone, and I'd have my freedom. I'd be able to get away and the cops should already be here to start taking away everyone else.

Tonight was the last night I would be in my own tower. The tower I built to pierce the heavens so everyone could bow to me. But my tower had to fall for God to be recognized.

Brandon shoved his arm into my throat, and I gasped for air. I was losing this battle because I didn't truly want to fight it. But as the light faded, and Brandon's sweaty battered face began to disappear, I heard Iyana's voice calling to me.

"Vito," she called, "please don't go!"

With every ounce of strength I had left, I fought for the knife I kept in my waistband. In a fluid motion, the knife jammed into Brandon's chest. His face pinched in shock and pain and his eyes squeezed shut.

"You… you stabbed me."

"I'm so sorry, Brandon." Tears rolled down his cheeks onto mine and he gasped for air. "You really were my brother, Vee. The only one I ever had."

"I know." I felt a lump in my throat forming as Brandon began to weaken.

"You'll tell Alex for me, won't you?"

"Yeah, I'll tell her the truth."

"I'm sorry I couldn't do it. I'm sorry I wasn't a good brother."

"You were the best." I forced a smile as Brandon began to tremble. I pulled the knife out, and he groaned and grunted.

"I love you, brother." I stabbed him once more, and he tensed before giving in to violent convulsions. When they subsided, I forced myself to lay beside him and let the last part of my connection to this world die.

Thirty-One

Iyana

Feb 4th | 8:27pm

"He's still not here," I complained as I paced back and forth. Logan was sitting in the driver's seat turning the knob on his police radio.

"He'll be here."

"What if he's dead?" I nearly shouted.

"Vee's not going to die. He's fine. Give him a few more minutes."

"Minutes?" I screwed my face up and folded my arms. "We'll wait here all night if we have to. I'm not leaving my husband."

"I care about Vito too," Logan said, looking out the open car door at me. "But he'd kill me if anything happened to you. I have to get you to safety."

"And where is that?"

"Away from here," he snapped.

I shook my head and walked around the back of the car. Denali had cleaned and dressed Hardy's wound. I was so relieved when he came stumbling through the door. But the relief was very short lived when he mentioned he and Vito had run into Brandon, and Vito was shot.

"How's he doing?" I asked as I glanced back at Hardy lying in the backseats.

"He's alright. He'll need to keep that wound cleaned, but he should really get some medical help."

"How, when we're in a gridlock? We don't have a doctor we can go to right now."

"Then the bandages will do. I'm just saying, it's not the best."

Denali, Logan, Hardy, even Challa, were all stressed, just as stressed as I was. I wanted to snap at Denali again, but I couldn't. She hadn't done anything wrong, and she protected me all the way down to the secret garage. I should be more thankful, but my nerves were getting the best of me.

"Hey guys, listen to this," Logan said from the front seat. Over the car speakers, there was a radio call coming in.

"We need backup at IncogVito Tower. The place is lit with gunfire and filled to the brim with bodies. We don't know who else is in there."

"Backup is in pursuit."

Logan lowered the radio. "This is the third call for backup."

"Which means cops are already here," I said as I came around the front. "Give me your gun."

"What? No. Iyana, you're not going back in there."

"They called for backup, Logan! Vito's guys weren't enough. Which means if a cop who doesn't recognize Vito picks him up, it's over."

"She has a point," Denali said as she stood beside me now.

"No." Logan shook his head, and the decision to leave Vito was eating away at him faster and harder than even me. He was flushed red, and his eyes were wet with tears.

"I have to get you to safety, that was his last order," he hiccupped.

"I'm not going anywhere without my husband." I took off for the black door across the garage as Denali and Logan shouted for me. My heart was pounding in agony as I traveled to the black door. No weapon, no radio, no earpiece. But that didn't matter. I would find him.

Snatching open the door, I found Vito standing there with one hand raised and the other clutching his shoulder. His face was bruised and bleeding, and there was blood all over him.

"Vito," I whispered.

He grinned. "You were coming to rescue me."

In my state of shock, it took me an extra second to realized that Vito was alive, and he was right before me, leaning down and kissing me. Stepping back, he lifted my chin and I could barely see him through my tears.

"We've got to keep moving," he said softly. "We'll have time to celebrate later."

He took my hand and led me back across the garage to the truck. Logan jumped out the front seat and embraced Vito for a moment. He squeezed him tightly, and Vito wheezed for air.

"You thought I was dead too?"

"No, boss," Logan lied through his tears.

Vito only sighed and ticked a brow before pulling me to the car.

"Where's the map I gave you, Logan?"

"Right here." I pulled it into the seat.

Vito leaned into the car, reading it over. Denali and Logan gathered around to join us in staring at the map.

"This garage is actually an attachment to my real garage. If we go through the door on the far left side, we'll hit my garage with all my cars. The only problem is we'll have to leave this truck here."

"What's on the right?" I asked.

"That's a trail that leads us right to the subway."

"How'd you do that?" Denali asked.

"I knew a cartographer and an architect once." Vito shrugged.

"Anyways," I elbowed him, "where are we going once we—"

The door to the garage flew open and a man was tackled by an officer. Two more came running to the door, and when they spotted us, they shouted, "Don't let them go!"

"Let's go for the trail!" I yelled.

Logan raced around the back and got Hardy up and they ran together across the garage. I whistled for Challa and he trotted beside me as we took off. When we made it to the door, I called, "I know which train to catch!"

"I'll be right behind you," Vee said as he pushed open the door. "I'm going to help Logan with Hardy."

I nodded and broke into a sprint with Denali right behind me and T'Challa beside me. The run was long, but I couldn't get my legs to slow down when the police were chasing us. Taking the trail was better than trying to get everyone into a car and get through traffic. Even though Hardy was slow, as long as we made it to the subway, we'd be able to lose the police.

I kept my chest up, and my legs pumped hard as there was a door coming up. I slammed right into it, bursting through it and into the crowd of people. I stumbled into a man who whirled around to snap at me, but my bleeding arm probably threw him off, and my pit bull panting beside me definitely shut him up.

"Come on," Denali grabbed my hand and pulled me along.

I waved at Challa and he made his way through the crowd. People were gasping and moving away from us and drawing attention. I loved Challa, but he was causing a stir.

"Where are the others?" I said as we walked through the crowd, trying not to look suspicious.

"I'm not sure."

"We can't get separated."

Behind us came a wave of screams as people began to move out the way.

"Police! Let us through!"

"Vito!" I shouted as the crowd wailed.

"Keep your voice down," Denali hissed.

"We've got to find them," I yelled at her. "Vito!" I cried again. "Vi—"

"Let's go," Vito walked up to me and grabbed me by the arm.

"Challa!" He trotted over and walked closely beside us.

We made our way through the crowd as the subway doors opened. People walked off while Vito, Denali, and I calmly walked on and took seats in the back. I tried not to be frantic as I searched for Logan and Hardy.

"No pets allowed on this train," a man said as he stared down at Challa.

"Excuse me, sir." Denali stood and stepped between us. "He's a special dog. He has to be with his owner."

"Calm down," Vito said as he slowly took my hand. "They're right in front of us and Denali can handle this."

Logan stepped on the subway with his hands in his pockets. Hardy, bruised and weak behind him, stepped onto the train holding his side. I wanted to believe this was over, but the stares from the people were making it more obvious that it was not over. Hardy was paling, Logan was sweaty. Denali and I had scrapes and bruises all over while Vito's face was a display of battery, and his shoulder was the evidence needed in court.

I counted the seconds until the doors closed as Denali and the man began to bicker. She backed him away from us, all the way through the cart, and just as the doors began to close, she shoved him off the subway. Gasps ensued and everyone began yelling at her.

"Should we help her?"

"Nah," Vito said, "it'll keep people from noticing Challa."

I took a deep breath and leaned against Vito's shoulder as I watched Denali argue with a crowd.

—— BT ——

"So where are we going?" Hardy tiredly asked behind us.

"We've been walking for a while now, Mrs. Gerardo," Denali added.

"Don't worry," I said. "We're here."

I walked up the steps with Vito by my side and we entered an apartment complex. The old brownstones were familiar, but the neighborhood seemed colder without Mom.

Inside was Bubba, the security guard. He took one look at me and exclaimed, "Iyana!?"

"It's me," I said with a smile.

The wide man came from around the desk and hugged me tightly. "I thought you were dead."

"Almost," I teased.

He glanced over my shoulder at everyone. "What's going on?"

"I'm here to see my father."

He nodded slowly without taking his eyes off everyone behind me. "Go right up. Don't sign the logbook."

"Thank you, Bubba."

He grinned widely as we passed by to the elevators. Bubba and I had always been friends, and when I told him I was moving out, he tried to bribe me to stay with cash, coupons, and dinner dates—although we never actually went on any of the dates.

We all piled onto the elevator in silence. I didn't know what to expect when I saw my father again. But home was the only place I could think of. I hadn't been here in ages, and I was certain Dad wouldn't mind the company since Mom passed. When the elevator dinged, I hesitated to step off.

"It'll be fine, Ana," Vito said beside me.

I nodded up at him and stepped off. Our echoey steps lingered as we made our way down the hall. I'd walked this hall many times since I was a kid. I remembered when I brought the last box from the apartment down this hall. I was alone then, doing things by myself. Now, Vito was beside me with Challa. Logan and Hardy were here, Denali too, and I wasn't alone anymore.

"One-forty-one," I said as I stared at the number on the door. "I hope he's home."

I reached forward and knocked on the door.

"Who is it?" a voice asked.

"Daddy? It's me, Iyana."

I heard him rushing through the place before he got to the door and ripped it open.

"Iyana," he stared at me and then at Vito. "What's going on?"

"I need some help."

He stuck his head out the door and peeked around. "Alright, come on."

Vito, Challa, and I all walked in, and Denali helped Logan bring an aching Hardy inside.

"Oh, baby," Dad said as he hugged me tightly. "I can't believe it."

"I know," I said as I squeezed him. "But we can only stay until morning."

"Why?"

"The police are after us," Vito said.

My father looked Vito over quickly. "You're the guy from the hospital, and from that event. You're the Prince of the City." He turned to me, pointing at Vito. "You married him?"

"Yes, Dad."

He rubbed tired hands over his face. "The Prince of the City is part of a gang." He glanced over at me. "Y'all been caught?"

"No, but we can't go back, and we've still got enemies."

"So you need to get out of the city?"

I nodded. "But we're too banged up. Just an overnight stay and we'll be gone."

He looked around the room at us and shook his head. "No, you all will need longer than a night."

"Normally, we would," Vito said. "But I can't put you in any more danger than I already have. If our enemies find out you're helping us, they'll come for you."

"You know he's got protection," Denali said.

My dad looked over at her, and then he gasped. "Dena? From The Club?"

Denali nodded and raced into his arms. I was scowling before I knew it and blew off a question before I meant to. "Are you sleeping together?"

Denali pulled away from my father and they each wore an expression of surprise. This was supposed to be a reunion between my father and me, and it was supposed to be a somewhat happy time despite the circumstances. Yet, with the looks on their faces, I think my indecent question sapped all the happiness from the room.

"No," Denali finally spoke. "I used to work at The Club when I wasn't working for Bridges. I needed money and would bartend. Mayor Walters would have meetings there quite often with members of all kinds of organizations who kept clean hands in the daylight but sullied them in the dark."

"Oh," I said weakly. "I'm sorry."

Denali waved a hand. "It's alright, Mrs. Gerardo."

"I didn't know you won the election," Vito said.

I realized that Denali referred to my father as the mayor. "Dad, you're the mayor?"

"All those meetings Dena mentioned helped me win the election and I can't back out now. All those people are counting on me."

Glancing over at Vito, he gave me a slow nod and I said, "Dad, you don't have to do it anymore. Brandon isn't after you anymore. You can stay at Gracie Mansion instead of here."

"I'm not here because I'm scared of Brandon, I'm here because I wanted to be here if you ever returned."

Tears pricked my eyes as my father smiled shyly at me. We'd been distant with everything that'd happened. We'd grown even further apart. But now, I was here and I couldn't even stay. I was causing more harm than good being here, but I'm glad I came home. I got to see my father one more time because, when I leave tomorrow, I won't know when I'll be back. If ever. The thought weighed on me, and the tears began to fall onto the old brown carpet.

"Don't worry," Denali said, grabbing my shoulder. "I'll stay with him."

"You can't," I said. "You worked for BT. Our rivals will come for you."

"They won't," Dad said. "Dena's always wanted to join the force. Now that she's been involved with gangs, she'll become an undercover cop. We need that right now." He puffed his chest. "As the mayor, I can make that happen for her."

Denali was glowing like an ember beside my father, and I could see now that everything would be alright. I didn't need to worry about my father because even though the distance between us had shrank, and I knew that tonight may be my last night with him, I could be okay with that because Denali would be here. My dad finally had someone he could depend on, and someone to be a friend. I think that's what he really needed.

"If you're the mayor," Logan said, calling my attention from my tear-stained hands, "that means you can cover this up."

My father's gaze narrowed on Logan. "I want to have little to do with this, but," he looked over at me, eyes softening now, "if it means saving my daughter, then I'll do what I can."

"And I'll be here to help. I know what needs to be kept a secret, and what can be public details," Denali added.

"Then make it look like we disappeared," Vito said.

"I can make it look like you never existed," Denali said.

"Thank you." I took her hands and she nodded.

"It's the least I can do for you." Denali had screwed up with Bug. But she'd protected me and was willing to stay behind to protect all of us, and my father. At the very least, I owed her respect and gratitude.

After a hot meal and a shower, I lay in my old bed with Vito. Dad was able to get a medic into the building without causing a stir, and he got Hardy all patched up, and nursed the rest of our injuries. Thankfully, my father was already making friends while in office—friends who could keep secrets.

I held the blanket to my chest as I stared up at the ceiling. The moonlight bathed Vito as he turned over to face me.

"Tell me where you want to go."

"What do you mean?" I asked. "Aren't we going back to California?"

"It's too dangerous right now. It's best if we lay low somewhere else."

"I see," I said, adjusting to face him. The swelling on his face had gone down, and he was left with a black eye and a busted cheek and lip. His skin was peppered with bruises and scratches, but he still looked as handsome as he always had, because every scrape and bruise was for me. Vito had done so much to save us, and even now, he was doing everything he could to not only protect me, and all of us here, but to protect my father too.

"I think I want to go to Hawaii," I said.

"Have you ever been?"

I shook my head against the pillow.

"Good. Then we'll go."

"What about you? Where do you want to go?"

"I want to go wherever you're going." He was silent for a moment as his bruised hand pushed loose hair from my face. "You're all I've ever wanted."

I couldn't find any words, so I snuggled against his chest and closed my eyes.

When the sun was traded for the moon, Vito and I got ready to leave. We'd have to stop by an ATM and a 24-hour store to get money and things we needed to head out of town today. But I couldn't leave without telling my father goodbye.

I've been through so much in the last seven months. A world of hurt, new realizations, love and experiences, but none of them compared to the feeling of freedom singing in my chest. My boat was capsized, but somehow, God found me favorable as I began to drown, and He saved me to bring Vito back to Him and others too. With the crumbling of BT, and hopefully Gang Grizzly, there'd be a lot less gang violence now. Maybe the city will remember the faith and cleave to it. Who knows? But my journey here in New York was finally over, and I had to start anew with God and Vito.

"Take care of her," my father said as he patted Vito's good shoulder. The two hugged and Vito took Challa and stepped into the hall to wait for me.

I gave Denali a hug and thanked her again for staying with my father. But tears returned as I embraced my father. I knew God would protect him, and even use him to make this city a better place. I just didn't want to say goodbye.

"This won't be forever," I said into his chest.

"It's alright if it is," he whispered, and I could feel my heart breaking. "Your safety is my top priority. I want you to live, Iyana, be happy. Don't waste your days worried about me, I'll be alright."

"I'm so sorry for everything, Daddy."

"There's nothing to be sorry for. Now, it's time for you to go." He pulled on my shoulders, and I looked up at him through thick tears. "Your mother would be so proud of you, baby girl."

I nodded. "I hope so."

Dad had changed. He wasn't a coward anymore. He'd finally become a real father to me.

For one more moment, I held onto my father, hoping that it wouldn't be the last.

"I'll always be right here if you ever return, and if you can't, you know my number."

"Iyana," Vito stepped back inside, "we need to leave."

I kissed my father on the cheek and nodded at Denali, then I looked back at him for the last time. "Goodbye, Daddy."

"Goodbye, Iyana."

Vito took me by the hand and led me out as I pulled the door shut. When we got downstairs, Bubba was asleep at the desk, but it was better this way than to say goodbye. And for just that instant, I understood why Kat couldn't bring herself to say goodbye to the rest of us when she'd left.

"Well," Hardy said as we stepped onto the sidewalk. "This is where we part."

"What?" Vito and I spoke at the same time.

"I've got to figure things out on my own."

"Why?" Logan asked. "C'mon, Hardy, what are you talking about?"

Hardy shrugged his shoulders which made him wince. "This isn't goodbye—it's just a break."

"Hardy, you know I'll take care of you. You don't need to go," Vito said.

"Vito, you've been better to me than I deserved." He took Vito's hand and gave it a firm shake. Logan looked upset, but he tried to stay calm as the two embraced for a while. I hadn't moved. I just watched the scene before me play out.

"Ana," Hardy said as he stood in front of me now. "Vito and Logan are going to take care of you until I find you again."

"I can't say goodbye to you too," I hiccupped.

"Good, because I'll be back." He leaned down and kissed my cheek. The warmth of his kindness bloomed where he'd pressed his lips, and when he pulled away, my heart had begun to miss him already. But, somewhere inside, I knew he needed this, and I knew this really wasn't goodbye.

"All you have to do is call, and I'll be there to protect you."

I laughed and wiped at my tears. "I don't think I'll need protection anymore."

"I hope so, because then you'll still need me."

I tightened my grip on Vito's hand as my heart continued to break. Without another word, Hardy sank his hands into his pockets and disappeared into the morning rush. The boy with the grin was finally becoming a man.

"Are you leaving too?" Vito asked after a moment of silence.

Logan sniffled and gave Vito a playful slug. "Whenever you're ready," he said.

"Good, let's go." Vito looked down at me, and after losing everything I had here in New York, I still found the strength to smile.

As we turned to start down the street, I whistled for Challa to follow.

Thank You... God.

Epilogue

May 15th | One Year Later

Alex

"Tobias, start the grill!" I called from the kitchen.

"Alright!" he called back.

I washed and dried my hands before carrying the tray of burgers and shrimp skewers out back.

"Happy birthday, Tobias," I said as I kissed his cheek.

"Thank you, Lex. You know I love your shrimp skewers."

"I made a lot today. And *I'm* grilling. I just need you to start it up."

"Fine, fine, but only because it's my birthday."

"Thank you, Papa," I said as I set the skewers on the grill table.

After having Ava, I returned to the Gerardos, and have been with them ever since. Dafni and I take care of Ava, and she thinks they're her grandparents. We don't tell her otherwise, because, what's the point?

I filed legal documents in April of last year to divorce Brandon. Turns out, the papers couldn't be served because he'd been killed. A large sum of money was given to me, and I was offered his property in New York, but I refused it and sold it back to the city. Since then, Ava and I have been here with the Gerardos, attending church on Sundays and Fridays as a family.

My relationship with God was finally getting better after I stopped waiting for Hardy or anyone to come save me. I became a mother and I had to learn to do things on my own. Ava needed me, *all* of me, and I needed her. She pointed me to God and made me realize more than ever that I was grateful to Him.

He comforted me as I eventually stopped crying over BJ and helped me learn what true love is. Through Christ, I learned that the love of God is what we should strive to gain. And when we do that, we learn to love other people and we learn the distinction between lust and love.

Learning the difference between love and lust reminded me every day of what could have been. But I didn't let myself linger on the past anymore. If I held on to every mistake I made, I'd never move forward. It was easier to let the past be a fragment of my imagination now. Learning the truth made me free, so I didn't have to dwell on the past.

Some days were harder than others, especially because not only did Vito save me and leave behind money for me, but so did Hardy. He left all his books to me, but thankfully I didn't need them. The Gerardos took great care of Ava and me, so I stored the books away for a time if I ever needed them.

"Lex, honey," Dafni said as she came downstairs with Ava.

"Mommy!" Ava shouted when she saw me.

I swooped her up and spun her. "Hi, baby," I said cheerfully.

"Momma, Grandma is hungry."

I fell back in laughter as Dafni took Ava from me.

"Sorry, Daf, the skewers always take a while to prep."

"It's fine." She waved a hand. "Go get changed, I'm taking Ava outside to see Tobias."

I nodded as the two of them strolled off toward the yard. Rubbing my neck, I tiptoed across the floor to the staircase when the doorbell rang.

"I got it!" I called as I jogged over to the front door and pulled it open.

Hardy

I stood there staring at Alex. I'd planned to tell her everything I felt. How I spent a year learning about love, and how to be a man, a real man, a *Christian* man. And in figuring this all out, I found out that I truly did love her. That what Vito said in the passageway was true. I'd fallen in love with Alex the moment I saw her because she was the missing part of me. God brought us together, but I wasn't ready before. I am now, and I hoped that she hadn't moved on. I was hoping she would understand me. But I don't think she did as she slapped fire from my face.

I placed a hand to my cheek as I looked back at her. Tears were rimming her eyes.

"I probably deserved—"

She flung herself into my arms and squeezed me tightly.

"I thought you were dead! I thought I'd never see you again!"

"I'm sorry," I said as I slowly wrapped my arms around her. I breathed in her scent, held on to her small frame. She was as beautiful as I remembered. Nothing had changed about Alex, except her new glow. She wasn't the fearful woman I'd left behind over a year ago.

"I didn't know what to do, so I stayed away until I could figure it out," I whispered to her. "But I thought about you every day, and every day, I tried to make myself a better man for you. I wanted to be here so badly, but I wanted to make sure what I felt wasn't lust. And I realized—"

"It wasn't," she said as she pulled back from my embrace. "We fell in love."

I stared at her because I had prepared to plead my case, not have her agree with me.

"I… I did… well, *we* did. We fell in love. And I have never stopped loving you, Alex."

She wiped at her tears. "And I never stopped loving you, Hardy. I still love you now as I did then. I just didn't know it."

"So, you'll marry me?"

I don't know where that came from, but the smile on Alex's face gave me an answer. I didn't have any money; I'd left it all to her in California. I didn't know if I'd return, so as a parting gift, I left her all my cash which meant I didn't have a ring—I'd been too broke to buy one before showing up. I'd worked a small job up in Maine, getting fish and lobsters off the coast. It was good pay, but I spent all my money getting to California.

"Sorry," I said, backing up. "I don't have a ring yet. I'm flat broke. But I'll get a job."

She began to laugh as she pulled me back to her. "I don't need a ring to marry you. I just want to be with you. Besides, I never spent a dime of the money Vito left me, or the money you left me. I was saving it for whenever Tobias and Dafni got tired of us."

Her smile suddenly dropped, and she stepped back from me.

"What's wrong?"

"I... I have a daughter."

"I know." I nodded. "Ava, I remember."

She looked me over quickly with one arched brow. "You want to be a father?"

"I want to be your husband, and I'll be whatever else if it means I get to be with you."

"But Ava's not—"

"Ava doesn't have a father. And now she does."

"You're sure?"

"Of course."

Before she could protest any further, I leaned down and lifted her off her feet. She flew into a flurry of giggles as I carried her over the doorstep, bridal style.

Cortez

"Ana!" I called as I tossed the ball to Challa. Digging his claws deep into the sand, T'Challa raced to catch it before it rolled into the ocean.

"Yeah?" she called as she walked down the stairs of our beach house.

Iyana wanted to live by the ocean, so I had a house built for her on whichever beach she wanted. It wasn't lavish like the tower, it was simple, the way she liked things. Our lives were different now. Since Dr. Walters got married and changed her name, Dr. *Ortega* was able to submit her research to a scientific journal and pass her board certification. It was hard to get her back into the program, but God favored my wife and me, and she was able to reenter.

But we were rich now. We didn't need anything. Still, we started a veterinary clinic here in Hawaii, just like in New York, to hide all our cash my parents sent after receiving a Christmas card from me with instructions. Iyana and I were planning to go see them this Christmas season.

"I can't wait any longer," I said as she walked up beside me.

She looked out at the ocean for a moment, the sun meeting the waves and exulting His passion for the ocean in pink and yellow hues. The waves seemed to like His touch as she danced back and forth in excitement.

"It's positive," Iyana finally said.

"You're kidding?"

She shook her head and looked up at me with a huge smile. "We're having a baby!"

Lifting her off her feet, I spun her in a circle as Challa barked at us.

"It must've been positive," Logan said as he came out the house. Logan worked at the clinic with Iyana as security, and he also lived with us. He's been struggling with the faith, but only because he has a vicious appetite for women. But he's learning there's more to the world than parties and sex, and it's been changing him.

"Yeah," I exclaimed as he hugged me.

"Congrats, Vee."

He was the only one who still called me Vito. He refused to call me Cortez because he said I had two last names for a name, and it didn't make sense. He preferred Vito, and he wouldn't let me forget it. But I know he didn't want to forget where we'd come from. It was his way of showing appreciation for me.

"I'm so excited," Iyana squealed. "We're having a baby!"

"Not me," Logan waved his hands.

"Yes, you." Iyana grabbed his hand and said, "You're going to be an uncle."

"Yeah," Logan thought for a moment, "I guess so."

"I can't wait." Iyana was beaming as she placed her hands over her belly.

A year ago, if anyone had told me that today I'd be standing on the beach with my pregnant wife, our dog, and my brother, I'd never believe them. But here I am, and it's all because of Christ Jesus. I'll never forget that.

The End

Thank you for finishing the series!

Want more Christian mafia romance? Check out the [Withered Rose trilogy](), a Christian romantic suspense series.

More books by A. Bean & TRC Publishing!

Christian Fantasy

[The End of the World series]()

[The Scribe]()

[Cross Academy series]()

Christian Science Fiction

[I AM MAN series]()

Christian Romance

[The Living Water]()

[Withered Rose Trilogy]()

[Fractured Diamond]()

Christian Children's Fiction

[Too Young]()

ACKNOWLEDGEMENTS

Jesus is the Christ, Son of the Living God. He is the One who gave me the idea and enabled me to write this story, thank you.

My editor, she's wonderful. My stories go from good ideas to polished books… thank you.

Follow me on Amazon to get updates on new releases, pre-orders, reduced prices on my books.

The Rebel Christian Publishing

We are an independent Christian publishing company focused on fantasy, science fiction, and romantic reads. Visit therebelchristian.com to check out our books or click the titles below!

   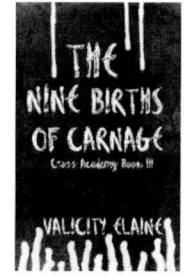
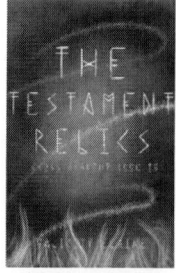  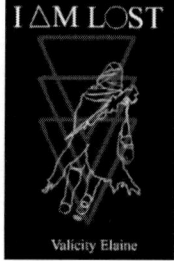 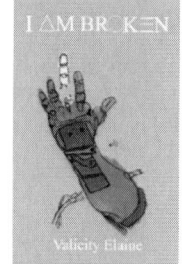
 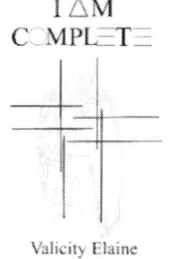  

Made in United States
North Haven, CT
18 January 2025